TRUESILVER

A TALE OF THE CHAOS WALKER REVOLUTION

GARETH IAN DAVIES

To the ones who stand up for those who've been beaten down

CONTENTS

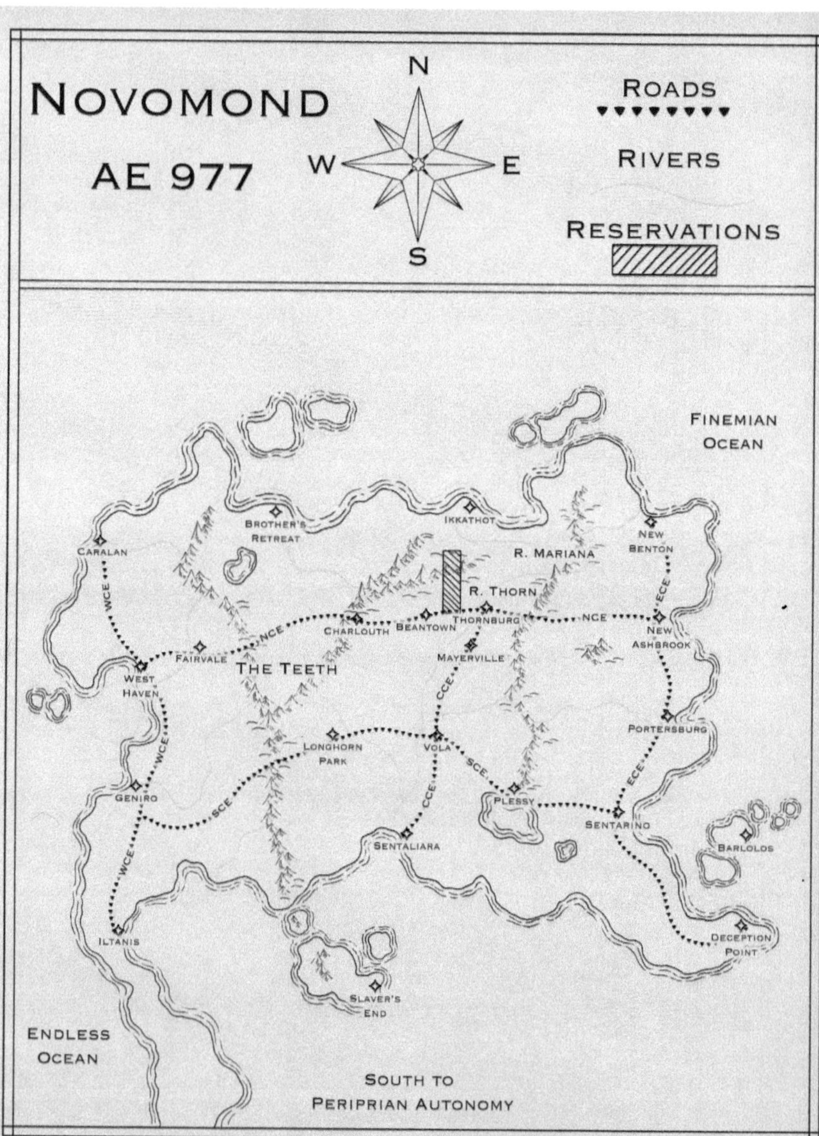

NOVOMOND
AE 977
N
W
E
S
ROADS
RIVERS
RESERVATIONS
FINEMIAN OCEAN
BROTHER'S RETREAT
IKKATHOT
NEW BENTON
CARALAN
R. MARIANA
R. THORN
WCE
NCE
CHARLOUTH
BEANTOWN
THORNBURG
NCE
NEW ASHBROOK
ECE
FAIRVALE
MAYERVILLE
THE TEETH
WEST HAVEN
CCE
PORTERSBURG
WCE
LONGHORN PARK
VOLA
SCE
GENIRO
SCE
CCE
ECE
PLESSY
SENTARINO
SENTALIARA
BARLOLOS
WCE
ILTANIS
DECEPTION POINT
SLAVER'S END
ENDLESS OCEAN
SOUTH TO PERIPRIAN AUTONOMY

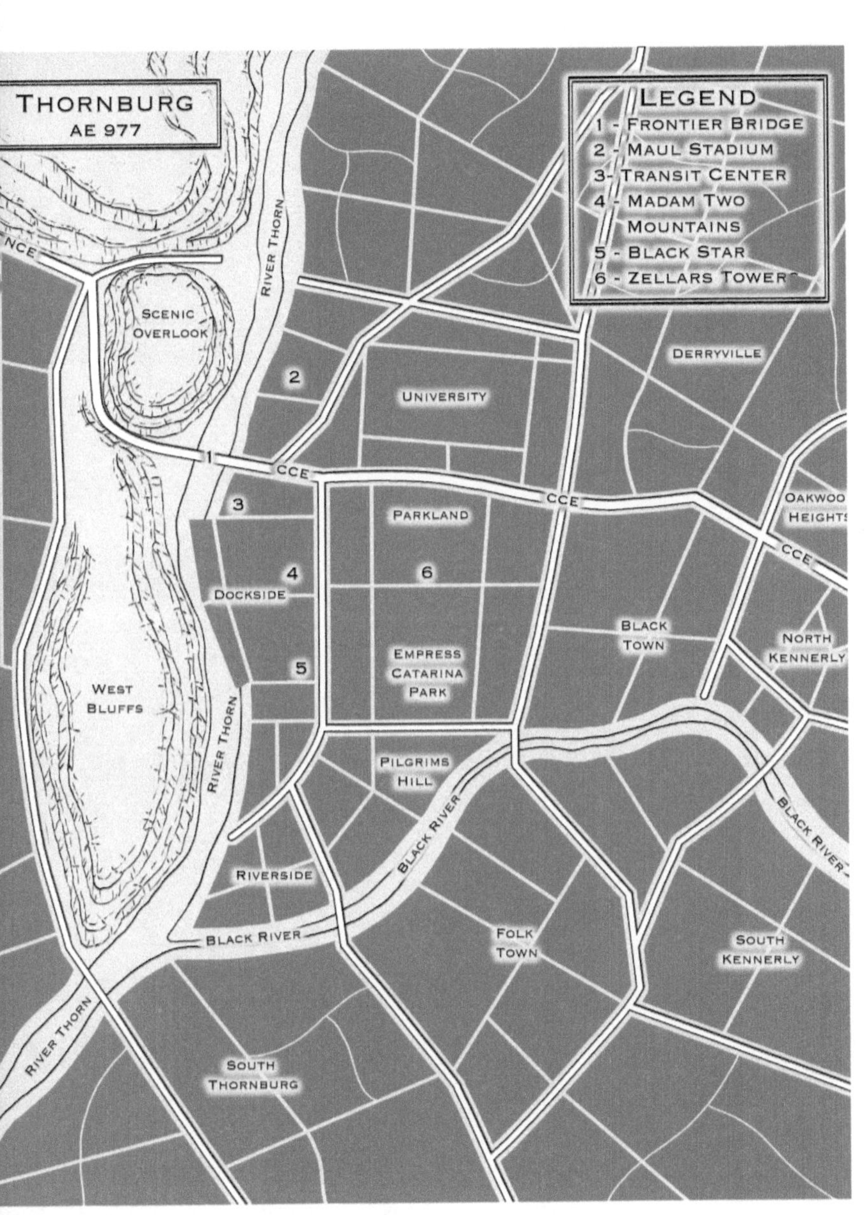

THORNBURG
AE 977
LEGEND
1 - FRONTIER BRIDGE
2 - MAUL STADIUM
3 - TRANSIT CENTER
4 - MADAM TWO MOUNTAINS
5 - BLACK STAR
6 - ZELLARS TOWER
SCENIC OVERLOOK
RIVER THORN
DERRYVILLE
UNIVERSITY
CCE
CCE
OAKWOOD HEIGHTS
CCE
PARKLAND
DOCKSIDE
BLACK TOWN
NORTH KENNERLY
WEST BLUFFS
EMPRESS CATARINA PARK
RIVER THORN
PILGRIMS HILL
BLACK RIVER
BLACK RIVER
RIVERSIDE
BLACK RIVER
FOLK TOWN
SOUTH KENNERLY
RIVER THORN
SOUTH THORNBURG

A Note on Time

The world in which the tales of the Chaos Walker Revolution takes place has many similarities to our own. It also has many differences, most of which I allow to emerge from the text. But since time is told very differently, using the metric system favored almost obsessively by the Empire, I offer this brief explanation.

Each day consists of 10 **tenths**, each consisting of 100 **hundredths**. Thus, a tenth lasts almost two and a half hours, and a hundredth roughly a minute and a half. Most people think in terms of **half-tenths** (just over an hour) and **quarter-tenths** (roughly half an hour). Instead of seconds, people use words like "tick" (from the few analog clocks still in existence), "moment", "breath" or "heartbeat".

There are no time zones. 0.00 is midnight in Earus, the city in the heart of the continent from which the Empire spread, but residents of Thornburg and New Ashbrook enjoy their evening meal around that time. The Day End Bell, a custom originating with Novomond's first settlers, is rung anywhere from 2.50 to 4.00 depending on how far west you go.

Instead of months and weeks, years are divided into **tennights**, with each day simply named after its number (e.g. Oneday, Twoday, Tenday etc.) The year ends at midwinter in the Northern Hemisphere, with five days (six in leap years) of **Festivus**. Calendar dates begin at the origin of the Empire.

Our story begins in the year 977 AE, on the date 977.17.3 (year, tennight, day) to be exact.

1

BLACK STAR

Jek One Raven and Ellin Two Water weren't looking for trouble that night. They were just trying to blow off a little steam. Final exams loomed with increasing menace, and after a hard afternoon's study, Jek suggested they head to Dockside.

"If I stare at these transmutation notes any longer, my eyes are gonna burn out," Ellin complained. "I just need to relax."

Jek grinned. "I know just the place!"

Bundling up against the late spring chill, they boarded the public bus to Thornburg's central transit center. They were the only two LightFolk passengers. The driver took their credit and didn't seem to mind, but they confronted more than one dark look from among the human passengers.

They sat near the front. Ellin gritted his teeth throughout the journey. Jek remembered that one of his friend's cousins had been raped and beaten to death by human thugs on just such a bus, five years before. The horrific incident dominated news cycles for just over a day, before sinking without trace. Had the perpetrators even been charged with a crime, much less convicted?

Righteous indignation about the murder of a LightFolk woman had faded almost as fast as the story. But Ellin and the Two Water clan hadn't forgotten. No LightFolk had.

As soon as the doors opened at the transit center, half a hectare of bleak concrete in the shadow of the Frontier Bridge, the two friends sprang from the bus and headed south at a rapid walk.

Squat, murky brick warehouses loomed over the first few blocks of waterfront, relics of the few functional docks remaining from Thornburg's heyday. One or two showed signs of life, even though the sun had set almost a tenth ago. Jek and Ellin kept their heads down. They didn't want to tangle with any dock workers.

"This way," muttered Jek as they reached another murky street corner. He turned left and led them into Dockside proper.

Since Thornburg's humble origins as a frontier trading post, those in search of high stakes and loose rules, free-flowing beer and fast women, looked no further than Dockside. Fur trappers, miners and explorers gravitated to the Thorn River, the Empire's first commercial artery in Novomond, even before its conquest of the continent was complete. Victory secured, the city expanded rapidly, but Dockside remained its beating heart.

Once, the working class district funneled wealth from ships and boats of all sizes to an ever sprawling, organic mishmash of warehouses, towering offices, and opulent mansions. Dockside kept little for itself, but the waterfront seethed with bars, brothels, and seedier establishments where you could acquire anything for the right price.

Then, two decades ago, civic leaders and property developers took note of the cheap, crumbling tenements blighting the river and swooped in. The few remaining cargo vessels now approaching the docks enjoyed a vista of gleaming, high end condo towers, a shield wall of stylish prosperity.

The seedy underside hadn't disappeared. It just moved a few blocks away from the river.

Jek steered them away from the brightest lights. He avoided the trendiest bars and restaurants, the ones with prominent displays of "517" signs in their windows. Technically, laws prohibited any business from discriminating against the Folk, but after a tempestuous campaign in the court of public opinion, Statute 517 had passed last year. It gave businesses the right to refuse service to those deemed "deleterious to the peace". In Thornburg, at least, that translated to "No Folk allowed".

"Who wants to party with a bunch of humans anyway?" Jek spat, noticing Ellin's fearful expression as they skirted a particularly raucous bar. A circular neon sign glowed red from the floor above, but Jek wasn't interested in the brothels where their people were used for whatever sexual pleasure humans could imagine.

He clutched Ellin's arm and dragged him down an almost invisible alley. "We're going to Black Star."

Every seedy neighborhood has a seedier end, disdained even by the purveyors of vice and ruin elsewhere. Fast food waste and mostly intact empty glass bottles carpeted The Mews. Its ill-lit cobblestone sliced through decaying brick terraces forgotten, or more likely ignored, by the property developers. Pungent odors of grease and bodily waste grew stronger with every step they took towards the single sullen street lamp. Its sickly yellow light reluctantly illuminated a battered wooden door, the black paint of a seven pointed star scratched and peeling.

Inside, out of the stink and decay, was a little better. No knickknacks or pithy signs adorned the dark walls, or hung from the stained drop ceiling. The cheap wooden tables and scuffed floor were clean, and the air smelled of beer that wasn't too stale. This early in the evening, only a sparse crowd of LightFolk nursed drinks. Some looked up as the newcomers entered, but none ventured any kind of greeting.

The black-stained wood front of the bar ran the entire length of the deep, rectangular room. Jek sank onto the nearest wobbly stool and had to grab Ellin, whose own stool almost tipped him off onto the floor.

"Nice," Ellin muttered. Jek couldn't tell if his friend was amused or disgusted.

The bartender, a burly LightFolk almost as wide as he was tall, gazed at them with coals for eyes within his pox-puckered moon of a face. He approached them from the bar's far end, with all the deliberation and personality of a cargo ship approaching its dock.

"IDs," he growled, in a voice as scarred as his skin. They produced their laminated cards, notarized by the Bureau of Folk Affairs, without saying a word. "Starshine Academy, huh? Thought you lot was too smart to come to a shithole like this."

Is he being ironic? Jek wondered. He bit back one of his wittier replies. "We got finals next tennight. Wanted to get as far away from school as possible for the evening, without leaving Thornburg."

The bartender snorted, and handed back their ID cards. "That, you've done. What do you want?"

"Two beers, whatever you've got fresh from the cask."

That earned another snort, but with humorless efficiency, their host produced two glasses of foaming brown liquid, thumping them down on the chipped stone bar top.

"Let me get these," Ellin offered, taking out his phone and looking for the tap point.

"Cash only," growled the bartender, sneering at the device. "We don't trace our customers here."

"I got it," said Jek, as his friend simply gaped in confusion. He slid out a pristine, uncreased bank note from his wallet, and tossed it next to their glasses.

The bartender's eyes lingered on the wallet as Jek replaced it in his pants pocket. "Wouldn't go flashing that around in here," he murmured, then turned his back.

"Friendly guy," Ellin observed, after they'd clinked glasses. He took a sip and grimaced. "What the fuck is this supposed to be?"

"It grows on you," Jek said, downing half of his beer at once. "Shit, I needed that. Hey, they've got a Three Rings table over there. Wanna go play?"

"And miss the fascinating bar conversation? Sure, if I must."

The circular table nestled at the back of the room, between the two toilets, at least one of which stank like it needed cleaning. The table was tavern size, two metres in diameter, which meant seven balls each. Jek had grown up with the full, three metre, eleven ball version, but suspected those skills would be more than balanced by the worn black cloth and, he suspected, uneven surface. As long as the randomizer worked properly, they'd still get a decent game out of it. He'd once played on a table that kept opening the same hole. It was still Three Rings, but the strategy was boring.

Jek gave Ellin the red balls, and off they went.

Ellin wasn't a bad player, but his accuracy didn't match his strategic acumen. He took his losses in stride, and dug out enough cash for another round. They were only vaguely aware of the bar filling up, as LightFolk workers from the docks and other menial jobs arrived to forget about their days.

But, as Jek drained his second beer, and contemplated a third, the buzz of conversation stalled. He finally noticed the decades-old playlist battling static from the bar's wall-mounted speakers, and looked up.

Three men stood just inside the doorway, surveying the silent room with amused disdain. They were human, not much older than Jek and Ellin. The cut of their collared shirts and everwool pants spoke of money and influence. Jek came from a prominent LightFolk clan, but nothing like that graced his wardrobe. He dismissed a sudden urge to tuck in his own shirt.

Ignore them. Whatever they're doing in Black Star, let them have their fun, so they can go laugh about it with their friends later.

He snapped his fingers under Ellin's nose, interrupting his friend's dangerous scowl.

"Hey. Your turn."

Ellin blinked, then met his eyes. Jek didn't like that look. They'd avoided trouble on the journey here, there was no need to start any now.

"Your turn, Ell."

Ellin took a deep breath. He tore his gaze away from the newcomers, who had been given a wide berth by other patrons as they ordered drinks from the no less taciturn bartender.

Ellin's next shot was wayward, and he stamped his foot before slumping into a chair in disgust.

Jek took a deep breath, studied the table, and calmly potted a blue ball. Then another. Ellin muttered a curse, and Jek shrugged as he ran the table.

"This boy knows how to play Three Rings."

Jek turned as he straightened up, setting the butt end of his cue on the floor next to his foot. The speaker was the tallest of the three humans, almost as tall as Jek himself. His pale face had a pinched look, narrowed blue eyes flanking his aquiline nose within a curtain of blonde hair. Thin lips curled within a square jaw narrower than typical for a human. It might have been a friendly smile, had the air of mockery not been so obvious.

Everyone's eyes were on Jek. The bartender drifted along the bar towards them.

"You guys want the table?" Jek asked, polite, not deferential. Definitely not deferential. "We just finished a game."

"So I saw." The speaker indicated his companions with a casual gesture. "My friends play, but their skills are lamentable. No, if I'm to enjoy myself, I wish to challenge you to a game, LightFolk."

Jek suppressed a scowl as his gaze flicked to the speaker's two companions. They were also blond, but thicker set, their otherwise pleasant enough faces twisted in predatory leers. He recognized the dynamic. He'd seen bosses and enforcers before, more often than he cared to admit.

Walk away. You don't have to play, you don't have to do anything these humans want you to.

But fuck that. He and Ellin had been there first. And he was tired of backing down to human pricks like this.

"Sure," he said with a jauntiness he didn't feel. "But only if I get a name."

The speaker's eyes glinted, but his smile broadened. "Fenner Castlewood," he announced, taking a blocky ring off his right index finger and stuffing it in a back pocket. "I'll take the reds your friend conveniently left all over the table. Care for a friendly wager?"

He's a Castlewood? Great.

But Jek couldn't back down now.

"I doubt I have anything you'd want," he said, arranging his blues in their crescent shaped starting configuration. He wondered how good his opponent was.

"Oh, I don't want anything you can't afford. First punch."

Jek blinked. "First what?"

Fenner grinned with what could only be called sadistic delight. "First punch. If you win, you get the first punch, see if you can put me on the floor. If I win, I get that honor. Let's bring some life to this dive! Your break, prim."

Jek forced himself to ignore the insult, and turned back towards the table. He'd faced down bullies before, but not a Castlewood, and not in a place he'd never expected to meet one. Could he talk his way out of this? The hungry glint in Fenner's eye suggested not.

Ellin perched on the edge of his seat and exchanged a mournful look with his friend, even as Fenner's companions stood flanking him. Low conversation buzzed around them, but few of the other patrons met Jek's eye for even a moment before turning away.

He was screwed.

Setting the cue ball on the center spot, Jek considered his options. The smartest play was to throw the game, or hope

Fenner was actually good enough to win, so that Jek could lose honorably. Take a punch, go down, and hope that would satisfy the smug scion of one of Novomond's wealthiest and most storied families. A few moments of humiliation, far away from his own kith and kin, in a place that kept its secrets close. It was the smart play.

He couldn't do it. Not without putting up a fight first, literally if he had to. He broke, and the players set up their Vanguard, the first three balls played before any rings were open. One of Fenner's reds encroached on the white circle painted around one of the holes, and with a muttered curse he reset that ball. Jek was fairly sure the mistake was deliberate, but that didn't mean he couldn't take advantage.

Books had been written about Three Rings strategy, and in recent years social media channels had posted videos of those and more. As with warfare, the strategies fell into two broad groups. When playing for fun, Jek enjoyed the thrill of a high risk, high reward attack, gambling on certain rings opening at certain times. Even when it failed, his opponents weren't always good enough to take advantage.

When the stakes were high, and if the other player was good or, as with Fenner, an unknown quantity, patience was key. Defend and probe, sometimes passing up easy rings as part of the longer game. He was good at it, but before all fourteen balls were in play, it was clear Fenner was too. The mistake had been an invitation to attack, which would have left the table open to running if Jek gambled wrong. The human's wistful smile was his only acknowledgment that his LightFolk opponent hadn't fallen for the ruse.

The game played out in a tense silence that soon infected the entire bar. No one left their seats, but other conversations died, or fell to whispers. The entrance door opened once, but the group of LightFolk laborers took one look at the situation and decided to take their meager patronage elsewhere.

Fenner appeared calm and unruffled, but his eyes narrowed to intense slits every time he played. Sweat beaded on Jek's brow, and his mind worked furiously to understand his opponent's tactics. They were both trying to set up a run, waiting for the other player to make the first mistake.

Jek made it. The cue ball clipped one of his own blues on the way back from the rail, and deflected into the open ring. He stared at the hole in horror, then stepped back from the table with a grim face.

It's for the best, he told himself, but couldn't make himself believe it.

Fenner grinned in portentous silence, before turning the randomizer and sinking his first red. Only an unforced error could save Jek now.

Fenner's second to last red lipped out.

That mistake had *not* been deliberate. It was the human's turn to look aghast, and he licked his lips before stepping away. Jek caught the look he gave his companions, and hoped Ellin was paying attention. Then he ran the table.

If anything, the tension in the bar ratcheted up a notch. How dare a LightFolk, a mere prim, defeat a Castlewood at anything?

"Well played," Fenner drawled, setting his cue back in the rack and turning to face Jek with a dreadful smile. From the corner of his eye, Jek saw Ellin stand, only for Fenner's friends to grab his arms with a warning not to interfere. "You get first punch. Put your cue down first though."

Jek hesitated, mind working furiously as he set his cue onto the table surface.

"And if I don't want to fight?"

Fenner's eyes glinted. "You made that choice when you accepted my challenge. First on their knees loses. Take your shot, prim. But you'd better put me down first punch, cos you won't get another."

Centuries of arrogance and contempt distilled into one little shit, facing Jek down like pre-pubes on the first day of school.

Suddenly, the thought of all the violence and petty indignities Fenner's kind had inflicted on the Folk seized hold of Jek's brain. To everyone's horror, not least his own, he drew back his fist and swung it with every shred of righteous anger and revenge at the human's jaw.

Yielding the first punch was one thing. Standing still, accepting it without taking evasive action was another thing entirely. Fenner swayed sinuously, and although Jek's knuckles made contact, it was merely a glancing blow. And he was extended, and ill prepared for the counterpunch. He flinched at the last moment, but Fenner's fist drove into his skull, just high enough that thicker bone absorbed enough of the impact to keep him conscious.

Jek staggered, but this wasn't his first brawl. He set his feet and blocked Fenner's follow up, landed another glancing blow that nonetheless forced the human back. The two circled each other, fists raised. Fenner's eyes narrowed with malice. Jek realized the only way he was going to walk out of Black Star was by putting his opponent on the ground. So be it.

"Stay back!"

From the corner of his eye, Jek saw one of Fenner's companions train a machine pistol on the bartender, who had advanced from behind his bar brandishing a wooden cudgel studded with iron spikes.

An intimidating weapon, an enforcer's weapon. A legal weapon.

The pistol was not, but since when had the same rules applied to the likes of the Castlewoods?

The third human held Ellin in an easy headlock, and his friend's frantic attempts to escape grew feebler by the second.

"Fucking prims," snarled Fenner. "You're all such a bunch of pussies. No wonder my ancestors—"

Jek attacked with a flurry of roundhouse blows that would have laid out most men within seconds. Fenner dodged and blocked them with contemptuous ease, landed a stunning counterpunch above Jek's left eye, then drove his fist into the pit of his stomach. Jek fought to stay on his feet, but struggled to breathe, and could do nothing but paw at Fenner's arm as the human grabbed him by the shirt and hauled him onto his toes.

"How disappointing. About as much resistance as your ancestors gave mine all those long years ago. I never understood why we didn't just wipe you out. You're not even good slaves."

Jek spat in his face. "Fuck you." Behind him, he heard a whip-like snap of bone, followed by Ellin's wail of agony.

Fenner didn't bother to wipe the spittle from his cheek. Almost in slow motion, he drew his fist back for a final blow, lips curled in a rictus grin of gleeful hate.

Was this all Jek had left? Spit and profanity?

No, of course not. He had one last card to play, one final recourse for a life threatening situation. All LightFolk did. The implications of using it were too terrible to think about. But as Fenner leaned into his punch, Jek had no time to think, only to act.

Closing his eyes, he summoned every reserve of energy he possessed. His whole body vibrated with it, as if he'd grabbed a live electrical wire and couldn't let go. Warmth flooded his chest and his ears roared, the roar of his ancestors. As he'd been trained to do, he wrapped the energy in The Word of the Mother and unleashed it.

The last thing he saw, through the blurred slits of his burning eyes, were the bloody remnants of what had once been Fenner Castlewood thumping to the floor.

An instant later, Jek's unconscious body joined them.

Only those slumped, or fallen, closest to the fistfight's horrific conclusion might have seen the pebble-sized globule of molten grey metal beading in the palm of Jek's outstretched right hand.

2

LATE NIGHT CALL

Xavier West's date wasn't going well. If he was being honest, the interruption from his ringing work phone was a mercy.

"Sorry, I've got to take this," he apologized, rising to his feet.

The pretty, but unimpressed, blonde with whom he'd failed to make sparkling conversation all evening rolled her eyes and picked up her own phone. Xavier turned away, looking for a more private spot in the busy steak restaurant. He wondered if she'd still be sitting there when he got back, and wouldn't blame her if she wasn't.

"What's up, Sharol?" He cupped his phone close to his mouth as he huddled by an indoor sourfruit tree that obstructed the corridor between the toilet doors. "I'm on a date."

"Really?" Amusement laced his young partner's deep, melodious voice. "How's it going?"

"Terrible. Absolutely nothing in common. So much for dating in my forties. I don't know what Alira was thinking."

"Your sister loves you, and wants you to be happy."

"She has an odd way of showing it. What do you need?"

All humor vanished. "Call came in. Bad one. How soon can you make it to Dockside?"

Xavier pinched the bridge of his nose as he considered. "Give me a quarter tenth."

He flagged down the waiter and asked for the check. "Sorry," he apologized to the blonde, who had paused during a text message and raised her eyebrows in inquiry. "Work, I'm afraid. Do you want anything boxed up? I'll call you a cab."

She shook her head. He wondered if she'd been texting Alira, demanding her own explanation for his sister's poor matchmaking skills. "Thank you, that won't be necessary. I already called one."

Despite his awkwardness, Xavier insisted on pulling out her chair and waiting with her at the front of the restaurant. She didn't object. She even repeated her assessment from the start of the evening, looking him up and down with a critical eye. He wished he owned clothes bought within the last decade.

"Work, you said? You're with the Bureau of Folk Affairs, right? What's so important at this time of night?"

"Nothing good," he muttered. Sure, now she showed a spark of interest in him, almost literally as the cab pulled up outside. With a perfunctory "Thank you for dinner," she turned her back and walked out through the door he held open for her.

Xavier breathed in, and regretted giving up smoking for the hundredth time. How much worse could this evening get?

He'd really have to stop asking himself questions like that.

Fluorescent orange police tape cordoned off the entire street outside Black Star. A chaotic jumble of police cruisers and ambulances throttled the street. Hordes of onlookers, visiting the dirty, dark backstreets of Dockside in search of one vice or another, battled frustrated police officers for a taste of that greatest vice of all: the sight, smell and sound of carnage, of sudden, grisly death and destruction.

Most of the crowd appeared to be human. He assumed all able LightFolk had already vacated the area, and couldn't blame them.

Xavier squeezed his car into a parking spot next to a fire hydrant two blocks away from The Mews. He jammed a wide brimmed black hat over his thinning hair before hurrying back down the uneven sidewalk. His politeness degraded with each step he forced through the mob, until he was practically beating people over the head with his BFA badge.

"What happened?" he heard a gruff male voice demand.

"Some fuckin' prim went berserk," another slurred, presumably the worse for drink. "Used their magic an' slaughtered th' whole bar. Humans too."

Brothers, I hope not.

Xavier found Sharol easily enough. Spiky green hair rose above the throng, her natural height increased by the thick soles of her riot boots. Her deep crimson jacket concealed a lithe, athletic figure, poised for action as her light, almond-shaped eyes surveyed the scene. Folk Affairs wasn't a bureau for the faint of heart, especially for someone rumored to possess Folk blood in their own veins. Showing a modicum of good sense, the muttering crowd gave her what berth they could, a pocket of free air amidst the booze and drug-tainted stink.

"I haven't been down here in a while," Xavier said, shouldering his way between a pair of heavily tattooed men he guessed were dock workers. They glowered at him, but kept their curses to themselves. "What's the sitch?"

Sharol gestured at the phalanx of emergency vehicles. Two gurneys prepared to load their blanketed contents into adjacent ambulances, as uniformed police officers milled around without obvious purpose. "Seven confirmed dead, almost twice that number wounded, some severely. I'm talking lost limbs here. Most are LightFolk." She grimaced, and swallowed as if nauseated.

"Most?" Xavier scanned the scene, looking for the officer in charge. He wondered if he would regret eating this evening. His steak hadn't been that great on its way down.

"Two of the dead are humans. According to the third, who probably won't last the night according to the single cop who'd talk to me, one of those is a Castlewood."

"Fuck. Relation to the senator?"

"Still working on that. But merely the name—"

"I know. Have you gone inside yet?"

Sharol shook her head, flashing a grim smile. "I was waiting for you."

Xavier held up his badge and flagged down a passing policeman, a wide-eyed kid who looked no older than his daughter. "Xavier West and Sharol Kostellan, Bureau of Folk Affairs. Can I speak to whoever's in charge here?"

"Umm, that would be Chief Detective Sorens," the youngster said, eyeing the badge. He offered nothing more.

Is this his first homicide? Or is it truly that bad?

"Can you take us to Chief Detective Sorens, please?" Xavier asked.

The policeman looked around, as if for permission or assurance. Everyone else was either too busy with the dead and wounded, or similarly dazed. He bit his lip and raised the orange tape. "He's inside. Come with me."

They followed his winding path through the shocked, the injured, and the first responders trying to help. Harsh white flashlights augmented the streetlamp's sullen glow, as medics examined and patched up injuries that, while not life threatening, were often grisly.

"These are the ones able to walk out," muttered Sharol.

Quiet orders and reassurances offset the sobs and moans of the wounded. The Mews stank of blood, shit, and fear. In one corner, near Black Star's guarded entrance, blankets covered the worst of a line of bodies and body parts. As they approached, two paramedics wearing blood-soaked green scrubs carried what was left of another victim through the door. The young LightFolk was missing his left arm and leg, and about a third of his skull.

The young policeman retched, although nothing came up. Xavier covered his mouth, but forced himself to watch as the paramedics laid the body down and covered it with what looked like a black plastic trash bag.

"Anything else I need to know before we go in?"

"Two things," Sharol murmured, as their escort stammered an explanation to his more seasoned counterparts at the door. "The perp is still alive, and he produced truesilver."

Xavier groaned, and suppressed an urge to turn around and run all the way home. "Double fuck. This gets better and better."

"BFA? This is a crime scene." A new voice emerged from inside Black Star. Xavier looked up to see a tall older man, whose pale, bald head shone in the interior's reflected glare like just another light bulb. Despite the evening's warmth, he wore black gloves and a gunmetal grey, ankle length trench coat. Deep set, almost colorless eyes examined the new arrivals with open disdain.

"I'm Senior Agent West with the Thornburg bureau. This is Agent Kostellan, my partner. The crime is why we're here. According to the statute—"

"I'm aware of the statute. Just because the law allows you to be here, doesn't mean you can obstruct my investigation."

Allows? Obstruct? Xavier bristled, but decided to let it pass. He needed to see inside the bar. "Detective Sorens—"

"*Chief* Detective Sorens."

"Ah, there's the introduction I was waiting for. We have no intention of interfering with your investigation. Investigate away! But we are required to assess the impact to the Folk community, and report back to the Senate. We can't do that from outside the bar."

Sorens's lip curled, and he looked like he wanted to defy what was obviously an inconvenient law. Then he turned towards someone else inside. "Gallish, can you spare a few moments to escort our *friends* from the Bureau of Folk Affairs, while they perform their very important official duties? Don't let them touch anything."

"I understand the LightFolk man accused of the crime is still alive," Xavier persisted. "We'll need to speak with him."

"Fine," Sorens replied, through gritted teeth. "But only if Gallish is present."

"Of course."

The Chief Detective stalked off without another word, to be replaced by another officer who couldn't be more different. Short, dark-skinned, sporting a faux-calfskin black jacket and tight fitting pants, Gallish peered at the newcomers with fierce curiosity.

"Chae Gallish," she introduced herself, offering a hand which both Xavier and Sharol shook in turn. "Don't mind the CD. He's just extra pissed because he got called away from his grandson's first birthday party."

"These things don't happen to suit our schedules," said Xavier. He didn't miss the calculating intelligence in Gallish's eyes, despite her overt friendliness. "May we come in?"

Gallish hesitated, then gestured for them to do so. "I hope you have strong stomachs."

Xavier gagged despite himself as the increased stench of blood and bodily fluids assailed him. Trails of viscera radiated in a bloody starburst over the floor, ceiling, and broken furniture, originating from a point near the ruins of a Three Rings table at the back of the room. Secondary starbursts streaked the far end of the bar, and what he assumed were doors to the toilets. A shocking amount of blood pooled near the table: several irregular crimson splotches, more than enough to kill a single person. Blankets and jackets covered suspicious lumps on the floor, denser towards the rear, but there was one, arm-shaped lump not five steps away.

One LightFolk perp was responsible for all this? Xavier thought he could guess what happened, but he needed to hear it from others before jumping to any conclusions.

"Holy Brothers," gasped Sharol, stumbling to a halt within a rare patch of clean floor.

Xavier turned to Gallish, who watched them through narrowed eyes. "All the dead and wounded have been taken away already? That was fast."

She nodded. "Many needed emergency surgery. Those with more superficial wounds are outside with the paramedics, and giving statements to my colleagues. I've seen some things in my time, but this…"

Gallish trailed off and gestured at the carnage. Chief Detective Sorens stood at the back of the room, flanked by two burly police officers, talking to someone Xavier couldn't see.

"What do we know about what happened?"

Gallish paused, likely considering how little she could get away with sharing. "Bar fight gone bad," she said at last. "An argument after a Three Rings game. LightFolk kid used magic." She waved her hand at the room, and this time it trembled, from fear or anger, or both.

There it was. The ultimate taboo. Xavier had only seen the results of violent, unsanctioned magic a handful of times. It never got easier.

"Agent West." Sorens turned around and beckoned Xavier with an abrupt gesture. "I want you to see this. For your report. Just you."

After exchanging a grim look with his partner, Xavier tiptoed carefully around the blood, gore and shattered glass to where the Chief Detective waited within a cluster of orange crime scene markers. Sharol followed anyway. As they approached, a fourth figure lay slumped on one of the few unbroken chairs. Blood soaked the young LightFolk's smart but simple clothes. It splashed his dark skin and soot black curly hair. When he lifted his head, slowly as if drugged, his eyes were so bloodshot they were almost entirely red.

"This is Agent West from the Bureau of Folk Affairs," Sorens said, brusque and dispassionate. He ignored Sharol. "Show him, before I take it into evidence."

The LightFolk simply sat there in silence. Bruises marred his face, and a knot blossomed above his left eye. Was that from the fight, or from afterwards? Xavier knew better than to ask.

"What's your name, son?" Xavier said, taking off his hat as he squatted awkwardly to face level. He would have to be the "good cop" here.

"Jek." The youngster's voice was barely a whisper escaping his swollen lips. "Jek One Raven."

One Raven? Worse and worse.

"What happened, Jek? What do you have to show me?"

Jek's bloody eyes appeared to focus on Xavier's, searching in mute appeal. "I thought he was going to kill me. I... I had no choice."

Then he dropped his gaze to his fist as he uncurled his fingers. Xavier gasped. That much truesilver from one LightFolk could only mean one thing.

"Death Curse," he muttered, before he could stop himself.

"See, you guys from the BFA have your uses after all," Sorens declared with satisfaction. He brandished an open evidence bag in front of Jek's face. "Put it in there. Then we're gonna haul your ass downtown. You're gonna find out what happens to prims who kill humans, who use a fucking Death Curse on a Castlewood."

3

BACK TO SCHOOL

Sorens promised to share the official police report with the BFA as early as the following morning.

Xavier did not interpret this as a good sign.

"Let's regroup in the morning," he told Sharol as they emerged from Black Star half a tenth later. Most of the ambulances were gone, and the gawking crowd had thinned. He yawned and rubbed his eyes. "They won't tell us where they're taking Jek. Maybe it'll be in their report. But all Chaos is gonna break loose tomorrow."

Xavier's phone rang moments after he'd merged his car onto the elevated expressway heading north towards his apartment. He groaned when he saw the caller ID: DeArei Bisset, Senior Administrator of the Bureau for Folk Affairs.

"I was wrong. Chaos found me already," he muttered, and answered the call.

"West? What the fuck is going on in Thornburg?" DeArei had a deep voice and, typically in his years of experience, an even temper. When she lost it, as often seemed to happen around Xavier, her menacing growl reminded him of his old boarding school principal.

He forced himself to take a deep breath, and switched his car into the highway's slow lane.

"I was planning to call you tomorrow morning, after we receive the official police report."

"Fuck the police report! I heard we've got a Death Curse on our hands, with human casualties."

How had she heard that already? "From who?"

She made a disgusted noise. "I just spent the last quarter tenth listening to Brogan Castlewood scream at me. Well, not scream. The senator never screams. He speaks the words, and it still sounds like he's screaming. He interrupted the opera... Fuck!"

Xavier bit back a complete lack of empathy for the ruin of his boss's evening's entertainment. If the fiery senator from Sentarino was making calls, the situation had already spiraled beyond his control. He doubted he'd ever see Jek One Raven again.

"What do you want me to do?" he asked tiredly. "Run damage control here in Thornburg? I'll reach out to the local LightFolk Academy and the One Water Elders in the morning, maybe put their truesilver production facilities on high alert. There are gonna be reprisals, you know that."

"I know. Did you meet the perp? This One Raven kid?"

"Briefly, yes."

"Is he a Chaos Walker?"

Brothers, this is getting out of hand.

"Chaos Walk is a DarkFolk movement, DeArei. As far as I can tell, he's just a scared LightFolk kid from Starshine who made a really bad decision."

A series of clicks and some scuffling echoed over the connection, then DeArei continued in calmer tones. "You understand these are the questions others are asking me. It's been almost a decade since the last Death Curse, but if Chaos Walk existed back then, no one but the DarkFolk knew about it. People like Senator Castlewood will connect the two, and use it to push their agenda. Things are about to get a lot worse for the Folk, Dark and Light."

"What can I do?" Xavier repeated.

"Clear your calendar. I want you in New Ashbrook tomorrow."

Xavier bit his lip before replying. He had mixed emotions about Novomond's capital city and the life he'd left there. He cleared his throat. "Don't tell me you want me to talk to the senator." He tried not to make it sound like a question. He wanted no part of Brogan Castlewood's latest tirade.

"Fuck the senator. Let him shit down my neck all he wants. I want you to spend time with the LightFolk co-principal of the Metropolitan Academy. If anyone can avert the worst of the carnage to come, it's Pralik One Raven."

The founders of the Metropolitan Academy had chosen its innocuous name to distract from the institution's purpose. Nestled in a relatively quiet enclave near the heart of the nation's capital, the three story building had initially housed a religious school of the now defunct Evonite sect. Streaks of soot-colored grime marred its once gleaming white stone exterior, and rendered most of the windows opaque.

For all that, his first sight of the early Earian architecture still impressed Xavier as he climbed out of his airport taxi. He wheeled his travel bag across the pitted sidewalk, stopping at the robust iron gate guarding the steps up to the grand double entrance doors.

"Xavier West of the Bureau for Folk Affairs," he introduced himself to the receptionist over the intercom unit. Why did they always hang the damn things so high? "I have an appointment to see Pralik One Raven."

The unhelpful crackle of static was his only reply. He was just about to repeat himself when another voice answered. "Please hold, Mister West. Someone will be with you shortly."

His sigh turned into a yawn. His alarm had roused him at 5:00 that morning, a half-tenth earlier than usual. He'd battled a swarm of business travelers at the understaffed and borderline dysfunctional Thornburg airport, only for a "minor mechanical issue" to delay boarding. A suspicious hint of airplane fuel permeated the full cabin during the tenth it took to fly to New Ashbrook. After stopping in the arrivals court to buy painkillers for his ensuing headache, he'd waited much longer than usual for a taxi into the city.

He could have sworn the day was half over. All he craved was a nap in a comfortable hotel room bed. Instead, he blinked fatigue and drizzle from his eyes and inhaled the familiar post-industrial tang of the city air.

The doors opened and a thickset man emerged. The nondescript black suit of a security detail clung to his muscular frame, tighter than necessary or likely comfortable. A holstered pistol jutted out from his right hip, and a walkie-talkie from his left.

The ensemble had the desired effect.

Intense gray eyes scrutinized Xavier from beneath a shock of black hair, shaved above jutting ears. The guard descended the steps, but didn't speak until he'd unlocked the gate and waved Xavier through.

"Arms out, please."

Xavier suppressed a sigh at his second full body frisk of the morning. "Is this standard procedure at the Academy? Or a recent development?"

The guard grunted as he patted down his visitor's legs. Xavier guessed it was too much to hope for sparkling conversation from the school's security staff.

He presented his Bureau of Folk Affairs ID card and endured the guard's careful scrutiny, even taking off his hat. He'd had a lot more hair in that picture. Finally, the guard nodded.

"Follow me," he said, and led Xavier into the two story entrance foyer.

It was much larger than he'd expected. Fluted marble columns flanked the three interior walls, forming colonnades around a central area strewn with sumptuous couches of a style briefly popular a hundred years before. The checkered tile floor gleamed in the soft radiance emitted by enormous spherical lamps, suspended from the ceiling high above. Everything was monochrome, blacks, whites, and shades of gray, as if he had stepped into a photograph taken during the couches' heyday. The faint scent of antiseptic reminded him of his own school days, as did the distant murmur of conversation, or rather instruction.

The guard gave Xavier a security pass, which he clipped to his suit jacket's lapel before following his escort down a broad hallway. He glanced inside the utilitarian school office, where a middle aged LightFolk sat behind a large desk. Her dark, almond-shaped eyes projected patience as she listened to the other end of her phone conversation. Meanwhile, a fair-skinned human woman of about the same age, who Xavier guessed might be the school nurse, knelt in front of a sobbing young girl. As he watched, she enfolded the student in a tender hug. The sight soothed him.

Opposite the office was a classroom, the door closed for a lesson. Xavier paused. The students standing poised behind reinforced glass shields looked a little older than their distraught counterpart in the office, maybe ten or eleven years. He was surprised to see a practical classroom so close to the office and main entrance, shields or no. The level of magic taught to this age may not be as risky as what the students would encounter during their teenage years, but all magic was perilous.

Sure enough, a flash of blinding light behind one shield preceded a shriek of agony. When his vision cleared, Xavier saw the teacher, a striking LightFolk woman no older than himself, dousing flames raging around a boy's face. The poor lad screamed in agony, even after the teacher healed his horrific burns.

"That one won't make it," observed the security guard. He and Xavier stepped aside as the harried teacher ushered the whimpering boy into the office across the hallway. Xavier raised his eyebrows in question, and the guard shrugged. "Second time this tennight. Doesn't matter who your family is. If you can't make truesilver, you don't belong here."

And then what? There were few options for a LightFolk who couldn't contribute to society in the only way society valued.

The second door down from the office sported a brass nameplate.

Pralik One Raven
Co-Principal

The inscription had faded a little, suggesting Pralik had held his position for some time. Xavier knew him by reputation, but they had never met. He did not relish this conversation as their introduction.

The door was half open, but the guard knocked on it anyway. He announced the visitor and stepped aside.

Xavier walked into a room best described as a library within a forest. Hundreds if not thousands of print books adorned shelves that were branches of one living tree, originating from a knotted trunk on the far wall. Its roots spread into a verdant moss-like carpet, before contorting into a desk supporting a flat screen monitor. He could see no electrical cables.

Slim leaves of iridescent silver green framed the living bookshelves, and reflected the soft glow of lamps similar to those in the foyer. Few of the books sported the simple modern bindings of those you could still buy in Novomond's few remaining retail stores. Leather spines of various dark hues blended with the woodland vibe as if it was the most natural thing in the world.

Looking equally at home was Pralik One Raven himself. The tall, lithe LightFolk stood behind his desk holding a phone to his ear, nestled in strands of shoulder length hair only a shade darker than his skin. Keen eyes flanked a thinner nose than was usual for his kind, but his traditional flowing robe of amber with jet black trim identified him as an Elder of the One Raven people. He acknowledged Xavier with a polite nod, but held up a slim finger in a request for patience.

"I understand," he murmured into the phone. "Give him the choice of rejoining lessons or recuperating in the office. I will contact his family. Thank you, Shala."

The phone disappeared within Pralik's robes. The LightFolk stared at the office's one window, its glass clean and clear despite what Xavier had seen outside. Then he emerged from his thoughts and turned to his guest. "My apologies, Mr. West. I take the struggles of my students to heart. Sit, please."

Pralik's voice was deep, resonant, and devoid of noticeable accent.

Xavier waved off the apology as he settled on a chair crafted from a whorl of tree root. It was surprisingly comfortable. "Xavier, please. I would expect no less from a co-principal and a *chiek'la* of the Folk. Your office is magnificent."

Pralik inclined his head in acknowledgement of the compliment, and perhaps Xavier's use of the old One Raven word for "elder". "I claim it is for the benefit of my students, an example of what may be accomplished using the Art by a skilled practitioner. Of course, most who graduate from my academy face tasks far more mundane, brute force labor to expedite the production of truesilver for the benefit of all. That is the Bureau of Folk Affairs legacy, is it not?"

"In return for retaining as much Folk culture as possible," Xavier countered, trying not to sound defensive. Pralik hadn't threatened him exactly, but there was a sharp edge to his voice. Old wounds ran deep. Just because the Elder facilitated the fragile peace between his people and their human conquerors didn't mean he harbored no resentment.

Another nod, tighter this time. "Of course. It is fascinating that creating beauty such as this produces more, and purer truesilver than menial tasks. Naturally, it pleases me also. I can sometimes forget that I live in the midst of the largest human city in Novomond, and believe myself roaming the pristine forests of my ancestors."

Xavier hadn't come to New Ashbrook to debate old iniquities. "What will happen to the boy? I heard this wasn't his only recent injury."

Pralik's expression turned grim. "Uncertain. He is One Sky, a prominent clan as I'm sure you know. They will not take his failure well. They will beseech me to keep him here, procure private tutors to help him keep up with his classmates. I may allow them to do so, for a time. The alternatives, as you know, are few."

Menial work, the tasks so low even the poorest humans would shun. Or options even more unspeakable. For a proud family from One Sky, that would be too much to countenance. Xavier pitied the boy.

"We've never met, Xavier West," Pralik continued, "but I know you by name, and a little by reputation." He gave a thin smile at Xavier's surprise. "My son and your daughter are classmates, it appears."

"At Segard Law School?"

"Indeed. Davek is one of the first of our people to study there. Segard is known as a hotbed of progressive ideas, including its support of LightFolk advocates for LightFolk affairs. I believe Davek has an interest in joining your Bureau when, and if, he earns his accreditation."

"I'm glad to hear it," Xavier said. He thought the barrier to a LightFolk becoming a lawyer might be insurmountable, but was too polite to say so. Even if it made sense at many levels. A LightFolk's career options had expanded beyond the truesilver factories in the last two decades, but he couldn't imagine the establishment tolerating one in a courtroom unless they'd been accused of a crime.

He wondered what Ariadne thought of the idea. She still hadn't responded to his messages, asking if they could have lunch or dinner later.

"We shall see. But you are here to discuss the unfortunate events in Thornburg, are you not? My time is valuable, and I'm sure yours is too. What can I do for you?"

Xavier shifted in his chair, steeling himself for the meat of the conversation now that greetings were over. "I hope you can help me do what is best for your people. The Folk, and the One Raven clan in particular."

Pralik's lips thinned. "Is it your intent to suggest we absorb all indignities and reprisals with our customary stoicism?"

"Not at all. While emotions are fraught right now, few would blame the entirety of One Raven, or the Folk, for the regrettable actions of one frightened young man. I believe you, and your fellow Elders, have an opportunity to speak for your people and your family. Cooler heads must prevail."

"Must they?" Pralik regarded his visitor in solemn silence for several awkward heartbeats.

Xavier squirmed in his seat, but forced himself to wait. To listen. Too often, the BFA tried to dictate specific actions to the Folk, the LightFolk especially. He hoped Pralik was as practical as his reputation suggested, and would arrive at his own solution.

With Xavier's help, of course.

"Regrettable, you say?" Pralik continued, eyes hooded. "Perhaps. Certainly, few would wish to see a Death Curse invoked against anyone, whatever the circumstances. I know only a little of Jek One Raven. Our mothers' fathers were cousins, once removed. I understand he was a promising student at Thornburg's Starshine Academy. Impetuous and foolish at times, but weren't we all? I also know, as do you, that his life is over. It remains only to see if the mob kills him before the Curse plays out."

"I met him last night." Xavier shared his brief encounter with the stunned teenager in the ruins of Black Star. "I understand that without adequate preparation and immediate attention, a Death Curse is as deadly to the caster as it is to the victim. I would prefer it run its course, and no spectacle be made of his death. I'm hoping you can help with that."

Pralik raised an eyebrow. "Indeed? How? Those few you speak of, who would blame me and all LightFolk for Jek's Death Curse, are both vocal and powerful." He gestured at his desk screen. "How many death threats do you think I have received since last night? How many have my students received? The entire Academy? My colleague, Co-Principal Vallance, stands before the Senate as we speak, petitioning for more security. That would be challenging at the best of times. I believe there is little chance of action when the most notable victim was the oldest son of one of Senator Brogan Castlewood's cousins."

Xavier shuddered. It had been a long time since the last mass casualty event directed at the Folk, especially LightFolk. Two, three years into his career with the BFA. Surely no one would attack a school, especially one patrolled by armed security guards?

Except shootings were not uncommon at human schools, classmate on classmates.

"I'll make a recommendation for more security on behalf of the BFA," he assured Pralik. "Here and other LightFolk academies around the nation."

"Thank you." Pralik's tone suggested he expected that would make little difference. He began pacing behind his desk. "I have discussed the situation with Loro One Water, the senior Elder of his clan in Thornburg, and with Varin Two Water here in New Ashbrook. Jek's companion was Two Water, and died also."

"I know. I called Loro from the airport this morning. I understand there is... tension between One and Two Water at present."

Pralik grimaced. "Loro wishes to present a united front, but I believe many One Water empathize strongly with their Two Water tributaries, including Loro's wife, Ajan, if I read between the lines correctly. They ask what would have led a young LightFolk man to break the ultimate taboo. Is that not something we should also discuss?"

"It is," Xavier acknowledged. "And I promise to do so. But there is a time and place for such discussion, if you really want to be heard."

The two men stared at each other in stony silence for several heartbeats. Xavier took a deep breath. "You think I'm giving you the run around, or looking for a quick fix at any cost? The Bureau has done that to the LightFolk often enough. I'm not. I want to help you and the Folk. I believe focusing now on what provoked Jek One Raven won't accomplish that."

Pralik held his gaze a moment longer, then sighed and rubbed tired eyes.

"Senator Castlewood has ramped up calls for greater control over my people's activities. More oversight of truesilver production, restrictions on employment, and movement. I even heard mention of curfews last tennight. He will use Thornburg to fan the flames of support in the Senate. What chances do I, and my fellow Elders, have to forestall even the worst of his designs?"

"What would your ancestors do?" Xavier asked.

Pralik cocked his head. "You wish to remind me of my ancestry?"

"Your people have customs, as do mine. In our past, problems like these were often solved in ways that allowed the offending party to retain honor. Senator Castlewood is a powerful man. I don't know him personally, but every powerful person I've ever met has been ruled by vanity. Perhaps you can appeal to it."

The One Raven Elder regarded Xavier with a thoughtful expression. "Perhaps we can," he agreed at last. His phone buzzed, and he frowned after glancing at the screen.

Xavier rose from his seat. "You're a busy man, Co-Principal One Raven. I won't take up any more of your time this morning. I'll be in town for three days. Please let me know if I can be of service."

"Thank you, Xavier," Pralik said, and extended his hand for a very human handshake.

4

DITCHING CLASS

Ariadne West witnessed murder for the first time two days after the Thornburg Death Curse.

She didn't think she'd led a sheltered life. Until her parents divorced when she was fifteen, they'd lived in Sandfield, a marginal suburb of New Ashbrook. Once a model for Novomond family life, many of the smaller homes crowding the deteriorating streets suffered from neglect. Those who could afford bigger houses further out from the city took their money with them, and businesses followed. The Sandfield Crossing Mall, one of the first and busiest in the nation, now lay derelict, home only to drug users and other criminals. She'd walked the streets with her high school friends and seen some shit. Done some shit too. Ariadne wasn't pure as the driven snow, no matter what her mother chose to believe.

But she'd never watched someone get killed in broad daylight. Right outside her North Embankment apartment building too. Mom would have a fit if she found out.

It was just after 5.50, three tenths into the new day, when she left for class. The on again off again elevator was off, so she hurried down four flights of stairs before they propelled her into the cool drizzle of Avon Avenue. She paused outside the building's double doors, preparing to head left into the heart of Embankment proper and walk the six blocks to Segard. Why was a crowd gathering?

To her right, at the corner with Empire Street, steps led down to the subway station. She often saw homeless Folk squatting on the sidewalk nearby, hoping to attract a few coins from the steady stream of commuters. They were mostly DarkFolk, lured from the poverty of the nearby Black Hills reservation to the smothered hope of a better life in the city.

That morning, Ariadne saw one such DarkFolk huddled over a tattered canvas bag, his bloodshot eyes peering up at a pair of belligerent human men not much older than she was.

"You stink, prim," the taller human spat, literally hawking a glob of phlegm onto the bag. He and his companion wore the collarless crimson shirts often associated with the Purists, a militant organization promoting ethnic cleansing of all Folk from "human cities".

"You're a fucking disgrace," snarled his companion, fervent eyes burning above a trim beard. "You and your kind don't belong anywhere near decent people."

Ariadne couldn't hear the beggar's mumbled response, but it enraged his harassers.

"Yeah? You got a death curse for us, asshole? Fuck you, prim!" The taller one kicked the DarkFolk in the head, so hard that the back of the man's skull ricocheted off the concrete slab of the wall behind him.

One or two onlookers gasped, either from shock or sick anticipation. The second Purist kicked the beggar's stomach, doubling him over. They kicked him again and again, his stomach, his head, his legs, his feebly protesting arms.

No one intervened. No one even said anything.

The attackers unleashed a frenzy of violence on the defenseless DarkFolk, and no one did a damn thing.

"What the fuck is wrong with you all?" Ariadne wondered, but not very loud. Certainly not loud enough for the Purists to hear. She turned and looked at the street around her, searching in vain for police or anyone who could and would help.

She dug out her phone and dialed emergency services, but by the time someone answered and demanded her name and location, the broken DarkFolk sprawled in a spreading pool of his own blood. The two redshirts strutted down into the subway with an arrogant, almost contemptuous glance at the crowd.

The taller man's eyes rested on hers for a moment. Her breath caught in the midst of her response to the emergency line, but he just favored her with a feral grin before vanishing out of sight.

"There's been an attack," she rattled out at last. Her phone shook in her trembling hand. "Someone's been hurt, bad. Maybe... maybe killed."

By the time a single police cruiser pulled up a few hundredths later, most of the crowd had dispersed, slinking away into the dispassionate morning. No one wanted attention, not from the police, and not from the Purists. Not for a homeless DarkFolk, who the world wouldn't miss anyway. Only an old LightFolk woman, bundled head to foot in a faded blue hooded cloak, kept Ariadne silent company as the beggar bled out onto the sidewalk.

The younger of the two officers sprayed a bright orange line around the victim and stood silent guard. Sirens heralded the imminent arrival of an ambulance. The second officer—no taller than Ariadne, but about twice as wide—offered what he likely thought was a comforting smile under a thick brown mustache.

"Terrible thing," he said, in the manner of someone missing their bus. "I'm sorry you had to see that, miss."

"There were two of them. I can describe them for you. The first—"

The officer held up his hand and grimaced. "In my experience, it's almost impossible to find these people. They just blend into the crowd."

Ariadne gaped at him. "But I can tell you what they looked like! Surely you can match that against a database—"

"Are you telling me how to do my job, little lady?" Any trace of conviviality vanished. He shook his head and stared at the corpse in distaste. "The number of tenths we'd have to sink into the effort, with little chance of success. It's not worth it. We've got higher priorities."

"Higher priorities than murder?"

"Keeping you safe. I don't expect people like you to thank me, but I do expect you to let me do my job. Thanks for calling it in."

People like me? People who give a shit if random DarkFolk are slaughtered on the street in broad daylight?

Ariadne quivered with fury as well as shock. The officer stepped between her and the victim, showing her his back. Her lips moved soundlessly as she tried to summon a reply.

A hand rested on her arm. She turned to see the LightFolk woman, staring at her in sad, silent entreaty.

The woman walked away when the ambulance arrived. She left Ariadne staring at the blood on the wall and the sidewalk, watching the paramedics load the corpse with emotionless efficiency, and smarting at the cop's casual indifference.

Alone, and not knowing what else to do, Ariadne continued on her way to class.

"In broad daylight? Holy shit, Ari! I would've been terrified!"

Maya Gortauld took Ariadne aside after their first lecture of the day. Property Law with the pompous Professor Cary was tedious at the best of times. That morning, his nasal voice washed over Ariadne like the background hum of city traffic, and she tapped listlessly at her screen keyboard. Maya sat next to her and stole glances of increasing frequency and concern.

Afterwards, she ushered her friend into a corner of the nearest common room and demanded an explanation.

"I *was* terrified," Ariadne confessed, bouncing on her toes as she surveyed the room. Bright, clean, utilitarian. A room with no opinions, that judged no one. A sprinkling of other law students huddled in small groups to study or simply catch up on each other's lives. In the far corner, politely shunned by everyone else, sat Davek One Raven and another LightFolk boy whose name she couldn't remember. She studiously avoided his gaze.

"Are they gonna give your apartment building extra protection?" Maya asked.

"From who?"

Maya bit her lip. An immaculate curtain of naturally blonde hair framed glacier blue eyes in a heart shaped face. Clothes from the latest designers hugged her svelte figure. She carried herself with effortless poise, a certainty that she not only belonged in any situation, but also commanded it. Ariadne often felt dumpy, her freckled skin and more pronounced curves overshadowed by Maya's glory, no matter how often her friend chastised her for talking nonsense.

Biting her lip that way likely endeared Maya to some of her many lovers. Here, though, Ariadne suspected she used it to give herself pause. She knew of her bestie's sympathies, and even if she didn't share them all, she respected them.

"It doesn't matter who the aggressor is if innocent people are hurt in the crossfire," Maya murmured. "I worry about you, Ari. Why don't you come stay with me for a few days? Let the bad buzz die down."

Ariadne forced a chuckle. "And get in the way of your love life? You'd never forgive me."

"You could always join in," Maya retorted with a flirtatious wink. "You know you're always welcome in my bed."

"That was just the one time. My college experiment." Ariadne blushed at the memory, but at least it was more pleasant than the image of the murdered DarkFolk on the sidewalk.

Maya grinned, then her expression sobered. She reached out and took her friend's hand. "I mean it. Stay a couple days. I'm here for you, Ari. I'll listen."

Ariadne took a deep breath. Maya's offer was tempting, not least because she lived less than a block from Segard's main buildings. "Thank you. I'll think about it. I will. But I don't want to run from what happened, either. This is the kind of injustice we're learning how to address. Maybe I need to experience it before I can truly understand it."

"There's my crusader," said Maya, with only a hint of mockery. She squeezed Ariadne's hand and kissed her on the cheek. "Message me, love. Anytime, anything you need. Okay?"

"I will. Thank you."

They exchanged tight smiles, then Maya straightened up with a dramatic flourish. Heads turned.

"I've got to run. Tort Reform with Gallagher, right after Property with Cary. Now *that* there should be laws against."

Ariadne brought up her schedule on her phone, even though she knew it well. Two more morning lectures before a group study session in the afternoon. Her heart wasn't in it. She shouldn't have come in, but she didn't want to be alone either.

She sensed she was being watched, and glanced at the far corner just as her phone vibrated. Davek turned his head a moment later to address his companion.

Unknown 1: Everything ok?

She permitted herself a half grin. She wouldn't be so bold as to include a LightFolk boy by name in her contacts. That would deter casual snoops, like Maya at least. She thought for a moment, then typed her reply.

No. Bad morning. Thinking of ditching.

She studied her screen intently, awaiting his reply.

Unknown 1: Ditch with me? Meet you in 50?

Sold

Ariadne gathered up her books and tablet, donned her jacket, and shuffled out of the common room. She ignored everyone, especially the two LightFolk in the corner.

Davek and his family owned a townhouse on Kulish Circle in the center of Oldtown, an easy half tenth walk from school. The park was the site of the first treaty signed two centuries before between the Folk and colonizing humans from across the Finemian Ocean. Today, it was pristine and peaceful. Residents, workers from nearby businesses, and occasional tourists enjoyed this oasis of green in the heart of the nation's capital.

Arriving early, Ariadne stood before the commemorative granite pillar in the exact center of the park. Decades of weather and official neglect had taken their toll on the bronze plaque celebrating the treaty, but she knew it failed to mention her ancestors had broken it within a decade.

When her phone vibrated again, she strolled north towards number thirteen. It was identical to every other narrow three story row house of golden brownstone, black door and window frames, and steeply pitched roof. Heart thudding in her chest, in anticipation rather than fear, she climbed the three steps from the cobblestone sidewalk and knocked on the door.

"I thought you were going to strand me out there," Ariadne said as she slithered inside. She took a deep breath of the fresh resinous air. It was what she imagined deep forest to smell like.

According to Davek, the Raven clans were famous for their connection to the natural world. That world had been invited into his family's home. Small trees masquerading as houseplants spread their dense leafy branches over its walls and ceiling, yet the hallway bathed in soothing yellow light from open doorways. She was always oddly disappointed not to hear songbirds or see them flitter from room to room.

Davek enfolded her in a warm hug. She rested her cheek on his shoulder and took a long shuddering breath.

"I heard what happened outside your apartment," he murmured in his lilting voice. "Do you want to talk about it?"

"I want you to hold me."

"I can do that."

They stood in silence for a while, his arms around her back, her hands on his chest. She could feel his heart's slow steady beat even as his breath tickled her forehead. He smelled of mint and fresh chopped wood. With each passing thud of her heart, she felt better, safer. She felt loved.

When he led her into the parlor and sat her next to him on the couch, she didn't object. Nor did she mind when he kissed her.

The thrill of his kisses never faded. Most of Ariadne's friends and acquaintances would disapprove, once they got over their shock. Only Maya, who she suspected had guessed something was going on, would refrain from condemning her outright. But as experimental as her own love life was, Maya might frown at what many considered a scandalous liaison.

Ariadne didn't care. None of her human boyfriends had lasted long, certainly not after the handful of times she'd capitulated to having sex with them. Sure, there was brief excitement and fulfillment, but after that? Nothing. No other boy would have asked if she wanted to talk before kissing her.

Davek's strong hand stroked the length of her spine, then strayed to her chest, cupping and gently fondling her breast. Even through the everwool of her shirt, the tips of his practiced fingers teased and tantalized.

"Are you taking advantage of a frightened young human girl, Davek One Raven?"

She grinned with mischief after breaking off the kiss. Brothers, he was beautiful! Eyes so dark brown they were almost black peered from beneath a mop of obsidian hair that framed the almost triangular face characteristic of his people. She loved his pointed jaw, his knife of a nose, and his soft skin the shade of worn leather.

"You're the one leading me into truancy, Ariadne West," he murmured. He held her eyes while he undid her top button. She trembled, needing this. Needing him.

"It was horrible," she said suddenly. Davek's fingers paused over the second button, and she mentally kicked herself, but the words were out now.

"My people suffer such every day, somewhere in this country." Davek's voice was mild, but she detected an undercurrent of outrage and anger.

"I know. I hate it. I hate the Purists and those who support them or stand by while they commit their atrocities. People like me."

She searched his face for the condemnation she deserved, but found only sadness. He kissed her, then undid her second button.

"What could you do, alone? Anyone capable of killing a defenseless man wouldn't let a single protestor stop them. It takes many of us working together to protect my people."

He undid another button, and slipped his hand inside her shirt. The heat of his deft fingers sent shivers across her chest. She began undoing the remaining buttons for him, as he brushed across the skin of her upper breasts and toyed with the strap of her bra.

Why that bra? You couldn't have worn something sexier?

"You're supposed to have protection," she murmured, unable to stop talking about it. She was nervous, always nervous with Davek, even more self conscious about her freckles and fuller figure than she had been with her prior, casual lovers. This wasn't casual. She didn't know what to call it exactly, but casual wasn't it. "The BFA—"

He kissed the swell of her breasts. She gasped, amazed by the way he looked at her, like she was the sexiest model who ever graced a runway.

"The BFA do what they can. Have you told your father about what you saw this morning?"

"No. I don't want him to worry, or want to see me again. One awkward dinner was enough."

"Awkward?"

Ariadne grimaced at the memory. She and Xavier had sat at a corner table in what used to be one of their favorite restaurants, struggling to find common ground that didn't reopen old wounds.

"It hurts him, returning to the city he grew up in, where we used to be a family together. And I'm not his little girl anymore."

"But surely he would want to protect you, if not the Folk. I never know exactly how much the Bureau of Folk Affairs is for us or against us."

Amid her need and desire, Ariadne surprised herself with the compulsion to defend her father. "He does care about the Folk, about what's right. We talked a lot about Thornburg, and what it might mean for humans and Folk alike. I guess it's a more comfortable subject than most others for us. He told me he met with your father, and suggested reparation based on ancient LightFolk custom. It might avoid even worse carnage."

"Xavier West suggested the honor killing?" Davek's eyes glinted, and suddenly he reminded her of a predator, a wolf defending its pack. And she'd literally bared her breast to him.

"Not that!" she gasped in a breathless rush. "Not the details. That was Pralik's—your father's—idea! And the Castlewood family refused the offer."

"They did," he muttered darkly. Then he seemed to remember himself. He kissed her breast again, warm lips lingering against her tingling flesh, while his hand searched behind her back for her bra clasp, and found it. "Do you wish to keep talking? Or would you prefer I use my mouth for other things?"

"I'm done talking," she said huskily. She carded his thick black hair with her fingers while he took her breast in his mouth, and she didn't resist when he slipped off her jeans and underwear too. His tongue trailed over her stomach, before nestling between her legs. She moaned and her head lolled to the side, her eyes unfocused.

Until she realized someone was watching them.

A tall, lithe young woman, dressed in a flowing ankle length robe of pale amber, stood in the open parlor doorway. Her brown face softened Davek's rougher edges, but the dark eyes that peered from beneath curtains of deep black hair burned with curiosity. Ariadne had never met Chiana, Davek's older sister, but didn't doubt this was her. She could have hoped for a better introduction than Chiana walking in as Davek went down on her.

"Davek," she whispered, tapping him lightly on the shoulder.

He raised his head enough to spy his sister arching her eyebrows, then muttered something along with an irritated wave. The door swung shut in Chiana's amused face.

The bead of truesilver produced by the spell was almost invisible in his palm, scarcely larger than a pinhead. But the liquid metal's vibration after he pushed it inside her was more than enough to make her come.

5

WALKING WITH CHAOS

Kit fisted the cheap, cream colored sheets and grunted as the second man entered her. His shaft was thinner and shorter than the man she straddled, so it wasn't as uncomfortable sliding into her ass as she'd feared.

This wasn't the first night she'd serviced these two men. She couldn't call them regulars yet, and hoped she never would. She paid as little attention to her clients' features as possible, especially their faces. It made it easier to forget afterwards.

Most paid to use her alone, demanding all that her young DarkFolk body had to offer for themselves. Five, six, sometimes seven in a night, nine nights out of ten. She'd do groups a handful of times each tennight, pairs of men, a man and a woman, sometimes more. It no longer bothered her. It no longer affected her in any way at all.

She gasped and moaned at all the right moments, and eventually both men pumped their seed inside her. No protection, of course. She was a whore, and no one paid to wear a condom when fucking a whore.

Besides, human men couldn't get Folk women pregnant. It was a well known fact.

There were many "facts" about the Folk that humans no longer questioned.

It would be their undoing.

The men pulled out of her, and she dismounted the one lying on the bed. She laid with her back against the pitted thin wall and watched them dress, ignoring her now that they had sated their desires.

"You wanna hit Duggan's for one more beer?" the first man asked.

"Nah, my crew are still working that window replacement job in South Kennerly. Fucking it up. I need to get out there early and knock heads together."

"C'mon dude, just one more beer. Fucking prims is thirsty work!"

"Fine. One more. You got the tab this time?"

"Yup." The first man, older with thinning sand colored hair, dug a hand into a pocket of his too tight pants. His buttonless shirt stretched over an unflattering paunch. He tossed a few bills onto the beaten old dresser next to the door, then sneered at her.

"Not bad, prim. Maybe we'll bring a friend next time, so they can do your mouth too."

She returned their gloating stares with a bland smile. They chuckled, and left.

Thank the Mother they were her last clients of the night. Madam Two Mountain closed her Dockside brothel as soon as the Day End Bell rang, at 3.00 Empire time.

The Day End Bell: another Folk tradition appropriated by their human conquerors to help make sense of their bizarre timekeeping system.

Kit washed up as best she could at the chipped sink in the corner, ignoring her reflection in the mirror above. She slipped into threadbare panties and her patched, clan agnostic black robe, then wrapped herself in a heavy cloak of the same color. Adding the cash from the dresser to the stack she extracted from under the thin mattress, she left her squalid room for the first time in four tenths.

Seven other DarkFolk girls, some older, some younger, lined up at Madam Two Mountain's table in the lavish entrance parlor. No one spoke as they handed over their night's earnings for their employer to take her cut. Old enough to be Kit's own mother, Madam Two Mountain's dark skin and flowing sable robe convinced most clients that she was Folk too.

Kit suppressed her disgust at the idea. If the Madam had been Folk, then Kit's clan would owe her allegiance, and the horror of what she did almost every night would be far greater. But the woman sitting in her comfortable chair, counting bills with satisfied greed, wasn't Folk, hadn't even been born on this continent. She was just another foreigner taking advantage of The Great Injustice.

"Eight fifty," Madam stated, no longer attempting to disguise the hitch in her accent. "Not bad, Kit. I need to send more pairs of clients your way. Those last two made a point to tell me how much fun they had."

Kit nodded and gave her the same bland smile as Madam slid three hundred dollars back across the table. "Of course," she murmured, realizing a reply was expected.

Madam dismissed her with a wave of a manicured hand. Kit Three Mountain stepped out of the brothel into the cool, night air, and hurried the five blocks to the transit terminal.

K'uelle ti-Lan'ot got on the bus headed to the Thorn River reservation.

She recognized other girls from the brothel, but no one acknowledged each other. K'uelle found a free seat near the back and waited while other DarkFolk arrived for their ride home. Whores and strippers mingled, in exhausted and defeated silence, with cleaners and dishwashers. No DarkFolk lived in Thornburg, not unless they were a slave in truth.

The bus shuddered into life after closing its doors, and limped along the two lane approach to the Frontier Bridge. Stark white light illuminated the suspension cables securing the triumphant concrete span of the city's main connection with the western half of the continent. After that? Nothing, not for hundreds of kilometres. At least, nothing that any civilized human would care about.

The journey to the reservation took over half a tenth. Despite the cold window rattling next to her, K'uelle snatched precious sleep. She needed her strength. Her night was far from over.

○⋯●

Many ti-Lan'ot and se-Perik families lived in isolated homesteads, scratching a living from the dusty, windswept soil that dominated the Thorn River Reservation. The triumphant Empire had rounded up ancestors of both clans from all but forgotten homelands to the east, and dumped them together.

As far as humans were concerned, Folk were Folk. The ti-Lan'ot and se-Perik may have allied to resist the invaders' violent overthrow of their way of life, but had little else in common. Consequently, those disinclined to grow desert corn or raise Black Kine chose to live in one of two shanty towns, named simply for their clans.

First Moon had yet to rise, and Second Moon's reflected light barely rivaled the brightest stars. The shacks and hovels of ti-Lan'ot City skulked in the darkness, neither threatening nor welcoming K'uelle as she stepped off the bus. Old model cars and rusting pickup trucks loitered among them like an unruly crowd on the edge of violence. She kept her head down as she hurried along the dirt streets, entirely bereft of lamp or candle light at this hour. She didn't need eyes to see. Her feet knew the way.

She unlocked the door to the one room structure she called home and slipped inside. Careful not to make a sound, she stood and allowed her eyes to adjust to the deeper darkness within.

Her people still built as they had for generations, only with different materials. Canvas and old growth heartwood had once dominated; now they applied their ingenuity to cheap processed fiberboard "donated" by the Empire.

It was less effective in keeping out the cold. K'uelle wrinkled her nose at the reek of burning kerosene from the cast iron stove in the middle of the dirt floor, even as she stretched out her hands towards its lingering warmth. Mingled with the noxious scent was the body odor and cherryweed haze of her snoring mother and the soiled underclothes of her infant daughter.

Biting back exasperation at Ai'aial's cherryweed-addled neglect, K'uelle knelt next to the low pallet on which S'ondra slept. For a moment, she simply listened to the soft rasp of her daughter's breathing. The one year old had thrown off some of her covers, perhaps upset about shitting herself, and frustrated her grandmother had been too stoned to clean and change her.

Even in the gloom, K'uelle could make out the strange birthmark discoloring the inside of S'ondra's left elbow. Her fingertips caressed the rougher skin, marveling how much warmer it was to the touch than the rest of the infant's arm. She gently dislodged the remaining covers, but S'ondra didn't wake until her mother wrapped her in fresh underclothes.

"Shh, dear one," K'uelle crooned. She lifted her daughter to her breast and rocked back and forth on her knees. The child emitted a couple louder wails, as if toying with the idea of throwing a tantrum. Fatigue and her mother's familiar scent won out.

K'uelle waited until the babe was sound asleep again, then settled her down in her cocoon of blankets. She wanted nothing more than to join her, sing her an old ti-Lan'ot lullaby or two, but she dared not. Not tonight.

It might have been different. Had K'uelle's husband and brother and eleven other men of the ti-Lan'ot lived, S'ondra might have a future. A poor future, perhaps, but a future other than slow starvation and eventual slavery.

K'uelle changed quickly and quietly, sparing no more than a weary glance of irritation at her snuffling, slack-jawed mother.

She pulled on a black tunic and breeches under her cloak, walking shoes, and the stick passed down to her from her own grandmother, carved with symbols few outside Thorn River could decipher.

She left her home and passed unnoticed through the outer streets, until the last stragglers of DarkFolk urbanization petered out. Only then did she lift her bright eyes to behold her destination.

Rising out of the patchy scrubland to the northwest of ti-Lan'ot City, the Mountain soared towards the sky like the first wave of a central plains dust storm frozen in time. Its stubborn basalt had resisted both the relentless western winds and the periodic frozen gales from the north. The city nuzzled its southern flank, as dependent on its shelter as a newborn calf drawing warmth from its mother.

K'uelle began climbing. There was no path, not yet, but the tumbled lower slopes were not so uneven to be unsafe for a careful traveler familiar with the journey. on-Vana had risen into a near cloudless sky above the dim glow of Thornburg to the east. There was light enough to reach the summit path. After that, instinct and conviction took over.

Humans would call it a trail. They would hammer lurid metal signs into the rock, warning of extreme difficulty and risk of death. They cheapened everything, the Folk and the very land in which they lived. This path had been inscribed over the increasingly sheer face of the Mountain like a love letter. Generations of Folk had nurtured that love even before the ti-Lan'ot arrived.

The Empire had driven out and all but exterminated the remnants of her clan's feared se-Lan'ot cousins during the first wave of human territorial expansion. The ti-Lan'ot would likely suffer the same fate before K'uelle's daughter reached womanhood. Until then, they maintained the path and paid the homage the Mountain was due.

on-Vana had traveled two hand spans before K'uelle reached the summit. In places, the path was gentle and broad enough to walk. At others, she clung to shallow crevices and slid over the cool rock face, embracing it like a forgotten lover. She was aware of, but not intimidated by, the dizzying drop behind. A playful breeze promised morning rain as it tugged at her. She endured. She always endured. The Mother would not be denied.

Five masked, cloaked and hooded figures awaited her on the windswept summit. She donned her own simple mask and hood, before climbing onto the flat top. She knelt before the tallest figure, who stood perilously close to the edge of the storm front. They laid both hands atop her head in benediction.

"Rise, child of Chaos," the Pathfinder murmured. A man's voice, she thought. Walkers didn't always shield their identities from each other. K'uelle was certain the Pathfinder knew each of them all too well, even though they remained entirely ignorant of each other.

Only the Pathfinder spoke. Others followed, and Walked.

She took her place alongside the two Walkers to his left, and waited for the last two to arrive. Soon, seven of them stood, shivering slightly in the northerly breeze, in a circle around the Pathfinder. He lifted his arms toward the newly risen First Moon, and they all began a low hum.

"You are the Seven," he declared, striding around the circle. "There are the Three, and the Seven, and the Thirteen. You are the Seven. *Aliach emor'i!*"

"*Aliach emor'i!*" Praise the Mother!

The Pathfinder stopped in front of K'uelle. He dipped his thumb into a tiny clay jar, then inscribed a sigil, a slanted half cross, on her forehead. From a bearskin pouch at his hip, he produced a strip of jerked meat and offered it to her. She opened her mouth and accepted it, wincing at the bitter taste as she chewed vigorously.

"In seven days, the hunter catches the hunted," the Pathfinder said, continuing his round. "se-Vana, Second Moon, smaller but swifter, ever pursues on-Vana, First Moon, their teacher and betrayer. Know you the story, children of Chaos?"

"Tell us the story, Pathfinder," they intoned.

"on-Vana once roamed the heavens alone, amassing all the knowledge of the world. After countless years of solitude, they grew weary. What was the purpose of it all? Those few of the People who sought its wisdom lived so fleetingly that knowledge was forgotten as quickly as it was learned. on-Vana yearned for a companion, a student who could truly appreciate and venerate them.

"Eleiach was a free spirit, born of Chaos, yet intrigued by Order and the many worlds of the cosmos. Wandering close to our world, they recognized on-Vana as a familiar spirit, and greeted them with respect. on-Vana basked in their polite interest, and implored Eleiach to tarry, with promises of shared lore and friendship. Eleiach agreed, accepting the name se-Vana, and stayed their restless heart.

"For age upon age, they danced the heavens together. se-Vana learned much from on-Vana, yet on-Vana had little interest in what they regarded as the simple wisdom of a wanderer. Soon, se-Vana longed for the wider reaches of the cosmos again, of which they had explored but a little. Where once they had venerated on-Vana's teaching and friendship, they now chafed at their possessiveness.

"'I wish to roam free, to resume my wanderings' they told on-Vana, who was most displeased.

"'Not yet' on-Vana begged.

"Every year, at Midwinter, se-Vana announced their intention to leave. Every year, on-Vana resisted, and used their superior strength to bind the wanderer to them. Teacher and student grew to despise each other, yet on-Vana could not bear the thought of being alone again.

"In the Year of Chaos, se-Vana demanded once more to be free. To their surprise, on-Vana agreed. Yet, they lied. As se-Vana sped on their way, eager to resume their explorations of the cosmos once more, they found themselves unable to break free of The World. No matter how fast they traveled, they found themselves back where they began, or near to it. Cursing on-Vana with every circuit, their closest approach lengthened every time.

"se-Vana vowed revenge. Using the last of their inner reserves, they altered their path, nearing on-Vana with every circuit. Alarmed, on-Vana deflected their closest approach, propelling them further away. Both were weakened by the exchange.

"And so it has gone ever since. Every Great Year, twenty three years of the Sun, se-Vana is repelled and begins their hunt anew. With each hunt, their closest approach grows closer still. One day, during the Year of Chaos Returned, they will catch their prey. Until then, each perigee thins the veil protecting The World from Chaos. Each conjunction brings a day of portents, of omens given and fulfilled."

The Pathfinder lowered his arms and gazed heavenward. on-Vana arced higher in the eastern sky. se-Vana prowled to the south, infringing on Mother's Necklace, confident in their ability to catch up with their betrayer.

Seven days. The buzzing in K'uelle's ears eclipsed the hum vibrating her lips. Every star, every pinprick of light, burned her eyes. Rain, smoke, and the growth of distant forests permeated the air that seeped into her flared nostrils. Flame lanced her tongue.

"You are the Seven. There are the Three, and the Seven, and the Thirteen. Seven Great Years ago, humans overran our lands. They made promises, and broke them. They promised shelter, and cast us out. They promised recognition and respect, and enslaved us. Then they promised dominance, and too many of us did not resist."

The Pathfinder held up a hand, and the humming ceased. Silence enshrouded the Mountain top, save for the low buzz of Chaos.

"You are the Seven. In seven days, seven Great Years since the Empire's Conquest, we shall resist. We resist! *Aliach emor'i!*"

"*Aliach emor'i! Aliach emor'i!*"

K'uelle joined the chant, screaming the words until her throat grew raw.

She resisted. For her dead husband and brother, for her despairing mother, and for her infant daughter who would never have a future. She embraced Chaos. She resisted.

6

THE SPIRIT OF EMPIRE

"Kelian authorities have downplayed the incident at the Kuvara flamestone power plant, claiming all safety features operated as expected. The aberrant behavior in reactor five's core was contained, and no one in the nearby city of over one million people was ever at any risk. The plant operators, Kelia Energitva, have promised to cooperate with state investigators in a full analysis of the incident before restarting the reactor. Meanwhile, all seven other reactors at the world's largest flamestone plant continue to run as usual."

"Now, let's go to Perry Agutter for a sports update..."

Xavier muted the volume, but allowed his hotel room's screen to display highlights of the annual college hoopball tournament finals, held this year in New Ashbrook. One of the arenas occupied an entire city block less than five minutes walk away, and almost every other hotel guest he'd seen had been a fan of one of the eight teams involved. He'd never cared much for the game, but found himself rooting for his alma mater, Washburn College, out of habit. The underdogs from what was now an exurb of New Ashbrook were knocked out last night by Calendia, the number one seeds. Bastards.

At least hoopball was a welcome distraction from post-Thornburg tensions and his return to the city he'd once called home. He'd welcomed taking his daughter out to dinner at her favorite restaurant, but had otherwise stayed in his room. The Mariana Elite Hotel straddled the border between the Embankment and Oldtown districts, both of which held too many painful memories.

His phone buzzed, the vibration taking it a tiny bit closer to the precipitous edge of the bedside table. He stuffed his toiletry bag into the middle of his folded clothes, then zipped up his carry-on before checking the notification.

DeArei Bisset had arrived, and awaited him in the restaurant downstairs. He sighed. He should have known he wouldn't escape at least one face-to-face discussion with his boss before heading back to Thornburg.

One final room check discovered no forgotten items. He scooped up his phone and room keycard, then steeled himself. He'd hoped the solution he'd suggested to Pralik One Raven would have satisfied his boss, but he caught the impression DeArei shared something of the LightFolk's displeasure.

"Maybe you dislike it out of habit," he said to no one in particular. "Well, let's get this over with."

As he rode down in the elevator with a pair of glum Washburn fans and their luggage, Xavier reflected on the meal with his daughter two nights before. Ariadne had greeted him happily enough. She'd regaled him with unremarkable stories about her law school studies and her second place finish in a recent fencing tournament. She'd asked him about the Thornburg Death Curse, and listened with polite interest to his careful answers. He knew she had strong opinions about the Folk, and how the Empire had treated them since the Conquest a century and a half ago. Yet, she refrained from anything more than mild indignance at what the One Raven clan had offered as reparations for their scion's unforgivable action.

He knew Ariadne had her secrets, and he respected that. He thought he'd surprised a blush on her face at the mention of Pralik One Raven, and he wondered at that. Perhaps it had just been a trick of the bistro's table candlelight.

He found DeArei digging into a plate of bacon and eggs at a corner table of the hotel restaurant. Once a college athlete, a marathon runner if Xavier remembered correctly, a series of recurring breast cancer diagnoses in her fifties had taken a heavy toll. Her tan jacket hung loosely on a sparse frame, but disguised how thin her arms had become. A midnight blue scarf wrapped her head where russet curls had once grown. It made her look paler than she really was. He knew she had little appetite, but forced herself to eat, to fend off the inevitable.

"Morning, West." She greeted him without warmth, simply gesturing to the opposite chair, before spearing another bite of bacon with her fork. "There's coffee in the pot, and the server is around here somewhere."

Xavier glanced around as he took his seat. He relied on breakfasts in these mid-level hotels to be as tasteless as their surroundings. The same meats, powdered eggs, and suspicious fruit complemented white walls and tablecloths with afterthoughts of color. He contemplated eating on the plane instead, then opted for a slightly stale Kelian pastry and cream cheese.

"Nice of Kelia to distract the world with a flamestone reactor accident," he murmured, pouring himself a cup of weak coffee. "Hopefully, it will push Thornburg down the news feeds for a while."

DeArei snorted. "I wouldn't count on it. If it happened at one of our reactors, maybe. Otherwise, it's a foreign problem that dumb foreigners halfway around the world have to deal with. I read as much in *Collette's Journal* on my journey over here. More flowery language of course."

"No doubt. To what do I owe the pleasure, DeArei? I have maybe a quarter tenth before I need to catch a taxi to the airport."

The Senior Administrator of the Bureau of Folk Affairs grimaced, then dabbed at her almost colorless lips with a napkin.

Only her vivid seawater eyes retained much of the spark of life. They imprisoned Xavier in their steely gaze.

"Jek One Raven is dead."

Xavier blinked. "That was a little faster than expected. Death Curses normally take most of a tennight to play out, although maybe that's a mercy in this case."

"You be the judge. His Death Curse didn't kill him, although I'm sure it was well on its way to doing so. Thornburg PD wanted to move him to a more private detention center on the city's outskirts. There was a 'lapse in security' during the transfer, and another prisoner sliced Jek's throat open."

"Holy Brothers!"

DeArei inclined her head. "An appeal to the Mother of the Folk might be more appropriate. The kid was a massive pain in the ass, made my life hell for the last three days, not to mention stirring festering resentment against the Folk, Light and Dark. He even forced one of his esteemed clan Elders to offer an old-timey honor killing to the Castlewood family. But he didn't deserve that. This 'accident' is as toxic as the one at the Kuvara power plant."

Xavier did not miss the glint in his boss's eyes when she mentioned the honor killing. He wondered if it would be worth trying to justify his action, then decided against it. He'd been a BFA agent for almost three decades. He knew as much about the Folk as any human in Novomond. He'd made a judgment call and what was really only a suggestion. Pralik had run with it. He'd gambled and won.

But the assassination of Jek One Raven didn't bode well. "I assume there's nothing to tie that prisoner to the Purists or anyone else."

"I doubt anyone is looking," said DeArei. "Too many people, not just the Purists, believe Jek deserved punishment for what he did, rather than the sad indignity of a quiet death alone, away from his family. Tensions are still high. Senator Castlewood appeared mollified in public by One Raven's offer, but I suspect he's still furious. I heard he's planning another speech before the Senate today, and I expect escalation rather than reconciliation. Outraged fury plays too well to his base."

"What will that mean? He's publicly disavowed the Purist movement, even though they act on a lot of his rhetoric."

DeArei glanced around and lowered her voice. "Castlewood believes in the Empire. Not just the oaths and the ceremonies, he believes in its righteousness. More than any other person alive, including the Emperor. Brogan Castlewood embodies the ruthless colonial spirit that drove our ancestors to expand their power from a small peninsula in Earia across half that continent and all of Novomond. History teaches us that you don't maintain that power by tolerating anything less than complete subjugation of those whose lands you colonize. The Emperor speaks of Empire, but it's men like Castlewood that make it happen."

She sat back and dropped her fork on her plate, curling her lip in distaste. Xavier hadn't expected a direct answer to his question, and nothing she'd said in hushed tones was new. Yet, she wouldn't have said it without reason. She scrutinized him while he chewed his last mouthful of pastry.

Xavier cleared his throat. "Do you think he'll propose more punitive legislation today? Something to advance that ruthless spirit of Empire, and appeal to the Purists and their ilk?"

She gave him a silent grim smile. That was all the answer he needed.

Life for the Folk, Light and Dark was about to get even more difficult.

Xavier's first instinct was to call Sharol and set up meetings with as many LightFolk Elders as possible on his return to Thornburg. Some had already sent him messages, expressing concerns over increased intimidation, seeking advice if not active protection. The Bureau for Folk Affairs was not a peacekeeping force. They couldn't deputize the local police or any branch of the military, although they could request such support from the Senate. In light of what Brogan Castlewood may or may not do later that day, Xavier suspected approval of such support would be tough to achieve.

The day was barely three tenths old, and he already had a headache.

He tried to rub the pain and weariness out of his eyes. "What would you recommend I do next?"

"I don't have to tell you to contact LightFolk leadership in Thornburg," DeArei said brusquely, unmoved by any show of trifling discomfort. "One Water clan are the heavy hitters, correct? See what they need, take their pulse. You might want to personally assess security at the city's truesilver facilities. How many are there in Thornburg? Two, I think?"

"Two for commercial development. A smaller boutique operation for specialized medical research and military contracts."

"Really? They flew that under my radar. Oh, and what about flamestone?"

Xavier flinched. "Flamestone? You want me to visit that hellhole of a mine? Or try to talk to one of the Three Mountain or Two Fire Elders? Not that any will listen."

DeArei arched a thin eyebrow. "Do you think the DarkFolk are exempt from reprisals? The Kuvara reactor incident had nothing to do with them, but flamestone was involved. Do you think the Purists will care? I've heard no accounts of unrest on the reservations—not yet. But I *have* received stories of harassment outside, especially in the cities. Beatings, some savage and even fatal. Doesn't your daughter live in North Embankment? Purists beat a DarkFolk beggar to death by the Avon/Empire subway station yesterday morning."

Avon/Empire? Xavier tried to recall exactly where that was in relation to Ariadne's apartment. It sounded awfully close. His daughter had said nothing about it to him, of course. He fought the urge to call or text her at the table, but instead vowed to do so in the taxi.

He glanced at his watch. "I'll see what I can do," he promised. "My taxi's due any moment. Any last word of advice?"

DeArei slumped in her chair, looking tired all of a sudden. "Don't forget we represent the Folk as much as we represent the Empire, West. If you haven't already, call Pralik One Raven before you board your plane. Call, don't email or text. Cultivate that relationship. Your instincts served you well in your first meeting. Use that."

Xavier nodded politely, even as dread settled over him like a dark blanket. He wasn't looking forward to talking to Pralik One Raven at all.

He bade his boss farewell, shrugged into his backpack and wheeled his carry-on through the busy lobby. The smiling valet opened the double doors for him, and Xavier emerged carefully onto the street. He blinked in the bright morning sunlight spearing through the skyscrapers lining the four lane road, and squinted in search of his taxi.

The guests with whom he'd shared his elevator ride were loading one bright green sedan in front of him, but a similar vehicle was just pulling up to the curb. "WEST, XAVIER" blinked in red LED from the upper windshield display. Xavier waved at the driver, who adjusted his sunglasses in what might have been acknowledgement before popping the trunk. Xavier stowed his luggage, but patted all his pockets before closing the trunk. He'd been paranoid ever since leaving his phone behind in a hotel room in Caralan last year.

He didn't notice the other passenger until he'd settled onto the back seat and closed the door. Sharing taxis in New Ashbrook wasn't uncommon, especially when heading to the airport. Xavier opened his mouth to offer a polite greeting to his companion, but no sound made it out.

Sitting next to him in the back of the taxi was Senator Brogan Castlewood.

At first glance, the man could have been any executive in a bespoke charcoal grey suit. Xavier had never met the senator in person, but there was no mistaking his bald head, close trimmed silver beard, and eyes so pale they only hinted at blue. He remembered reading that, in his youth, Castlewood had played the Maul, the most brutal and consequently popular sport in the Empire. He'd been good enough to turn professional after college, but turned that down to work for, and then run, his father's shipping conglomerate.

Thirty years later, the bespoke suit jacket couldn't disguise his muscular frame. The large hands resting in his lap hearkened back to past savagery, now replaced by rhetoric on the Lesser Senate floor. The smile of a jungle cat spread across his face, suiting his rumbling baritone.

"Xavier West. I apologize for intruding on your ride to the airport this morning. I was hoping to keep our discussion private. I assume you know who I am."

"Senator Castlewood." Xavier took a breath, and composed himself. "We were just talking about you."

"Oh? Nothing too derogatory, I hope." Castlewood didn't ask who Xavier had been speaking with. He either knew or didn't care.

"I wouldn't say that. We're simply assessing the developing situation, and the likely actions of the major players."

Castlewood grinned. "I'm flattered you consider me a major player. Would I be correct in guessing your breakfast companion was DeArei Bisset? Your boss and I have had some colorful discussions over recent days."

"I think she described it as you shitting down her neck."

The senator's eyes flashed for a moment, and Xavier wondered if he'd pushed too far, but then the man's grin turned into a rueful chuckle, and he spread his hands in apology.

"I must confess to having taken an overly strident tone with Mrs. Bisset. If you have ever watched me speak or debate, you know I am a passionate man. Passionate about the Empire, and passionate about my family. I knew Fenner Castlewood. A brash and, I'm afraid to say, spoiled young man. Not my kin's best and brightest, but my kin nonetheless. No one should die the way he did."

Xavier inclined his head in respect. "On that, I think we all agree."

The driver suddenly hit the brakes with a muffled curse. Castlewood frowned, and glanced at his watch. A Parisi, if Xavier didn't miss his guess. It was worth most of Xavier's annual salary.

"We'll get you to the airport in time," Castlewood assured him. "This is still safer than taking the subway. Where was I? Ah yes, DeArei Bisset. She's a good woman with a tough life and a tough job. Despite my rudeness, I respect her. The Bureau of Folk Affairs must be a thankless place to work. You're trying to govern the ungovernable. Yet, every so often a stroke of genius emerges. When I heard you were the architect of Pralik One Raven's offer of a LightFolk honor killing, I knew I had to meet you."

"I'm hardly the architect. I merely suggested Pralik remember his people's traditions."

Another frown, this time for Xavier. "Don't sell yourself short, Mr. West. I abhor false modesty. You may not have laid out all the details, but yours was the kernel of the idea, without which the situation would no doubt continue to be far more volatile than it is. The Empire needs men like you."

The senator didn't reach out and touch him, like a Church of the Brethren minister bestowing benediction, but Xavier couldn't help but stir with pride.

"Thank you. I appreciate the recognition, but I'm sure you had another motive for giving it to me in person."

"Of course." Castlewood's eyes narrowed and grew intent. "Despite your best efforts and those of Pralik One Raven, the situation remains dangerous. My constituents, and those of many of my fellow senators, continue to express their concerns. Everyone worries they may be the next victim of a rogue LightFolk Death Curse. It is my job to ease those concerns."

"Do you also hear from LightFolk constituents fearing recrimination?" Xavier asked. "I just learned that Purists murdered a DarkFolk beggar a stone's throw from my daughter's apartment. And that was not an isolated incident."

Castlewood made an irritated gesture. "Regrettable, of course. Your daughter should not have to endure such ugliness so close to home. But all the more reason to impose additional measures to improve security for everyone. I will be proposing such measures on the Lesser Senate floor today. I could use men like you within the Bureau of Folk Affairs, who have the ear of influential LightFolk, to ensure their cooperation. Can I rely on you, Mr. West?"

Xavier didn't answer immediately. Glancing out the front windshield, he saw their car approaching the highway exit for the airport. He wondered what "additional measures" Castlewood intended to propose, and suspected it meant nothing good for the Folk in general.

The BFA's mission was to facilitate integration of both LightFolk and DarkFolk into the Empire, not to police them. His job promised to become far more challenging.

"I will do what I can to preserve peaceful relations between us and the Folk," he said, choosing his words with care. "I assume I must wait along with everyone else to learn what your proposals are?"

"Why give away the surprise?" Castlewood said with a thin smile. "I or my office will be in touch."

The taxi finally rolled to a halt, occupying one of the free slots at the New Ashbrook airport's busy passenger drop-off point. The driver popped the trunk. Xavier began to open his door, then turned back to his companion.

"I mean it, senator. Peaceful relations. That goes both ways."

Castlewood regarded him impassively. "Have a safe flight, Mr. West. I hope for your cooperation. Do not make the mistake of withholding it."

7

LEAVETAKING

"Stop fidgeting, Davek," Pralik One Raven said under his breath, jaw tight.

The young man tugged at the collar of his ceremonial amber robe and scowled. Yes, the gilt edge stiffened the fabric, and if you slouched in your seat like Davek did, it would scrape the underside of your chin. But he was no longer an unruly child, unable to master his emotions. Nineteen summers marked every boy of the Folk as a man, at least in the eyes of the clan.

Laida, Pralik's wife, leaned in from Davek's other side and whispered in his ear. Davek straightened and slowly dropped his hand into his lap. All expression leached from his face. Tension between the two had risen over recent months, for reasons unclear to Pralik, but Laida still had a way of bringing their son to heel when necessary.

Pralik tried to catch her eye, but his wife focused on the shaman. Chiana, to her left, gave every sign of following the ceremony, but the amused twitch of her lips betrayed her.

He suppressed a sigh. For twenty years, he and Laida had done this, wrangled their surly, impatient son and his supercilious older daughter to the annual Leavetaking ceremony. At some point, he'd thought it would get easier.

The joys of being a parent, especially in this modern age of casual distraction.

The soft thumping of eleven skin drums drew his attention back to the shaman. Naked but for a black loin cloth, the old ascetic writhed in a slow, sinuous dance, made jagged by the hard lines of his bones and angular tattoos. Pale blue smoke wafted from five braziers spaced equally around the central circle, and Pralik wasn't the only one to cover his mouth and cough discreetly as the acrid fumes swept over the celebrants.

The ceremony had been designed for an outdoor setting, where Mother's wind could take up the people's offering and disperse it far and wide as She saw fit. More justly, it was hoped, than the Empire had dispersed the Folk themselves after the Conquest. But the city of New Ashbrook no longer permitted open-air Folk ceremonies, forcing them inside "temples" such as Emori Cadrach instead. From the outside, the iconic circular dome impressed. Inside, its hollow interior swallowed chant and drum alike, as lifeless as one of the humans' stone tombs. The irony in relocating a ceremony commemorating Leavetaking to such a space was bitter indeed.

And soon, even this might be taken away by the their longtime conquerors.

"One and sixty and one hundred years," the shaman intoned, his clear voice smothered by dull echoes. "We have not forgotten the lands we once called home. Our feet remember their hills and soil. Our bellies remember their crops and kine. Our ears remember the song of bird and stream. Our eyes remember the trees and the sunrise. And our hands remember the building of homes along with the spears that defended them. Before the Empire forsook their oaths."

As Pralik's attention wandered, so did his gaze. He'd attended over four decades of Leavetaking ceremonies, and knew the tragic story all too well. Meanwhile, another tragedy had, he suspected, only begun to unfold. Who among the LightFolk would weather the storm?

The Two Water clan would fancy their chances. Varin Two Water's tall lanky frame and bald scalp loomed through the smoke amid the navy blue robes seated across the circle. A strong, some would say obstinate leader, he clung to the old ways, and his clan's youth followed his lead. Liurin, the shorter and quieter of the male Two Water *chiek'la*, huddled in a seat behind Varin and smiled at some secret thought. Pralik had heard rumors of discontent between Two Water and the One Water clan, to whom they owed allegiance. He noted that the latter's small New Ashbrook contingent had chosen to observe Leavetaking elsewhere. That situation bore watching.

Sunward around the temple sat haughty Shalae One Sky, surrounded by her considerable extended family and her two diffident fellow *chiek'lai*, Arae and Eglente. Pralik made a mental note to avoid Shalae at all costs following the ceremony. Her nephew's struggles at the Metropolitan Academy required discussion, but not here. The cracks in One Sky's pride needed no further widening, today of all days.

Istilla One Raven caught his eye a few seats to his right. Her voluminous robe swaddled her short, slight frame almost as if she were a newborn, but the *chiek'la* had seen more of these ceremonies than almost anyone present. Wisps of white hair escaped her hood. Keen eyes yet burned beneath her wrinkled brow, glancing at Pralik for a moment before turning back to the shaman. Istilla would advocate retrenchment, guarding the few traditions and scraps of honor the LightFolk still possessed. She had endured many indignities in her long life, and claimed she and her people were stronger for it.

The third and final One Raven *chiek'la* was an entirely different story. Flanking their clan's contingent to the left, Khavrik sat with a straight back between his strikingly beautiful wife, Aviara, and their bemused young son, Turik. Khavrik's quick mind balanced a volatile temper, but his charm and physical prowess endeared him to those of the clan who sought respect and a better life for their people. He backed his passionate eloquence with deeds, helping Aviara run several charities for LightFolk youth and homeless, while overseeing the city's largest low-income housing program.

There was a lot to admire about Khavrik, yet Pralik could never bring himself to like the man. He reminded him, uncomfortably, of Varin Two Water. When their eyes met, the younger Elder's lip curled even as he nodded his respect. They were neither enemies nor rivals. They simply didn't get on, and tended to avoid each other.

The ceremony concluded with everyone rising from their seats, turning their backs in unison on the shaman and ululating drummers. Lowering their heads in silence, the clans trudged towards the exits, filtering down the aisles between the seats, not looking back until they crossed the threshold of the inner doors. The shaman crouched in silence, forehead pressed to the stone, shoulders bowed as if under the weight of everything the Folk had lost—or had ripped from them.

Davek let out an exasperated sigh as they passed into the outer corridor. Painted motifs crawled over the walls, pretty but dead without magic's glow; to Pralik they were empty masks. He spared another irritated glance for his son, who now waved at friends in the distance, then turned to Laida.

"I need to talk to Istilla and Khavrik. Do you wish to wait for me? Or shall I see you back at the house?"

Laida smiled, lighting up her elegant face, still as youthful to him as when they'd courted five and twenty years ago.

Five and twenty? The ceremony must be getting to me.

"We'll wait. Yours isn't the only important conversation to be had today. Stop it, Chiana."

Their daughter rolled her eyes. "Must you?"

Laida's smile tightened, and she drew herself up straight. She still fell well short of Chiana, who had inherited her father's height. "This is the perfect opportunity to meet potential matches. The Mother knows you do little else to meet eligible men."

"Maybe I've already met them, and found them wanting," Chiana muttered. She scowled down at the floor, kicking at a stray pamphlet.

"Certainly you won't endear yourself to anyone by sulking. Please, let's not argue about this today. Can you indulge me introducing you to one young man at least?"

Chiana sighed. "Fine. Who did you have in mind?"

Laida brightened. "I was thinking Bilarek, Tanik and Oalla's boy. I heard he's taking on a greater role in Tanik's clothing business."

"Bilarek? That crow fucker? You must be joking."

Laida flinched, then glanced around nervously to see if anyone had heard that gravest of insults. Davek chuckled, earning himself a furious glare.

"Chiana, that was mean-spirited and highly inappropriate," Pralik admonished. "You may not enjoy your mother's matchmaking, or care for those she wishes to introduce you to. But you *will* do her the courtesy of accepting it with good grace, especially if you want us to consider your own wishes on the matter."

It was Chiana's turn to flinch. "My own wishes? Father, rest assured I will have every say in whom I court and whom I bond, if anyone. And it would help if we didn't waste time on boys with a reputation for cheating and, so I hear, roughing up their dates. Is that what you wish for me, mother?"

"Of course not!" Laida hissed, then visibly gathered herself. "I have not heard such rumors, but I do not wish to dismiss them either. If you would only talk to me, *en'aia*! I will not ask you to talk to such a boy, but if not him, then who? I only seek to guide you towards a suitable match."

"Does that apply to Davek as well?" Chiana asked with a sly look at her brother. Pralik thought he caught a flash of alarm in his son's eyes, before he assumed the bored, mocking expression the siblings typically reserved for each other.

"I haven't begun courting yet, dear sister," Davek said. "I'm focusing on my studies."

"Oh, is that what you're focusing on?"

Someone cleared their throat behind Pralik. He turned to see Khavrik waiting a discreet distance away, politely ignoring his fellow Elder's squabbling family. Khavrik's long lustrous black hair cascaded free of his now lowered hood, accentuating his rugged good looks. Only a partially raised eyebrow suggested any amusement at what he may or may not have heard.

The man was insufferable. Pralik had never been so glad to see him.

"Istilla awaits us," Khavrik said mildly, gesturing back inside the temple's heart. "If you can spare a few moments, there are things we should discuss."

Pralik excused himself from his children's bickering and his wife's rising temper. He followed Khavrik through the interior doors, which the other man closed behind them.

The shaman and other celebrants had vacated the central circle, and an eerie hush enveloped the domed chamber. Istilla stood next to the dais, supporting herself with a *balkua*, the traditional two-handed walking stick favored by their ancestors. Barely half Khavrik's stature, she radiated the authority of decades. And she got right to the point.

"The Senate votes today on the so-called Castlewood Plan," she said in her crackling voice once the two men halted beside her. "There is little doubt of the result. Castlewood and his faction have been paving the way for such measures for many years."

"Purists," spat Khavrik.

"Some. But many others are frightened, for themselves or of those to whom they are beholden. The outcome is clear. The question is how should One Raven respond."

"What choices do we have?" Pralik asked. "In the popular mind, we bear responsibility for the atrocity in Thornburg. Our offer of reparation merely deflected the worst of the backlash."

Khavrik snorted. "And played our hand. I still say we turned too fast to appeasement."

"I suspect it made little difference in the end," said Istilla, peering up at Khavrik from above her sharp nose, a mother bird scrutinizing a wayward chick. "There has been talk of curfew before. Now the Senate is establishing one. There may be some truth to Brogan Castlewood's claim that keeping our Folk off the streets in the dark hours would keep them safer."

"Unless of course they are assaulted in their homes, as happened last night in Kentwich. Are our people supposed to endure violence, even death, rather than flee to the streets for fear of arrest and imprisonment?"

"Khavrik has a point," Pralik put in, seeing Istilla's eyes flash. "Let's not pretend the proposed curfew is anything but a curb on Folk freedom of movement. The real danger is our meek acceptance, followed by a reduction in Purist violence. That will only help convince the Senate, and the human public, that the curfews should be extended beyond the proposed one year term, and made permanent."

The younger man inclined his head at the support, then turned back to Istilla, whose lips were set in a grim line. "Exactly. Increasing the frequency of inspections of our schools and truesilver factories was inevitable. I dare say they'll extend that to my housing program soon enough. If they don't find anything, they'll just twist that to justify maintaining the new regimen."

Istilla shook her head. "I don't doubt what you say is true. Perhaps the same will happen with these new Ceremony Permits." She scowled, as if this was the greatest affront. "Today's Leavetaking might be the last one we ever hold without asking permission first."

"Permission!" Khavrik growled, clearly struggling to hold his temper. "Will we soon need permits to eat with our families when we honor the Mother?"

"That would be absurd," said Pralik. "Have either of you spoken with other clans? What are their positions? I know Two Water and Two Eagle are outraged, mostly about the curfew. Varin Two Water claims his clan will ignore the curfew, and urges us to follow suit."

"Good for Varin," murmured Khavrik.

Istilla harrumphed. "With all due respect to Two Water, but they are a smaller clan. Varin wishes to be the catalyst for major clans, such as One Raven, to elevate his own standing. His vanity may be his undoing."

"Vanity?" Khavrik retorted. "Did you not hear what Pralik said? If none resist, these crackdowns will become permanent. Varin Two Water and his clan deserve our support. Did you know one of their own died at Thornburg too, a friend of Jek One Raven?"

"I am well aware," said Istilla. "But I have heard rumors that Chaos Walk has grown in favor within Two Raven. Given the new outright ban—"

A city implodes, homes and offices crumble, skyscrapers collapse. Dust and debris billow up and out, enveloping all. Thousands upon thousands of people, humans and Folk alike, sliced in half as if by a giant scythe. No screams, no time to even draw their final breath. Blood and smoke and a sickly green glow that enshrouds the wreckage, cooling to a malignant red as the heavy air clears.

"Pralik?"

Istilla's voice echoed dully as if Pralik's ears still rang from the explosion. He staggered, dizzy and blinded by the sudden light of the temple. Khavrik caught him before he fell, and guided him to a chair. Pralik slumped in it, heart racing, and pressed a palm to his suddenly throbbing head.

What in Mother's name was that?

"Pralik?"

He raised his head, blinking as he met Istilla's concern and Khavrik's curiosity. The vision had lasted only moments, yet it had scoured him of vitality. It was some time before he could summon the strength to talk.

"I'm well," he gasped. "Just..."

He paused. Was he ready to admit what he had seen? Would Khavrik perceive it as weakness, and use that against him? Would Istilla see something more sinister, possibly a True Seeing?

If so, it would be the first in almost a century. And his lineage, as far as he knew, carried no history of the True Sight.

"Just lightheaded," he finished, close to his normal, calm voice. He managed a weak smile. "Laida only just recovered from a nasty cold. Perhaps it has awoken in me. I should go."

"Very well," said Istilla, although her shrewd eyes showed she wasn't fooled. "But we should continue this conversation when you are sufficiently recovered. One Raven needs our leadership."

Pralik glanced at Khavrik, who stood tall, face impassive. "Thank you. Perhaps tomorrow evening. In the meantime, I think we should consider reaching out to our cousins on the reservations. One Snake, Two Eagle, and other DarkFolk deserve a voice too."

Davek waited for the restroom door to close before emerging from his stall. He hadn't used it, but washed his hands anyway. He was refreshing his mop of dark hair, teasing strands to fall over his forehead just so, when Khavrik entered.

The LightFolk Elder stood by the door, effectively blocking it. He cut a dashing figure. Davek wasn't the only young LightFolk entranced by Khavrik's charisma, his passion for their people, and the way he made others feel heard and worthy.

Davek's own father meant well—he could acknowledge that—but he was too old-fashioned, too cautious. One Raven needed strong, visionary leadership, especially now.

"What do you have for me?" Khavrik asked in a low voice. His eyes were distant, as if distracted. His right eyebrow, the one interrupted with the burn scar, twitched lazily.

Davek inwardly cringed, fearful of wasting the Elder's time. "It is as we suspected. The BFA agent indirectly suggested the honor killing."

Khavrik's gaze narrowed. "Xavier West?"

"Yes. I heard it from his daughter. They discussed it over dinner, after he met my father the day after Thornburg."

"Xavier told his daughter he'd encouraged a One Raven *chiek'la* to propose an honor killing? Something we haven't done in decades?"

Davek licked his lips. He needed to be careful. The wrong words at the wrong time could do more harm than good.

"Indirectly. She said he'd told my father to consider Folk traditions when considering what reparations to offer the Castlewoods. I think the honor killing itself was dad's idea."

Khavrik exhaled, and a frown darkened his features. Davek hesitated before asking his next question. "Did he not discuss it with you first? With you and *chiek'la* Istilla?"

"Of course he did, boy," snapped Khavrik. "None of us would dare take such action alone. Mine was the only voice against. Istilla supported him."

The air crackled with tension. Davek held his breath until Khavrik sighed and rubbed his eyes.

"Forgive me. I already have much to think about, and this complicates matters. It is not your fault, Davek. Are you still close to this girl?"

"Ariadne? The BFA agent's daughter? Yes, we're, um..." *Dating? Fucking?* Davek couldn't for the life of him think of a word that wouldn't infuriate Khavrik.

To his surprise, the Elder chuckled and favored him with a knowing grin. "The bravest of us must sometimes commit to tasks we or others consider abhorrent. This is not such a task.

I am not one of those sanctimonious traditionalists that would denounce you for dallying with a human girl."

Davek grinned back, basking in his mentor's camaraderie.

Khavrik glanced at the door. Voices grew louder outside. "Learn what you can from her, for as long as she's useful, for as long as her father has Pralik's ear. I want to know as much about what Xavier West is telling my fellow Elder as possible."

8

NO WAY HOME

K'uelle sensed menace in the night air as soon as she slipped out onto the poorly lit street.

Tensions still simmered in the wake of the Black Star atrocity—sure, that counted because it happened to humans—but this was different. Every shadow leered. Every doorway yawned with an unspoken threat. Every building loomed with ill intent, crowding the sidewalk as she hurried towards the transit terminal.

The Thorn River reservation bus waited at its usual stand, under erratically flickering fluorescents. A handful of other DarkFolk, including two other whores from Madam Two Mountain's brothel, approached from various directions. Several other buses parked at adjacent stands, all but one dormant. Far to K'uelle's right, mostly elderly human couples thronged a modern, luxurious tour bus, departing unusually late for another distant city built on stolen land.

They weren't the problem. She couldn't see the problem, couldn't tell what had stirred the hackles on the back of her neck, and raised gooseflesh on her arms. The danger—for danger it surely was—concealed itself, for now. Waiting.

One more night. Tonight, then one more night. That's all I have to endure.

K'uelle thought she glimpsed a pair of figures lurking in the darkness behind another bus. She wanted to dismiss them. Perhaps they were kids, or a drunken couple stealing kisses or copping feels in as unromantic a location as Dockside could provide. More likely it was a Shade dealer, selling their latest wares to a desperate addict, but something about the furtive way the pair had withdrawn from sight alarmed her.

She glanced at the yellow LED clock above the bus's front windshield as she climbed the steps inside. Five hundredths until it left. Five hundredths wasn't that long.

K'uelle slumped into a seat near the back and peered through the dirty window. An irregular smudge directly in front of her face obscured her view. She tried to look around it, then realized it was growing, that it wasn't a smudge at all. It was a mob.

They issued from the mouth of Frenton Street, the main artery through the heart of Dockside, like ants teeming from a nest. The flickering nearby lights made it hard to tell, but she guessed that thirty or forty masked, dark-clad figures marched on the transit terminal, towards the reservation bus in particular. She caught noises of alarm from outside, from the luxury coach, but they had nothing to fear. The fear was meant for the DarkFolk.

"Close the door!" someone cried from nearer the front of the bus. Others took up the cry, as K'uelle stared in mounting horror. Perhaps the driver wasn't paying attention, studying his phone right up until the last moment before leaving. Maybe he was too stunned by the sight of the approaching mob, too slow to react—or perhaps he was part of it, a co-conspirator.

The door didn't close in time. The pneumatics engaged with an apologetic hiss as the first arms reached for the bus and jammed the door. Hands clawed in the air, like the horned trout writhing in the bottom of her uncle's canoe when he'd taken her fishing as a girl. Passengers stood in front of her, blocking the sight. Some yelled at the driver. Others began screaming.

"Drive! Get us out of here!"

Fear spiked within the DarkFolk trapped on the bus, a shared adrenaline rush that also swept up K'uelle. Most passengers were women, who understood all too well their likely fate at the hands of a rampaging mob. A few male voices urged them to the back, and what glimpses she managed of the chaos up front showed four or five determined men bracing themselves for the inevitable breach. Older, frailer men, men reduced to washing dishes or cleaning filthy bathrooms for as little money as their human employers could get away with.

They were valiant, but without magic, they didn't stand a chance.

Even as the first masked men surged through the broken door onto the bus, K'uelle flinched from a loud thump behind her. At first, she thought someone had thrown something against the bus. Turning, she saw a woman whom she recognized as another of Madam Two Mountain's whores, grappling with the emergency exit. The hatch swung partially open, then stuck. She slammed her shoulder into it, to no avail.

This was no time to follow the rules. Too much was at stake.

"Back, sister!" K'uelle cried, stretching her hand towards the faulty exit. Her surrounding passengers recoiled with wide eyes as they understood what she was about to try. Couldn't they understand what would happen if she didn't?

A Death Curse wasn't the only spell available to them, and in the cacophonous chaos of the bus, who would ever know?

K'uelle embraced the Mother, muttered the words under her breath, and *pushed*.

The hatch flew fully open, rebounding against the side of the bus in a shattering of glass.

"Go!" she cried.

The woman who'd started opening the emergency exit was first to recover. Flashing K'uelle a wild grin that mingled terror with elation, she jumped out. A mass scramble ensued, and those hesitant to make the leap were shoved out ruthlessly. Howls of anguish and defiance assailed K'uelle from all sides, their individual voices lost. It was as if the bus itself roared with agony and rage.

When her turn came, K'uelle had only a moment to assess the situation outside. The sterile overhead lights strobed over people struggling or writhing on the ground in pain. At least two DarkFolk were being dragged away, to where their assaulters had room to do what they would. She couldn't see anyone running free. The mob was thinner here, but that wouldn't last long.

K'uelle sprang down, landing poised between two masked men, both a head taller than her. She knew their kind. She serviced them every night, but tonight she fought back.

She still held her connection to Chaos, granted to her through the grace of the Mother. She wanted to sweep away these human dogs, clutch their throats with invisible hands of power, and cast them into the nearby river. She was not strong enough for that. She couldn't save them all, but she could maybe save herself. She was one of the Seven.

Both assailants crumpled as they reached for her, as if punched in the stomach by a man twice their size. K'uelle dodged around them, seeking the quickest path through the carnage. On a nearby bench, an older woman beat at her rapist's chest with ineffectual fists. The masked man crushed her throat with one hand while pinning her hips down with the other, the top half of his pale hairy buttocks gleaming in the strobe light.

She couldn't save them all, but she couldn't abandon them all either.

A word of power. A surge of energy. A howl of agony. The assailant rolled onto the ground, clutching his groin as blood fountained through his fingers. His victim recoiled, pulling his severed member out from between her legs and flinging it away with a strangled sob. Her wide eyes met K'uelle's, too shocked for thanks.

Get out of there.

Gripping her left hand in a fist, K'uelle nurtured the pain and kept her head down, slipping away like a ghost. She avoided the other bus, whose boarding passengers had scrambled to take shelter inside, leaving suitcases strewn around the concrete. That left only one option: the river.

She emerged from the transit terminal's dispassionate lights and plunged into the relative darkness of the docks themselves. Avoiding the occupied bays and their inevitable security, she slipped from one shadow to another. She'd put two city blocks between her and the beleaguered reservation bus when she abruptly realized two things.

She was being followed—and someone was waiting for her.

The soft footfalls of her pursuers finally eclipsed the jeering and screaming of the mob attack. K'uelle spun, prepared to wield the Chaos she still held. She relaxed as she spotted two other DarkFolk women following in her wake. The one she'd savagely rescued from rape stared back at K'uelle with grim determination. The other, limping as if she'd twisted an ankle in their frantic escape, was Shilaiyo, a girl she'd gone to school with in ti-Lan'ot City. K'uelle couldn't remember much about her, other than she lived with her grandparents in a homestead in the foothills outside the city proper. She was fairly sure Shilaiyo didn't work for Madam Two Mountain, but in Thornburg there were always other brothels willing to buy DarkFolk flesh.

Shilaiyo's frightened eyes widened further as she spotted something over K'uelle's shoulder. From the end of the street, heading back into the heart of Dockside, a human woman approached, one palm raised in greeting. Her black hoodie had peeled back slightly, revealing a hint of spiky green hair, as she spoke low and urgently into a cell phone. Behind her, an unremarkable mid-sized car parked at the broken curb, skulking in the gloom enveloping two derelict warehouses ignored by gentrification. Standing next to the car was a figure wearing a wide brimmed hat and a calf-length coat.

"Peace!" The newcomer's eyes scanned the street behind the fleeing DarkFolk as she greeted them, searching for further pursuit. "My name is Sharol. I mean you no harm. Is there anyone else with you?"

K'uelle didn't answer, so the older woman did. "No. Only we ran this direction."

Sharol nodded, then beckoned to them. "Let's get out of the open. The police are on their way, but I imagine that's not much comfort."

K'uelle wanted to keep running, to put as much distance as she could between her and the mob or any other human, but she couldn't run forever. She couldn't swim across the river, nor could she walk all the way to the reservation. Although suspicious of their savior, she acknowledged wisdom in taking a moment to assess her options.

One more night. I just need one more night.

The man in the hat didn't move as they passed him, seeking the deeper shadow between the car and the warehouse's crumbling brick edifice. K'uelle caught pale eyes gleaming under the brim of the hat, but the rest of his equally pale features blurred into a scruffy beard. Sharol stopped to confer with him, and K'uelle strained to hear their quiet conversation. In the distance, sirens wailed.

"Do you see any more?" The man's low baritone reminded K'uelle of her father, despite the strange nasal accent.

"No. Maybe some fled in other directions. I hope so. This is worse than Ajan One Water feared. Where are the fucking cops?"

"Taking their sweet time. Your intel was good, Sharol. I'm glad you reached out to One Water while I was in New Ashbrook." The man shook his head and glanced back at the three wary DarkFolk women. "Shit. I just can't believe..."

"That so many of our fellow humans are this bigoted and cruel?" Bitterness laced Sharol's words. "If there's one thing about this job I dislike, it's that I see more of that crap than ever before. They hate us too, by the way. I've been called a sympathizer, shill and worse... Finally! I hope there's someone left to save."

K'uelle glanced down the street as flashing red and blue lights swarmed the transit terminal like a nest of night hornets. She glimpsed several silhouettes of masked men fleeing the scene, and raised up on the balls of her feet, prepared to run. Sharol and her companion saw this too.

"Time to leave," he announced, turning to K'uelle and the others. "My name is Xavier. You have no reason to trust me, but I want to help. Get in my car, and I'll drive you wherever you want to go. Somewhere safe."

The three DarkFolk women looked at each other. Shilaiyo took a hesitant step towards the car, but the older woman shook her head.

"No offense, but I used up all my trust for humans some time ago. I'll find my own way."

She raised an eyebrow at K'uelle in invitation. K'uelle froze, unable to decide. The excruciating pain in her hand made it difficult to think.

The older woman shrugged, then turned and faded into the shadows.

Sharol opened the rear door and ushered Shilaiyo inside just as the man climbed into the driver's seat.

"Are you coming too?" K'uelle asked her, searching her face for any hint of deception. Sharol's skin was too light, but the shape of her eyes and contours of her chin reminded K'uelle of her LightFolk kin.

Sharol waved her phone. "I called it in. I need to go down there and talk to the police." She glanced inside the car, then back at K'uelle. "You'll be safe with Xavier. He's a good man. I swear it, on my honor."

Fighting the urge to flee, K'uelle slid cautiously into the car's back seat.

The human man, Xavier, had removed his hat, revealing short untidy dark hair just starting to thin on top. He pulled out into the street, made a U-turn and then drove a couple blocks farther down the riverfront before turning again. Only then did he switch on his lights.

"Thorn River?" he asked, glancing at them in his rear view mirror.

"ti-Lan'ot City," K'uelle confirmed, and he nodded, driving down another narrow, quiet side street.

Shilaiyo trembled, shock and fear catching up with her. Wincing, K'uelle slid the rock chip into her jacket pocket, hoping no one caught its fading green glow. She took Shilaiyo's shaking hand in her burned one and offered comfort she didn't really possess. Shilaiyo slumped against her, resting her head in the crook of K'uelle's shoulder.

Xavier drove in silence as he maneuvered his vehicle onto the highway leading to Frontier Bridge. K'uelle was grateful for that, at least. The less said, the better. She was one of the Seven.

He broke the silence with a soft curse as the elevated highway swung in its final arc towards the bridge. More red and blue lights heralded a line of police cruisers blocking off the westbound lanes, ushering all traffic onto the last exit ramp this side of the river. K'uelle held her breath, fearing a checkpoint, fearing an interrogation, fearing...

But no. A bored officer wearing a fluorescent orange vest waved them towards the exit ramp, and Xavier didn't stop to ask why the bridge was closed.

"Now what?" K'uelle asked. "Why can't we use the bridge?"

"I don't know," Xavier admitted. "I don't want to draw attention by asking. We could head south, I guess. The next bridge is almost a hundred kilometres away, near Mayersville. Or you could hole up somewhere in the city tonight and try again in the morning. Do you have a place you can go?"

"No."

Even if Madam Two Mountain would open her door to them, K'uelle wouldn't trust her. There was nowhere else, no other sanctuary. She spent as little time in Thornburg as possible. She rode the bus in from the reservation early in the afternoon, sold her body for the rest of the day, then rode another bus home. She wanted no part of the city humans had built with her people's blood on their hands.

Shilaiyo only whimpered, burrowing against K'uelle. She'd been brave or scared enough to run, but she had nothing left.

Xavier drove in thoughtful silence, keeping to quiet side streets, turning often so that K'uelle soon lost her sense of where the river lay. Finally, he glanced back at her in the mirror.

"I have an apartment, not far from here, near the University. You're welcome to stay there for a few hours, then I'll try to get you back home tomorrow."

Every instinct told her to decline. She didn't know this man. He may not have been part of the mob that attacked the bus, but who knew if his motives were honorable? Why would they be? His kind viewed hers as scarcely more than animals, to be used as slave labor or cheap pleasure, then herded back onto the reservations, out of sight and out of mind. Humans weren't kind to the Folk, to DarkFolk especially.

But she was tired, and frightened, and her hand really fucking hurt.

"Very well," she said with a determination she didn't feel. "Thank you."

The height of the office and residential towers tapered off as the elevated highway wound from downtown through the inner suburbs. It amazed her how many lights still shone even in the dead of night. Were humans so afraid of the dark?

To be fair, they had reason to be.

Xavier parked underground, in a featureless concrete chamber below his five-story apartment building. It smelled of gasoline and garbage, and the clanking elevator reeked of stale sweat. Not so different from ti-Lan'ot City, just with electricity and without open sky.

They crept along a dim, carpeted hallway until he stopped in front of a black door on which the numerals "403" were stenciled in white. He waved a plastic card at a small metal box beneath it and ushered them inside.

"My guest bedroom is through there," he murmured, gesturing at a closed door to his right. "And, um, my room is next to it if you want to take separate rooms. I'll sleep on the couch. Sorry about the mess."

Shilaiyo clung to K'uelle in silence, shy or terrified or both. K'uelle gazed around the apartment's plain white walls, the combined living and kitchen area alone twice as big as the home she shared with her mother.

But this wasn't a home. There were few signs of life other than a pair of framed pictures on one wall—one of a younger Xavier and another of a girl with an awkward smile whom she presumed was his daughter. A taupe couch faced a flat screen TV, like the ones in the bars she passed on the way to work. Between them squatted a glass-top table strewn with half-empty glasses of water, a large square box smelling faintly of cheese, a lightly crushed beer can, and a glossy paper information packet from a company called Novomond Micro. The fancy electric cooktop looked unused. It was a place to live, not a home.

"We'll share," K'uelle told him, a mix of defiance and gratitude in her tone.

He simply nodded, then grabbed a couple of towels from a nearby closet and pressed them into her arms. "Use the bathroom, freshen up. Help yourself to water or anything from the fridge. It's rather bare, I'm afraid. I'll set an alarm, and we can be off at first light, if that's okay."

K'uelle returned the nod then held the bedroom door open for Shilaiyo, who slunk inside immediately.

"Wait," Xavier said as K'uelle made to follow. He rummaged through a few drawers in the kitchen island, then produced a small metal cube, about the length of her thumb. He took off the lid and offered it to her, his face expressionless.

Carefully, she took out the chip of flamestone from her jacket pocket. Its sickly green glow had long since faded, but it remained warm to the touch. She dropped it into the box without comment. Xavier replaced the lid, and set the box on the countertop.

"Let's take care of your hand before you sleep," he murmured, too soft for Shilaiyo to hear. "I've heard flamestone burns are painful."

9

UNEXPECTED GUESTS

Xavier rose early the following morning, well before the watery spring sun penetrated his living room's uneven blinds. In truth he'd slept little. It had been a while since he'd hosted female overnight guests, platonic or otherwise.

He crept to the bathroom and took a quick shower, clucking his tongue at the debris surrounding the vanity sink. He collected stray bottles of hair restorative and turned their labels to face the mirror. He'd long dreaded the day male pattern baldness would strike, but none of the miracle cures offered by retail pharmacies helped delay the inevitable. Hats were becoming a more essential part of his wardrobe.

Neither of the DarkFolk girls had visited the bathroom that he could tell. If they had, they'd stolen silently through his apartment during one of his very few periods of fitful dozing. If not for the low rasp of someone snoring, he might have believed he was still alone.

His surprise guests made Xavier at least as uncomfortable as they had to be, hiding in a stranger's apartment. A human, just like the vicious assholes who'd attacked the bus. Or hopefully not like them, but a human nonetheless. He tried to remember the last time he'd so much as spoken to a DarkFolk, other than one of their wary, stone-faced Elders. He felt even more awkward than he had on that recent date he kept trying to forget.

These girls weren't much older than his daughter. Attractive, if the severe angles of their dark-skinned faces were your thing. There weren't many reasons for girls like that to be in Thornburg after the Day End Bell. A pang of pity shouldered aside his selfish worry about what the neighbors would think.

Xavier hoped none of his neighbors would be any the wiser. The sooner he and the DarkFolk got on the road, the better.

Even as this thought crossed his mind, the guest bedroom door opened. The short-haired DarkFolk girl, the one with the puckered, crescent shaped scar at the base of her pointed chin, emerged wrapped only in a towel. And, of course, the bandages swaddling her left hand. She paused when she saw Xavier watching her. He detected no fear, no brazenness. She evinced no emotion at all.

"I may use the bathroom?" she asked, her hand resting on the door handle behind her. The words sounded oddly formal in her deliberate, clipped accent.

"Of course. I tried to tidy up a little. Single guy living alone, you know."

Why the hell had he said that? Especially given the profession he suspected she followed.

She gave a thin, mirthless smile. "You did not expect company, and now there are two DarkFolk whores sleeping in your bed."

"I... That's..." *Dammit, pull yourself together, man!* He inhaled slowly. The room still smelled like pizza. "No, I rarely have company, but that's a me problem. I don't wish to make this any more uncomfortable for either of us. Please, use the bathroom, you and your... your fellow guest. The shower runs hot, just so you know."

She nodded gravely, then closed the bedroom door. She was almost to the bathroom when he cleared his throat.

"I left the ointment and fresh bandages by the sink. If you need help, let me know."

She inclined her head, and for the first time he thought he spotted a spark of emotion in her eyes. Gratitude? Sorrow? Then it faded, and she slipped into the bathroom.

He pushed away the images the running shower summoned, picked up the Novomond Micro information packet and pretended to sift through it. The Thornburg location of the truesilver microchip conglomerate had accepted his short notice inspection the day before with good grace. At least its human management team had. Ajan One Water, clan Elder and senior LightFolk liaison at the factory, had bristled at her people's implied shared responsibility for the Death Curse incident. Xavier had assured her that was not so, and made an effort to single her out in his commendation of the well run operation. She wasn't impressed, but he couldn't please everybody. Some days, he wondered if he pleased anyone.

Hadn't Ajan been the one who tipped off Sharol to the reservation bus attack?

He lost track of that train of thought once the shier DarkFolk girl took her much briefer turn in his bathroom. She wouldn't even meet his eyes until both girls were dressed in their threadbare black cloaks, ready to leave.

Xavier laid out a selection of fruit that hadn't turned overripe, and defrosted a few Kelian pastries he discovered in the back of his freezer. The girls tucked in with relish, although neither finished their pastries. Maybe he hadn't defrosted them all the way.

"We need to get going," he told them. "Sharol, my partner from last night, just texted me. The city reopened the bridge an hour ago. I don't think anyone's looking for you, but the sooner we get you back to Thorn River, the better."

Thanking the Brothers that none of his neighbors appeared during their descent to the underground garage, Xavier ushered the two DarkFolk girls into his car and headed out into the early morning traffic. Peak rush wouldn't hit for another quarter-tenth or so, but long lines of brake lights greeted him as two highways merged within sight of the Frontier Bridge.

"Why are you driving us back to the reservation?" asked the girl with the chin scar. Neither of them had volunteered their names, and he hadn't asked. It was better for all of them that way. "Why not take us to the transit terminal, so we can take the morning bus home?"

Xavier glanced at her in his rear view mirror. She cradled the steel cube safeguarding her chip of flamestone in her lap, covering it with her freshly bandaged hand. She stared intently at the mirror, while her companion gazed with apprehension at the towering office buildings looming over the highway. "You want to take a bus to Thorn River? After last night?"

"No. I am just surprised. You do not have a job to go to?"

"Ah." He rubbed his chin. His beard itched worse than usual this morning. "I do, but it takes me west also."

She narrowed her eyes. Other than the few isolated mansions of the rich and antisocial scattered over the arid hills west of the river, there weren't many places a human would go to work. But, perhaps acknowledging he hadn't inquired about their backgrounds, she changed topic. "Did your partner say what happened last night? With the bus?"

"She did. No deaths, that's the one piece of good news. Many passengers were hospitalized, some with serious injuries. At least one of the attackers too, who almost bled out after his victim fought back." He thought he saw the corner of her mouth twitch. He sighed. "The DarkFolk men were beaten. Most of the women were raped, and beaten too. The police arrested a handful of those involved, but most fled before the cruisers arrived. We'll see if they have any luck tracking more down."

She sniffed in dismissal. "They all wore masks and hoods. They were ashamed of their own humanity. Unless betrayed by others, the police will not find them, even if they bother looking."

Xavier wanted to counter her cynicism, to assure her that there were honest men and women in the police force, that not every human was a prim-hating bigot. But that was exactly what a prim-hating bigot might say. Sometimes, he'd learned, it was better to keep his mouth shut.

"Justice will find them," the DarkFolk girl continued, so soft he almost didn't hear. They were the last words spoken until he approached ti-Lan'ot City with the rising sun at his back.

State police had set up their blockade less than a hundred paces before the reservation police checkpoint on the southern outskirts. Xavier showed his ID to the bored youngster who tapped on his window. The officer peered into the back seat and Xavier managed a wolfish grin and a sly wink. The youngster sneered in disdain, then waved them through without a second glance.

Xavier thought calling the largest community of ti-Lan'ot DarkFolk a city was generous. The low, utilitarian blocks lining the handful of dusty streets would have looked shabby even in one of Thornburg's poorer neighborhoods. The jumble of building materials might have been scavenged from that human metropolis's construction sites, but there the resemblance ended. The bus depot was simply a larger open space next to a ticket office composed largely of rusting corrugated steel.

The quiet girl got out of the car as soon as Xavier unlocked the doors. He decided to stay inside. He didn't want to earn them more unwanted attention than they may already receive.

The girl with the bandaged hand unlatched her door, but paused before opening it. She bit her lower lip as if struggling with something.

"Thank you," she said at last. Then she lowered her head, wrapped her cloak tighter, and walked away.

10

THORN RIVER MINE

Xavier couldn't stop thinking about her as he drove to the mine. He spared the deteriorating road surface some attention—the last thing he needed was a flat tire in the middle of the reservation—but replayed the night's events over and over again.

Why had Sharol insisted he accompany her to witness the bus attack—had she anticipated refugees, or actually believed he could prevent the next atrocity? She'd worked for Folk Affairs long enough to know better.

Would Senator Castlewood take any positive action? Not a chance. After all, technically the DarkFolk were breaking curfew. What did it matter that their work and their employers demanded they take a bus home after the Bell?

Even now, Xavier danced around the truth of his fascination—her pain, his guilt, and the way she refused to break.

I don't even know her name.

He guessed she was a prostitute. Her dullness of expression did not derive from dimwittedness, he felt sure. No practitioner of magic capable of producing a chip of flamestone and enduring the torment of its aftereffects was dim. She simply withheld her emotions, lest they drive her to despair or worse. He'd seen it before.

She's young enough to be my daughter. She's someone else's daughter. What drove her to such a life?

Unfortunately, there were too many reasons that might drive a pretty reservation girl to sell her body. Or, better stated, there were too few other options.

He needed to get out to the reservations more often. Even in the current climate, things needed to change. Folk were people too, no matter what the Purists claimed.

The road wound around the eastern edge of the massive escarpment, shielding ti-Lan'ot City from the cold northerlies, then fell in beside a railroad track that sliced through arid scrubland dotted with struggling homesteads. Many of the single-story houses still showed heartwood framing and white-daubed walls, but few were in good repair.

Xavier missed trees already. He would have to drive half a day westward before seeing many of those again.

Tumbled hills reared ahead, their bare russet-colored slopes blotched with black, as if burned or diseased. A forbidding chain-link fence twice as tall as a man stretched in a wide loop, crossing the rails and skimming the road, which turned west before dwindling into little more than a rutted track. As Xavier approached the gate, three monstrous diesel engines breached the barrier, hauling a line of open freight cars whose far end disappeared into the exhaust haze.

Coal, the lifeblood of the Empire's heavy industry, was the second most important product of Thorn River Mining Company.

Two human guards waved him to a halt. Unlike the bored occupants of the state police reservation checkpoint, these men meant business. Clean shaven, clad in sleek gunmetal gray company uniforms and equipped with half an army's worth of lethal weaponry, they stared impassively through insectoid sunglasses as he showed them his identification.

"Xavier West, Bureau of Folk Affairs. I have an appointment with Director Latham." He brought as much dignity and authority to his statement as he could, but failed to impress either guard.

"Wait," one said tersely, fingering a military-grade assault rifle.

The other conducted a brief conversation over his two-way radio, then approached the driver's side window and held out his hand. "Director Latham is expecting you at the Command Center. I need your phone."

Xavier blinked. "Why?"

"Condition of entry. Phones and other unauthorized electronic communication devices are not permitted onsite. You won't miss it—there's no service close to the mine shafts anyway."

He exchanged Xavier's surrendered phone for a neon pink visitor badge and a hanging decal for the car. "Wear that badge at all times. It contains a radiation monitor. If it starts fading to white, you're in trouble. Don't wander."

With that warning delivered, the guard stepped back and waved Xavier through. The gate slid shut across the roadway behind him. He couldn't shake the feeling he was visiting a friend or relative in jail. He couldn't fault the security so far.

The Command Center consisted of a squat prefab trailer built from dull gray composite. Aesthetically uninspiring, Xavier knew the material was supposed to resist stray radiation from residual flamestone particles. A massive fan lodged in one of the walls filtered out particulates.

The risk to a short-term visitor like him was minimal, or so they said, but for those working daily near the shafts, it compounded. Xavier still felt uneasy.

Director Harran Latham greeted Xavier with the forced smile and careful patience of someone indulging a troublesome relative. "We're always happy to see our friends from the Bureau," he said, a bushy mustache hiding most of a smile that didn't reach his watery eyes. His grip was firm, and his tall spindly frame loomed over his guest like a spider welcoming the fly into his web. "Is this inspection part of the Castlewood Crackdowns?"

Xavier raised an eyebrow. "Is that what they're calling them?"

"Kinda catchy, isn't it? They can play politics in the cities. We've got a real operation out here. No fucking Chaos Walker bullshit in my mine. You'll see. Put these on."

He shoved a stack of safety equipment at Xavier. A pair of scratched plastic glasses rattled inside a grubby hardhat that had once been white, which rested atop a heavy vest matching the pink of the visitor badge. Every human outside, in or close to the mine, wore the same, only their vests were dark green. He stuck out like a sore thumb, but he knew that was the point.

"I can spare you half a tenth," Latham said, as Xavier hurried to keep up with the director's long strides. "Our next shipment is due out by end of day, and I'm told we're behind schedule."

He gestured to a much shorter train waiting in a siding near the pithead. One modest diesel locomotive could pull this load with ease, each of the three cars consisting of narrow cylinders supported by an elaborate steel gantry. Two were already sealed, but a hatch in the top of the last in line yawned open, awaiting its precious and toxic cargo.

Xavier shuddered, recalling the faint green glow of flamestone in the hand of a young DarkFolk woman.

"Does much news of the outside world reach the mine?" Xavier had to yell over the alarming rattle and creaks of the elevator, as their cage descended into darkness. He tried to ignore the slow buildup of claustrophobic panic. "Do your workers know about what happened in Thornburg? About the Crackdowns?"

Latham chuckled without humor. "We don't run a news service here, agent. No phones get service or even last long in and around the mine. That said, word gets out. My staff rotate in and out in tennight shifts, and some are too talkative for their own good, but what are the prims gonna do? This is their home.

They live here, and live under our rules. No Chaos Walker crap here, I guarantee it!"

That was the second time Latham had brought up Chaos Walk. The ancient DarkFolk religion, undergoing a recent resurgence, particularly among the youth, threatened to encourage resistance to human authority, or so the Empire claimed. Brogan Castlewood's new legislation banned it outright, but the DarkFolk working the mine were prisoners in all but name, isolated from even their kin on this benighted reservation. They couldn't practice Chaos Walk in secret, surely. Not with what Xavier suspected were long, brutal workdays and supervised communal living.

What was the director hiding?

The elevator cage rattled alarmingly as it shuddered to a halt at the bottom of the shaft. Bright LED lights hung at intervals around a roughly circular space the size of Xavier's apartment. The harsh reek of burnt wood tainted the still air and caught in his throat. He covered his mouth as he coughed and wished he had thought to bring water.

Latham spared him a condescending glance and gestured towards one of the five passages leading away from the chamber. "This is our most active vein. Low-level stuff. Fodder for the less skilled prims."

Xavier winced at the epithet, but chose not to take issue with it as he followed the director down a scantily lit tunnel. Narrow gauge rails split the middle of a mostly straight passage, just wide enough for the two men to walk side by side. The gradient wasn't that steep, but Xavier marveled at the strength involved in pushing a laden cart of coal back up towards the pithead. Though, that might be preferable to carrying flamestone.

At one of the few remaining mines that employed human workers, Xavier might have expected to hear hammering, drilling, or shouted orders. Here, only a hint of murmured chanting reached his ears.

His skin prickled. Even sanctioned magic disturbed him, whether it hung in breathtaking displays in Pralik One Raven's office or chewed through recyclables in the soulless LightFolk truesilver factories. Magic was wild, alien, and the Empire had crushed it and its practitioners for a reason. Yet truesilver and flamestone were now the Empire's lifeblood, feeding its electronics and insatiable hunger for power. The entire world craved what only Folk magic could produce.

Xavier suspected it was the only reason any of the Folk had been left alive.

"Say again?" Latham held a two-way radio up to his ear, frowning as he tried to decipher the static-ridden squawks from its speaker.

"... op... can proceed... rized?"

"Yes, dammit! I'm in Eda tunnel with a BFA inspector. When I get topside, I wanna see you bring up the rest of my quota."

Static roared from the radio and Latham turned it off in disgust. "One of those smart guys they say we've got needs to invent something that works down here," he muttered.

"What's going on?" Xavier asked.

"Major op in a different vein. We don't use it much, all the easy stuff was exhausted long ago. That one's too risky for casual observation, but you can see some of the prims before you leave if you like. Make sure they're well cared for and all."

Latham's tone was mocking, but Xavier thought he sensed a thread of unease beneath it. *The sooner I get out of this mine, the better.*

A sudden flare of lights ahead revealed a small crowd of people huddled at the current end of the tunnel, just behind a row of rail carts. Two wore the dark vests of human company employees, doing little but watch seven DarkFolk standing in a tight circle. No safety vests or other protective gear for them, just simple shirts and pants of dull brown. DarkFolk naturally resisted the chronic effects of flamestone, or so it was claimed.

The DarkFolk lowered their heads in meditation. Lips moved in unison, summoning their magic. They were all men, of different heights, but features too similar to distinguish in the dark. Each man raised their right arm until fingers touched in the middle of the circle. A heavy steel box lay open on the floor beneath them.

One of the employees—prison guards, Xavier couldn't help thinking—glanced at Latham, who waved impatiently. The employee aimed his flashlight at the box and turned it on and off three times.

Xavier knew what to expect, but couldn't help cringe as the chanting increased in volume. He gasped as the air vanished, sucked from his lungs and the tunnel alike, then slammed back in a pulse of acrid fire. The rough rock at the end of the tunnel simply melted away, silent, leaving black nuggets and chips of coal tumbling onto raw stone.

Xavier blinked and staggered, covering his nose and mouth to protect himself from an eruption of dust that never actually happened. Heartbeats later, it was as if the tunnel had always stretched fifty paces farther, its floor more than ankle-deep in coal.

Magic. After all the times he'd watched it remake the world in front of him, some stubborn part of him still refused to believe it was real.

The DarkFolk slumped as one to the ground, but not before they'd each dropped a sizable chunk of flamestone into the metal box below. Xavier wondered how badly burned their hands were.

The company employees rushed to close and lock the box, its lid clunking louder than any other sound he'd heard down here. Only then did they check on the workers, examining their hands, breaking out canteens of water from a nearby pallet.

"See?" Latham said, already turning for the surface. "Perfectly routine. Give them a few hundredths to catch their breath, then they'll load the coal. Remarkably resilient, these prims."

Xavier stared for a few moments longer. A few of the DarkFolk looked up at him with wary eyes. Eyes that held little hope for their own betterment. Eyes that counted survival as the best of a meager set of unappealing options. Only one, a younger man towards the back of the group, showed any life, tilting his head in what might have been pride, or even defiance.

"Come on, agent," called Latham. "Some of us have a transport to oversee."

Coughing as coal dust caught up to him, Xavier turned. Latham was fifty paces back up the tunnel already, past the rail carts.

The deafening explosion tore through the side wall, shredding the Thorn River mine director to pieces before he knew what was happening.

Then the roof came down.

11

ATONEMENT

"Because it's wrong!"

Ariadne struggled to keep her temper, but honestly, why couldn't people see what was right in front of them?

"Are you arguing from a moral standpoint or a legal one?" Professor Kent demanded for the second time. He ran a hand through his silvering, sand-brown hair and peered at Ariadne over his stylish bifocals. "They are not the same thing."

"Why not? What's the point of the law if it's immoral? How can we justify legalizing clear discrimination against an entire subset of our population? Because that's what it is: discrimination!"

Maya laid a hand on Ariadne's arm as she rose half out of her seat. Most of their fellow students goggled at her outburst, but she noticed more than a few smirks and eye rolls, mostly from the boys. Good old misogyny was still alive and well in this most prestigious of law schools.

Ulysses Kent frowned. He cultivated a roguish, flamboyant reputation, appearing approachable but dangerous. Especially to his female students.

"I am not disagreeing with you, Ariadne. Not all laws are agreeable to us on a personal level. Some of you, perhaps, may one day influence or make those laws. Until then, as those charged with interpreting the established laws of the land and keeping citizens of the Empire safe, how should we reconcile ourselves with laws we find distasteful?"

Distasteful? Curfews and curbs on Folk traditions. The singling out of an entire demographic as second-class citizens of the holier-than-thou Empire.

This rationalization, this lack of outrage, infuriated Ariadne.

"Interpretation is everything," Maya volunteered, sitting up straight and tossing her hair. "Laws are designed to accomplish specific goals. They're rarely so detailed that those on all sides of the ethical and political spectrum can't support interpretations that achieve those goals in ways acceptable to them."

Kent rewarded her with an indulgent smile, and Maya beamed. Could she make it any more obvious? Ariadne loved her best friend, but right now she resented the preening and attention seeking.

Just shut up and fuck him, if you aren't already.

Ariadne bit her tongue and lapsed into sullen silence as others joined the debate. Well, it was hardly a debate. No true opposing views emerged, only nuanced variations of the position Kent espoused. Sociology of Law was a class where currying favor with the professor was particularly important.

"Ari! Wait up!"

Ariadne paused at the top of the Grand Staircase, whose marble steps spiraled in opulent majesty to the lobby two floors below. Maya hurried down the corridor from Kent's lecture theater, dodging other students in far less haste to reach their next destinations. She clutched her backpack to her chest, probably to stop her boobs bouncing.

Brothers, Ari. Bitch much?

"Hey Maya," Ariadne said in a neutral voice. "I'm heading out to the Quad to get some air."

"Join you?" Her tone was earnest, almost wheedling. Most days Maya was a comfort, sometimes Ariadne's only comfort. Not today, but Ariadne simply nodded and set off down the stairs, forcing the other girl to keep pace.

"I wasn't trying to steal your thunder," Maya murmured as they reached the second-floor landing.

"I know what you were doing," Ariadne snapped, before she could stop herself. Maya flinched, but kept walking. Ariadne sighed. "Sorry, I'm being a bitch this morning."

They reached the lobby in silence, then Maya shrugged into her backpack and took Ariadne's arm. "The crackdowns really bother you, huh?"

Ariadne waited until they emerged into the cool sunlight of the Quad. Red brick paths crisscrossed the close-cut grass of the perfect square at the heart of Segard Law School. All the benches and most of the lawn were already occupied, some students taking an early lunch, others just enjoying what they thought of as the open air. But there were no trees, no flowers, simply four tubs of dejected ornamental bushes at the square's corners. The inside of Davek's family home was closer to nature than this.

As if her thought summoned him, she saw her clandestine lover sitting on the grass towards the far left corner. His LightFolk friends, Keralek and Jair, flanked him as usual, resting their feet on their closed book bags. Only those paying close attention would notice the barely perceptible buffer of open space between them and their fellow students.

Ariadne ground her teeth, wondering what Davek would have added to the discussion in Kent's class, and whether anyone would have listened.

"Don't the crackdowns bother you?" she asked Maya, forcing herself to face her friend. She hoped she wasn't blushing, or if she was, that Maya would interpret it as the lingering heat of passionate opinion.

"Of course they do," Maya said, squeezing Ariadne's arm. Her brow furrowed. "Or at least, most of it does. Restricting traditional Folk ceremonies is petulant, and the curfew is outrageous. I'd be surprised if those aren't challenged in court.

But I don't think it's unreasonable to call for closer inspections on the truesilver factories and flamestone mines."

"What do you think they're going to find? And what exactly are they inspecting? Production practices, or workers' activities and personal lives? Those aren't inspections. That's harassment."

Now Maya looked troubled, and her gaze drifted to the far corner of the Quad. "If that's true... but Chaos Walkers are dangerous, Ari. If they infiltrate—"

A chorus of yells cut her off. Ariadne's head snapped around to see five students crowding Davek and his friends. Davek had jumped to his feet and was nose to nose with the ringleader, a gawky young man with tight brown curls and tanned skin, whose handsome face twisted in a snarl. Ariadne recognized him from one of her classes, but didn't remember his name. She hated him instantly, especially when he shoved Davek in the chest hard enough that only his companions prevented his fall.

"Oh no you fucking don't," she growled, shaking free of Maya and striding across the grass.

"Ari, wait!"

But Ariadne didn't listen, or wait for Maya to catch up. She still loathed herself for standing by while Purists murdered a DarkFolk beggar in broad daylight. She was damned if she was going to stand for racist bullying in her own school.

"You don't belong here, prim," Curly sneered, to the obvious enjoyment of his smirking friends. Ariadne ignored them as she approached, sparing more of her irritation on the gawps and inaction of the surrounding students. "No human citizen of the Empire will ever listen to a LightFolk lawyer. If you want to practice on the reservations, or keep your people from breaking curfew, go ahead. But you shouldn't take a place at Segard from someone who's gonna be a real lawyer."

"I could say the same about you, Menzies," Davek retorted, his body shaking, fingers flexing in and out of fists. He ignored Keralek and Jair, who were trying to tug him backwards, away from the confrontation. "I'm surprised they haven't flunked your dumb ass yet. You couldn't prosecute a traffic ticket."

Menzies' eyes bulged and he bared his teeth, drawing back his right fist. "How dare you talk to me like that, you little prim sh—"

His head rocked on his shoulders and blood sprayed from his split lip. He staggered from Ariadne's sucker punch, and she landed another blow, then a third, beating him to the ground. Menzies tried to protect his head as she fell to her knees, pummeling him in a merciless frenzy. Other hands clawed at her, trying to pull her away. She fought them off too, for as long as she could.

She wasn't just fighting for Davek. She wasn't just fighting for the LightFolk or the DarkFolk. She fought for a poor, defenseless man, down on his luck, not harming anyone, who'd been murdered in front of her eyes. She hadn't done anything about it then, but she was sure as shit making up for it now.

"Ariadne!"

It wasn't until Davek's urgent voice pierced the chaos that she realized she was screaming as she battered Menzies, in plain sight of dozens of other students. Her bloodied fists dropped to her side, and she stared panting at the boy curled up in a fetal position before her.

Davek dropped to his knees beside her and gripped her trembling shoulders. Just like that, her adrenaline-fueled rage subsided, leaving horror in its wake. What had she done?

Menzies groaned and rolled over onto his side, uncovering his face. Blood poured from both his lip and a distinctly broken nose. He looked up at Ariadne, but his eyes were unfocused, no trace of arrogance or contempt or even fear. Two of his friends dropped to the ground and tried to haul him up, but he couldn't, or wouldn't, stand.

"You'll pay for that, you crazy fucking bitch!" another spat. "When his father—"

"Oh no."

Suddenly Maya was there, planting her feet between the speaker and her friend, hands on her hips. He took a step back, for all that Maya was a full head shorter than him. "Don't pull the 'his father' card on us, Jordan, you spineless weasel. You and Menzies think you can run your mouths without consequences? These are the consequences. Deal with them like the 'men' you seem to think you are."

Maya turned her back on Menzies and Jordan, dismissing their mute indignance. She held a hand out to Ariadne, awe and compassion softening her smile. "Come on, love. Let's get you cleaned up."

Ariadne found herself walking back through the Quad between Maya and Davek. Dully, she registered the wary, astonished looks from everyone they passed.

Inside, Maya steered them to the nearest women's bathroom. She exchanged a shrewd, understanding look with Davek, who let go of Ariadne's other arm. He opened his mouth to say something, then grimaced, before fading back into the crowd.

Maya set Ariadne in front of a sink and ran both faucets. "Hold your hands under the water," she commanded. Ariadne did as she was told. She stared at her reflection as if she didn't recognize the girl looking back. Maya dabbed at her face with a wet towel, wiping spots of blood off her skin. Her friend was calm and tender, and offered no judgment. That, more than anything else, stopped the shaking and slowed Ariadne's heart rate.

Once the water ran clear, Maya dried Ariadne's hands and took them in her own. "Are you okay?"

Ariadne took a deep, shuddering breath, then wrapped Maya in a fierce hug. "I'm better, thank you, hon. 'Okay', might be pushing it. I made at least one enemy today."

Maya snorted. "Menzies deserved it. I don't care if it was LightFolk he was bullying. A bully is a bully, and that prick, Jordan... Don't worry about it. What are they gonna do?"

That question was answered a half-tenth later, when the police arrived.

Segard Law School hosted a police substation, a small office in one of the secondary buildings making up the civic campus. The two assigned officers dealt mostly with keeping students safe from unsavory trespassers, and occasionally with matters of petty theft. They didn't have anything like a holding cell, so the officers who came for Ariadne took her to the main Embankment police station several blocks away.

Her racing pulse and righteous anger, which Maya had so lovingly and effectively soothed, reared up once more. She didn't resist, even as they slipped the cuffs over her wrists. The woman and two men who accosted her as she emerged from the school's main entrance were polite but firm. No one was interested in making a scene, but Ariadne seethed in the back of the police cruiser.

"I've got you, love!" Maya promised as the door closed. Through the mercifully tinted window, Ariadne saw her friend stab at her phone and begin an animated conversation.

"What exactly am I being charged with?" Ariadne demanded after they'd parked behind a dingy stone building whose unremarkable classic Earian flourishes must have been added as an afterthought. "'Assault' is a very broad term."

"Second Degree Grievous Bodily Harm," said the burly, short-haired female officer. The name "BRADY" was stenciled on the badge pinned to her chest. Her junior counterparts hovered either side of Ariadne as she exited the car, and failed to intimidate half as much as Brady did. "Let's go inside and book you."

"GBH? That's outrageous!"

Brady paused before the station's rear doors. The ruddy-faced look she gave Ariadne wasn't unfriendly, maybe even betrayed a hint of sympathy. "May I remind you of your right to remain silent?" she murmured. "Your accuser can afford the best lawyers. Given where we apprehended you, I'm sure you understand what that means."

It meant that fucking Menzies—she didn't even know the jerk's first name—had the upper hand.

Damn it! I should have punched him harder.

Ariadne took a deep breath, then gave the officer a curt nod of acknowledgment.

Brady took her inside and logged the ludicrous charge. Her only audience in the surprisingly dim booking area were two pale, thin men in plain, mismatched clothing. They sat opposite each other, cuffed wrists in their laps, and watched the process with curious dark eyes. She guessed they were brothers, but she spared them only a moment of attention.

Now she was inside the police station, the reality of her arrest sank in. She fought a rising panic.

"You'll need to stay here until we can find a judge to set bail," Officer Brady told her. "That may happen this afternoon, but there's no guarantee. Is there anyone you need to call?"

I could be locked up overnight in a police station holding cell? Holy Brothers!

"Umm, yeah," she stammered, then steeled herself. "I want to call my dad."

"You don't have to tell me who," Brady said. She led Ariadne down a short corridor, whose brighter lights revealed chipped floor tile with scratches and dents in the walls.

In a small, windowless room towards the end, sat a narrow table supporting a corded phone. Brady unlocked Ariadne's cuffs and waved at the scuffed wooden chair next to it. "We have to leave the door open. I'll give you a few hundredths."

The police had confiscated her backpack and phone before putting her in the car. She remembered very few numbers off the top of her head, family mostly. And Maya, but Maya was already doing whatever she could on her behalf. Bailing her out was unlikely to be one of them.

There was only one choice. Ariadne picked up the receiver, waited for the dial tone, and punched in the digits for her father's cell phone.

She composed herself as it rang, trying to imagine how she would break the news or what she would ask for. *Come and get me, Dad?* That sounded pitiful and also implausible. He was halfway across the country, in Thornburg. Even willing, he would struggle to make it to New Ashbrook that day.

By the sixth ring, Ariadne realized her father wasn't going to pick up, even before the subsequent click and his awkward voicemail greeting. "Hello! Um, this is Xavier West. I can't answer right now and, um, so leave a message and I'll call you back. Oh, and a number too. Your number. Um, thanks."

She stared bleakly at the receiver for a few moments, then replaced it without saying a word. The prospect of confessing her arrest over a phone conversation was horrifying enough. She couldn't leave a voicemail. What number would she even give him?

She tried again. "Come on, Dad," she murmured, glancing at the room's open doorway. This time it picked up on the second ring, but her momentary relief soon evaporated.

"The number you have called is currently unavailable. Please wait and try again later."

What the fuck does that even mean?

Ariadne thought furiously. She knew her father sometimes visited the DarkFolk reservations as part of his Bureau of Folk Affairs job. They often received shitty cell service. There was a big reservation near Thornburg, wasn't there? He'd told her, maybe more than once, but it was a detail she'd never been sufficiently interested in to remember.

She tried one more time, hoping to reach his voice mail again and leave a generic "call me" message. No luck. Xavier West, senior BFA agent, was unavailable. She'd saved his partner's number and the Thornburg BFA office in her phone, but a fat lot of help that was now.

Ariadne stared at the blank wall ahead and racked her brain for an option other than the obvious one. The one she really didn't want to take.

She had no choice.

Fuck.

She punched in the numbers with reluctance, bracing herself for what was sure to be as unpleasant an experience as her arrest.

A young woman's clipped voice answered. "Hello? Senator Braeyer's phone."

"Hi, Val," Ariadne said. "Can I speak to my mother, please? It's urgent."

12

BLACK ROSES

Davek still shook with repressed fury, almost a quarter-tenth after his confrontation with Aleister Menzies and Ariadne's shocking intervention. He locked himself in a stall in the nearest bathroom, assuring Keralek Three Raven and Jair One Water that he'd see them later in their Tort lecture. He wasn't at all sure he'd make it.

He knew his secret human lover had saved him from making at least one poor decision. Any poor decision at Segard would likely see him suspended, or even expelled, in the current climate. The three LightFolk were pioneers, the first of their kind to qualify for a new scholarship offered by one of the college's more progressive benefactors. Expectations for their future legal careers were modest, but all revolutions started small.

Davek longed for more.

So he'd stood there and soaked up as much of Menzies's bigotry as he could before his waspish tongue got the better of him. What would have happened if Ariadne hadn't smacked the arrogant prick in the side of the head? Nothing good, not for Davek at any rate.

Ariadne. She'd assaulted a fellow student for him. Pummeled the mouthy bastard into a whiny ball on the ground, while his so-called friends stood around in frozen shock. As had Davek and the entire quad. He'd actually had to stop her, or how far would she have gone?

How much trouble was she in?

He'd wanted to thank her, no, to protect her afterward. His feelings toward Ariadne were complicated, to say the least, but she'd stood up for him in a way no human ever had. But Maya stepped in instead, of course. Maya, her best friend. Maya, the brilliant student and everyone's crush, even some of the professors. Maya knew best, and bloody Maya always got her bloody way.

Maya was right. Davek couldn't be seen to be anything but grateful for Ariadne's inexplicable actions on his behalf. He didn't know what the blonde suspected about her friend's reasons or their relationship, but the wordless look she'd given Davek in the lobby afterward spoke volumes.

You shouldn't be seen with her. Especially not now. Go. I've got this.

The restroom door opened and feet shuffled over the scuffed white tile toward the urinals. Davek seized control of himself. He couldn't skulk in this stall all day.

Maya was right. He hoped she did, in fact, have this, but he couldn't face a Tort lecture either. He was fairly sure Menzies was in that one too, or would be if his public beating allowed. What pleasure Davek might derive from gloating over the bully's comeuppance would be more than offset by the dark looks and potentially worse harassment he'd endure.

Slipping through the corridors as invisibly as he could, Davek hurried to Theater Four, hoping to catch Professor Kovic early in her preparations.

Serala Kovic was the only tenured female professor at Segard. She had one of the most brilliant legal minds in the Empire, and needed every bit of it to prevail in a male dominated profession. In some ways, many of her peers and students resented her as much as Davek and his LightFolk interlopers. Yet, he expected no sympathy. Kovic survived by being tougher than any of her male counterparts, and less compromising.

But Davek had to try. Simply skipping her lecture would not go unnoticed.

Luck was on his side, insofar as he discovered her alone in the smallest, mustiest theater in the college. With her silver hair pinned in a rigid bun, she reminded him of a bird of prey as she frowned down over her beak of a nose at her laptop. He stopped just inside the doorway, and tried to think of the right words.

"Yes, Mr. One Raven? Are you as shocked by your unprecedented enthusiasm for my subject as I am? You're almost ten hundredths early."

"I, umm..." Davek stammered, then tried to cover that with a sheepish grin. "I just came to tell you I'm not feeling well. I'm going to head home. Can you give me the homework assignment so I can work on it later?"

The professor's impatient expression turned shrewd. "Avoiding fisticuffs in my lecture, Mr. One Raven? Very wise. A one-thousand-word analysis of Becker and Joievier, chapter seven, in my email inbox by Eightday evening."

Davek suppressed a groan. How could he make "this is the most boring book I've ever read" last a thousand words? But he forced a grateful smile and withdrew, before any of his classmates arrived.

He kept to the stairs and quieter side corridors, and so was still in the building when his phone buzzed. Sheltering behind a venerable display case featuring images of famous alumni, he dug it out of his faded everwool pants and squinted at the screen.

OALiA.

The sender was a meaningless four digit number, the kind used by automated systems to broadcast appointment notifications or weather alerts. But even anonymized, Davek knew who this was from.

"Oalia" was a name for the Mother in the almost defunct old tongue of the One Raven clan. His ancestors had used the name for the Mother's protector persona. It was rarely uttered these days, only in desperate appeal. Most believed that Mother's aspect had failed the people one hundred and sixty one years ago.

The lower case "i" was not a typo. It was the message.

Davek backtracked to the mailroom, a dingy, ill-lit cube near the administration office. Rows of faded steel mailboxes stacked atop each other on every wall. Even in this modern era, when class schedules, exam results, and most other pieces of Segard business were available online, all students were assigned a physical mailbox. Sometimes the administration chose to send information the old-fashioned way just to keep students on their toes.

Davek sat on his haunches and searched for the five-digit numbered box. It sat in the bottom row midway along the back wall. The advantage was that his body naturally shielded its contents from the doorway, but he glanced over his shoulder before opening it all the same. He was alone.

Inside the shoebox-sized cavity lay a standard cream-colored envelope stuffed with what felt like multiple sheets of paper, possibly of different sizes. Curious despite himself, Davek turned the envelope over, but the outside was completely blank. He slid it inside his backpack, locked his mailbox, and stood up before replying to the text: "*XX*".

Requested action acknowledged and performed.

Davek dug out his mirror-shade sunglasses and left the building as quickly and invisibly as possible. He was just debating where to await his next instructions when his phone vibrated again. An address and a time.

He knew better than to map the address on his phone. Fortunately, he knew the general area: Bottleworks, a former industrial district where gentrification efforts had not so much stalled as collapsed. Lots of working poor lived there. Lots of LightFolk. And he had just over a half tenth to find the address and deliver the envelope.

If he hurried, he had time to go home and change into something less "preppy". What usually allowed him to blend in at Segard would have the opposite effect on the streets of Bottleworks. And, failing invisibility, blending in was important.

Drops of rain splashed his face as Davek entered Kulish Circle. He skirted a tour group as they listened to lies and misrepresentations. He didn't entirely blame the young human docent; they were educated and trained to believe the Empire's version of events, which is exactly what their customers wanted to hear.

He slipped into his family's house as quietly as he could. His father would still be at Metropolitan Academy, and he'd hoped his mother was out on her social rounds, but apparently those rounds had followed her home.

The chink of porcelain and light melodious laughter greeted him from the parlor. He risked a glance inside as he headed for the staircase. Five other One Raven matrons sat in a circle around their coffee table, which was laden with cups, saucers, and several plates of cakes and sandwiches. His mother presided from her usual armchair, a gaudy creation of forest green velvet and brass studs, reading aloud from a book. He noticed the other women, arrayed on the matching couch and loveseat, each had their own copy of the same book. They hung on Laida's every word.

By the Mother and her Children, a book club tea party? Could they imitate the Empire more if they tried?

Davek seethed with suppressed resentment. He understood the expediency of fitting in, but to embrace their conquerors' customs so shamelessly mystified him.

Careful where you sit, ladies. I fucked an Empire girl on that couch only yesterday.

He avoided the creaking steps and made it to his upstairs bedroom unobserved. Dumping his backpack onto the bed, he shucked out of his college threads and replaced them with a plain white T-shirt and jeans of faded black denim. His old matching denim jacket had failed to keep pace with his teenage growth spurt, but it sported a large inside pocket, into which he slid the unmarked envelope.

He checked his watch. Barely a quarter tenth until the drop off. He grabbed a battered black peaked cap and headed for the front door.

"Davek?"

Shit.

His mother stood in the parlor doorway, carrying a teapot on a silver tray. He noticed the teapot's blue and white design was based on Kelian motifs, and his irritation deepened.

"Hey, Mom," he said, forcing a sheepish grin. "I didn't want to interrupt your reading."

Laida, wearing one of her most elegant robes, favored him with an indulgent smile. She raised an eyebrow as she took in his clothes. "I take it classes are over for the day?"

"Yup." For him they were, anyway. "Gotta go help a friend with a thing, then I've got a Tort paper to write."

"You'll be wanting dinner in your room then?"

Several of her friends giggled, and Davek understood she was playing to her audience. Fine, two could play at that game.

"No, Ma," he replied in his best long-suffering teenage boy voice. "I'll come down for dinner with the family, but I gotta go."

As he escaped out the front door, he heard one of the other women proclaim "Boys! They only think with their stomachs!"

"But he's studying at Segard Law School! You must be so proud, Laida!"

He closed the door. He didn't want to hear it.

The raindrops had joined forces into a light shower, even as shafts of sun still fought with the growing cloud cover. Davek jammed the cap over his head, grimacing over what it would do to his hair, and headed for the river.

Kulish Circle nestled among the fringes of Oldtown, a district of respectable residential neighborhoods that bordered the Mariana River. Named for the consort of Emperor Justice III, whose armies first overran One Raven's ancestral lands and those of other clans up and down the east coast of Novomond, the Mariana sliced New Ashbrook roughly in two. Tourists generally stayed on the north bank, which hosted the business and main shopping districts, as well as the most affluent homes and communities.

On the south bank, toward which Davek walked at a pace bordering a jog, lay what had once been the industrial beating heart of the nation. Bottleworks and its peers may have declined from their heyday over fifty years ago, but sprinkled between and around the warehouses, docks, refineries, and old coal power stations were the homes of working communities. Most LightFolk lived there, along with their poorer human counterparts. For all that they shared circumstances, the two groups kept to themselves as part of a frail, uneasy truce. Especially these days.

Gusts of wind tossed rain at Davek from all directions as he sped across the iconic Bottleworks Bridge. The first suspension bridge opened in Novomond had been photographed from all angles, and saw more municipal investment than the district after which it was named. The sour reek of cooking yeast greeted him on the southern shore, likely from the cluster of squat warehouses comprising the Pioneer Brewery, still one of the world's largest. Other than a handful of more adventurous tourists sampling the tasting room, and local hipsters patronizing the handful of trendy riverfront restaurants, the shabby streets were empty.

Davek paused on the first street corner, made sure of his bearings, and plunged into the heart of the neighborhood. In six short blocks, shabbiness descended into disrepair. The first apartment buildings promised little luxury or space, but retained their dignity. All too soon he passed tenements whose boarded up windows sported increasing amounts of spray painted graffiti, sometimes artistic, but mostly territorial. Some structures, obviously closed or derelict, stood like a row of broken and decaying teeth, awaiting repair or demolition that might never come. Cracks and potholes scarred the road, while weeds ran rampant around and between the uneven, broken slabs of sidewalk.

Tourists rarely ventured this far. If they did, the two bleak tower blocks flanking the deteriorating road at the Sixth Street intersection would repel them. The developers had bestowed the name Paradise Gardens on the city's first low-income housing project three decades ago. New Ashbrookers assumed that was an inside joke. Weeds aside, there was little green and no gardens in evidence among the brutal slabs of soot-darkened concrete. It was certainly no one's idea of paradise.

An eerie hush permeated the eastern tower as Davek reached its dilapidated forecourt. The peeling paint above the grimy glass of the entrance doors, miraculously still intact, confirmed his destination: "PARADISE GARDENS EAST".

He licked his lips and hesitated. Cool rain still fell in the middle of a workday afternoon, but he'd expected to see some signs of life. He'd feared having to avoid gangbangers skulking outside the brightly tagged walls, or lurking in the gloomy corridors within. He feared the silence even more.

Davek's vibrating watch startled him. He'd set the alarm before leaving his house. Three hundredths before drop-off. He glanced at the dull, battered door of the nearest elevator, took a deep breath, and headed for the stairs. They wound up the outside of the tower, open to the air, and puddles of what he hoped was just rainwater gathered on every landing. But no one could pay him enough to get in one of those elevators.

He was young and fit, but he needed a moment after reaching the ninth floor. A moment was all he had. Steadying his breathing, he shuffled down the exterior hallway until he arrived at a plain door of faded red with "907" stenciled on it at head height. He knocked twice, paused, then knocked twice again.

The door opened silently into darkness.

Davek knew better than to stand on the threshold gawking. He stepped into the apartment with confidence he didn't feel, past the hulking figure holding open the door. They were almost as broad as they were tall, clad head to foot in black. Before they closed the door behind them, cutting off the little reluctant light filtering into the room, Davek noted the simple cloth hood and mask covering their head and face.

A Chaos Walker mask.

His heart beat faster, but it was as much excitement as fear. The recently banned Chaos Walk tradition—or "religion" as the Empire would have it—had its origins in the time before LightFolk and DarkFolk. Before the Empire's conquest, Folk were just Folk. The clans did not always get on, and fighting or even petty wars were not unknown.

After the Conquest came the Great Division, after which those clans that became DarkFolk preserved the old ways without compromise. Chaos Walk crystallized what it meant to be Folk, where their people had come from, and who they were now. Despite recent Empire propaganda, few LightFolk expressed any interest in it, having embraced the customs and culture of their conquerors in order to survive.

Some compared it to the Purist movement within the Empire, but Davek recoiled at the idea. Purists like Aleister Menzies were reactionary, racist bullies in search of a flag to wave while intimidating those they felt threatened by. Chaos Walk was all about pride in being Folk, and the righteous struggle for dignity and equality. Those were the reasons he attended Segard after all, to become a lawyer and strive for justice for his people. Chaos Walk was another aspect of that struggle, and Davek found it fascinating.

The Walker didn't speak. In the last of the exterior light, they gestured toward a barely visible doorway leading toward the heart of the apartment. Davek took his cue, and tiptoed carefully toward the slightly less dark rectangle within the wall of black ahead. The apartment appeared devoid of furnishings, but it stank of bleach over an unmistakable undercurrent of stale vomit.

As he reached that interior doorway, very conscious of the Walker looming behind him, Davek recognized another source of light. Dim, orange, and flickering, it buffeted the shadows heroically. A candle flame.

He spotted the source as soon as he stepped into the next room. It was difficult to judge in the gloom, but glimpses of wall cabinets suggested this might have been the kitchen. Its only other furniture was a small table upon which the candle stood, next to a vase holding a single rose. On the other side of the table sat another figure, taller than the first, but masked and clad in black just the same. Another Chaos Walker.

Davek halted before the table and tried to remember the protocol he'd been taught. The uncomfortable silence stretched, then the seated figure made a small gesture with their gloved hand toward the other chair. Davek sat and waited.

The Chaos Walker didn't move again for several heartbeats, then slowly drew the glove off their right hand. A man's hand, definitely, turned palm upwards. Another pause, then the air hummed and Davek's skin prickled. A whispered rustling filled the air, then new stems branched off the rose—two, three, four—lengthening into vines that stretched toward the four corners of the table. Abnormally long thorns scratched the surface until, with a final surge of energy, the vines burst into clusters of new roses. Black roses.

The vines grew quiescent and the air stilled. Davek swallowed and nodded.

The Chaos Walker curled his fingers into a fist before Davek could see what lay within. He didn't need to. He didn't want to. He drew the envelope from his jacket pocket, laid it on the table, then stood up and left.

He barely noticed the rain on his entire walk home.

13

SAVIOR

Darkness. Utter silence. The acrid stench of smoke. Dust or soot filling Xavier's nostrils and coating his tongue.

Was he alive? Or had he been condemned to one of the afterlife's Punishment Realms?

Xavier groaned, more to prove that sound was possible than in the hope of any response. He lay on his side, his left arm trapped underneath, jagged rock digging into his clothes and skin. His right arm was coiled over his head in protection, which must have worked if he was recovering consciousness. His legs...

He couldn't move his legs.

Adrenaline pulsed through his veins. His deepest fear of being buried alive, born from a prank by a childhood friend whose family ran a funeral parlor, erupted from its shallow grave in his mind. He couldn't move. He couldn't remember how to breathe. His heart hammered like an oncoming freight train. He couldn't move! He couldn't—

Xavier's gaping mouth caught enough of the unseen, swirling rock dust to trigger his body's reaction, bypassing his paralyzed brain. He gagged, then inhaled a double lungful of bitter air. Huge wracking coughs followed, making him flop like a fish freshly hauled from the water. Fierce pain flared in his right ankle and shin, and his head swam.

He passed out for a time.

When consciousness returned, like a persistent unwelcome house guest, light flooded in. And someone was touching him.

Xavier flinched from the hand on his shoulder even as he sought the source of the dull red glow. For a moment he feared fire, but no, the glow was steady. An emergency lamp perhaps.

Who's touching me?

He twisted his head upward to see the silhouette of someone kneeling next to him. He couldn't tell if it was one of the company employees or a DarkFolk miner. All he could really see was an intense pair of eyes. Their owner held his gaze while barking something unintelligible over his shoulder.

DarkFolk, then.

"You are alive." The miner's halting deep voice scratched as if from a throat injury, or years of yelling over machinery. "This hurts?"

Surprisingly gentle fingers probed the length of Xavier's right arm. He winced as they found a sensitive patch just above his elbow.

"No. Not really." Xavier could barely summon a whisper, but the DarkFolk nodded before tilting his head.

"Legs trapped. Rockfall."

Xavier could feel an immense weight over his feet and shins, although not much sensation in those body parts themselves. He tried to wriggle free, only to be rewarded with another spike of agony.

The miner rested a hand on his shoulder. "Do not move. It will not help. Save strength."

"What happened? Latham... Who else is alive?"

Xavier thought he heard a snort of disgust. "One company man, buried. Dead. The other, free of rock but not awake. Head wound."

"And the miners? Are you all OK?"

There was a long pause. "We are alive. For now."

For now. Xavier didn't like the sound of that. "There was an explosion."

"Yes. There was a working in another tunnel. Bad place. Unstable."

Latham had been determined to make his quota. Had he taken a risk and paid the price?

The image of flying rock shredding the director's flesh flashed in front of Xavier's eyes. He closed them and shuddered.

Assuming it was the source of the explosion, how close had the other vein been? Could a force that powerful have left anything of the tunnel on the other side of the rockfall under which his legs were trapped? Was there another way out? How long would their breathable air last? What were the chances of another explosion?

They were alive, for now. But was there any hope of staying that way?

The horror of spending the night in jail, even in a holding cell at a police station, settled over Ariadne like a shroud.

She sat on a hard wooden bench in the corner of a cold concrete room, knees drawn up under her chin to make herself as small as possible. Not long after the taciturn Officer Brady locked the barred door behind her, she heard a distant commotion. Female voices yelled, male voices barked commands. Another door banged open, and two young women, scantily clad under thigh length jackets, struggled in the grip of the same male officers who'd arrested Ariadne. The women cussed and graphically demeaned the size of their captors' genitalia, but they ended up in the cell with Ariadne all the same.

"Fuck you!" screamed the taller woman, a bleach blonde who might have been pretty once. Thinning hair and the distinctive pink tinge of her sclerae betrayed her addiction to Shade. The Kelian drug still ran rampant on the streets of Novomond a decade after its introduction as a post-surgery pain killer. "We're just trying to make a living, you tiny dick fuckwads! I gotta pay rent tomorrow."

"Cops don't have dicks, Belle." The redhead didn't look at her companion, but called her reply down the hall. One bare arm stuck out of her jacket, its pale skin streaked with horrific scratches. "Especially the male ones. Don't know why they try to get off harassing prozzies."

Once it became clear their torrent of abuse would draw no further reaction, the pair finally seemed to notice Ariadne. The blonde, Belle, narrowed her eyes and took a step towards the corner. Ariadne cringed.

"Nothing to be scared of, precious. What do these bastards have you in for? You don't look like you're in the biz."

"Got in a fight," Ariadne mumbled. The last thing she wanted right now was to strike up a conversation with a Shader prostitute. She tried not to judge sex workers, even though the idea of selling her body for a living revolted her. But Shaders were notorious for violent mood swings, especially when deprived of their next fix. She was trapped in a cell with two of them, and they'd been screaming their heads off for the last several hundredths.

Belle stared at the soberly-dressed young woman hugging her knees in the corner of a police cell with evident skepticism. Then she lost interest, laid down on the opposite end of the bench, and appeared to fall asleep.

Her companion, however, was far more curious. The redhead manufactured the kind of smile she might use on prospective clients and sat down next to Ariadne, close enough for their thighs to touch. "Some things are worth fighting for," she purred, resting a hand on Ariadne's knee. If she saw the other woman flinch, her pink eyes showed no sign. "Say, do you have any Shade on you? Just enough to tie me over until Gregor gets here to bail us out."

Ariadne leaned as far away as the cold walls would allow. "Sorry, I've never tried it. I don't do drugs."

Her denial didn't appear to register. The redhead stroked her knee absently for several awkward heartbeats. Then, as if someone flicked a switch, her eyes bulged and her caressing fingers dug painfully into Ariadne's thigh.

"Fuck!" she shrieked. Before Ariadne could begin to defend herself, the redhead sprang to her feet, spun around, and drove her fist into the middle of the wall. Knuckle bones broke with a sickening crunch, and droplets of blood splashed over Ariadne's astonished face. The redhead stood still for a breath, staring at her ruined hand, then collapsed onto the floor next to her oblivious companion, howling in agony.

Ariadne leapt to her feet and hammered on the iron bars. "Help! Please, for Brothers' sake, help!"

Get me out of here! I'll do anything, please!

It was no use. No one was coming to bail her out.

But then someone did. Someone she never expected.

As Ariadne stared down the hallway, clutching the iron bars and resting her forehead against them like the wronged prisoner in every cop show she'd ever watched, two officers appeared at the far end. One was Brady, accompanied by one of the male cops who'd joined her at Ariadne's arrest. Ariadne stepped back as they approached the cell door.

"I didn't expect you to join in the ruckus," Brady said as the other cop unlocked the door.

Ariadne gestured behind her, to where the redhead slumped, clutching her hand and whimpering. "She hurt herself, bad. Broke her hand, I think. Punched the wall," she added hastily. They wouldn't suspect her of beating up a drug-addled prostitute, would they?

Brady smiled grimly and pointed up at the ceiling above where Ariadne had been sitting. A camera lens peered from behind a black wire mesh guard. "These aren't the first Shaders we've had in our cells. It's not even the first time for these two."

She spat on the ground, and Ariadne flinched. "Fucking drug is bad news. These two don't have long left."

The male officer knelt next to the redhead, showing no resentment at her recent verbal abuse. With surprising tenderness, he cleaned her hand with antiseptic wipes from his first aid kit, then wrapped it in gauze. The woman burst into tears.

"She needs a doctor," he told Brady. "At least two fingers broken, maybe three."

"Make the call," she said, then turned to Ariadne. "I'm gonna escort this one out."

Ariadne blinked. "Out?"

"Bail has been posted, Ms. West. You're free to go."

Dumbfounded, Ariadne followed Brady down the corridor. She hadn't made any more calls, and she doubted her mother had had a sudden change of heart. So who...?

Two LightFolk waited for her at the front desk. She didn't recognize the older and taller of the pair, although he was striking enough that she'd never have forgotten him had they met before. Long black hair framed a handsome triangular face, his flawless skin darker than the average LightFolk. What looked like a burn scar split his right eyebrow in two, and lent him a roguish air. He wore a loose amber colored shirt, unbuttoned at the collar, and sleek everwool pants of a stylish cut. He gave her an easy smile in greeting, but his eyes burned with curiosity.

The second LightFolk was Davek.

Ariadne stopped dead and gaped at him. His smile was awkward, but genuine. She guessed he was happy to see her, but embarrassed by the circumstances.

No more embarrassed than I am, trust me.

"Davek?"

He straightened up with an insouciant grin. "Hey, Ariadne. Sorry it took so long. This is Khavrik One Raven. He's a clan Elder, just like my dad."

Khavrik stepped forward and offered his hand, palm down. She recalled the custom, a formal greeting between clans. She turned her right hand palm up and laid it on top of his. His smile could set hearts ablaze.

"The clan recognizes its allies, Ariadne West," he said in a melodious baritone. He waited for her to blink, then withdrew his hand, leaving hers dangling in air for a moment.

"Why...? How...?" *Smooth, Ari.* The two LightFolk waited in patient silence for her to speak. *Pull yourself together, girl!*

"Thank you," she finally said, clasping her hands together to prevent them wandering aimlessly. "I thought I was gonna spend the night here. Thank you."

· Khavrik nodded. "Of course. Let's get you home, or wherever it is you wish to go."

She didn't miss the twinkle in Khavrik's eye or Davek's sudden embarrassment. Nice. But she refused to be ungrateful. She lifted her head high and met the Elder's still curious gaze. "Home sounds great."

Two vehicles awaited them outside. The lights of the modern black sedan flashed in response to the key fob Khavrik brandished. The flatbed truck next to it might have rolled off the assembly line before Ariadne was even born. Dull red and brown were the predominant colors, but body panels and, presumably, other parts had been replaced haphazardly throughout its life. An older LightFolk, tufts of white hair clinging to his liver-spotted scalp, stood next to it wearing the simple blue overalls of an auto shop mechanic.

Khavrik murmured a few private words into the older man's ear, then pressed a wad of bills into his hand. The mechanic handed over a ring of keys, then walked off without so much as a glance at Ariadne.

Khavrik tossed the keys to Davek and smiled. "I'm needed elsewhere. Return the truck tomorrow morning. And give my regards to your father. I hope you're not too late for family dinner."

Davek snorted, then helped Ariadne climb into the truck's passenger seat. The cab was cleaner than she expected, although several rips in the leather bench exposed wisps of foam stuffing. The pungent odors of gasoline and unfiltered tobacco assaulted her nostrils as Davek slid behind the wheel. She couldn't wind down the window fast enough.

Driving through the heart of New Ashbrook was a novel experience. Taxis were a rare luxury, usually reserved for the rare late night out with Maya and friends when the subway seemed too risky. Dusk had fallen by the time Ariadne's rescuers arrived, but there was daylight enough for her to see the streets change character, and the people with them. They skirted Segard, fighting stop and go traffic as hordes of commuters poured out of tightly clustered skyscrapers crowding the venerable law school. She didn't see many other private cars among the buses and taxis until they reached the urban foothills of North Embankment. There, six- and seven-story office buildings allowed the day's last few rays of sunlight to illuminate a dense quilt of commerce and residence. Few pedestrians paid any mind to the old truck trundling past. Everyone had their own business to mind.

"How did you know I needed bail?"

Davek started, lost in his own thoughts. He looked as if he'd forgotten why he was driving a beat-up flatbed with a human girl as his passenger. "Sorry, Ari. What?"

"I only called two people. My dad never picked up and my mom refused to help. So how did you even know where I was, let alone needed bail money?"

He grimaced. "Maya told me you'd been arrested. I... I wasn't home and didn't get her message until a tenth or so ago. She hadn't heard from you and wondered if I had. I got worried. Khavrik, um, he knows people, and I asked him to help. I hoped he'd find out where you were. I didn't expect him to post your bail."

Ariadne frowned. She knew there was more to the story than that. "Khavrik is another One Raven Elder? Like your dad?"

"Yeah." Davek's skin was too dark to flush, but his shifty eyes betrayed embarrassment. "Dad's too busy with preparations for the Hunter's Moon Festival tomorrow, assuming we're allowed to have it."

"But Khavrik can spare time and money to bail a random human girl out of jail?" Ariadne persisted, refusing to be redirected.

They stopped at another red light, and Davek looked at her. Truly looked at her. He took her hand and stared at her with heart-stopping intensity.

"He did it for me. For us. You stood up for me. Do you know how rare it is for a human to take the side of the Folk against another human in public? You got arrested for it. As far as Khavrik was concerned, we were in your debt. And now the debt is paid."

"Nonsense," Ariadne murmured, swallowing. Her throat was so dry.

She stroked the back of Davek's hand with her thumb, and tried to ignore the desire stirring within her. Suddenly, she needed his arms around her, his body inside her, in the worst way.

Davek licked his lips, which didn't help. "Why wouldn't your mom help you?" he asked, a clear effort to distract them both. It worked. There was no surer way to smother Ariadne's smoldering passion than to talk about that woman.

"I've told you who she is, right?" she said, as Davek nosed the truck through another intersection. Only two blocks from her apartment building now. "She's our senator, representing New Ashbrook North. She and Dad raised me in Sandfield, middle class back then, now on the way down. But Mom always wanted to be one of *them*, one of the elite. Got ambitious, made connections, even as she neglected me and divorced my dad. Twenty fucking years of marriage, and suddenly he wasn't good enough. But she thought I was. She still claims she pulled strings to get me into Segard."

Ariadne wanted to spit out the sour taste that invaded her mouth. Davek gaped at her, his diversionary tactic having exceeded both their expectations. He halted the truck in a no parking zone in front of her apartment building, leaving the engine running.

"That's bullshit, of course," she muttered. "Segard has more integrity than she ever had. Dean Collins made a point to tell me they'd admitted me *despite* her interference, not because of it. But I'm sure she still parades my status as a Segard Law student in her political and social circles. So I must have shocked her this evening when I explained her perfect daughter had been arrested for attacking another student, and could I have some bail money, mommy, please?"

Ariadne barked a laugh, totally without humor. There'd been nothing amusing about that phone conversation.

Really, Ariadne, I expected better of you. You're a student at the most prestigious law school in Novomond, not a trailer park brat brawling in the dirt to impress potential mates. I think a night in jail would help you remember that. I'll send someone over in the morning.

Bitch.

Ariadne squeezed Davek's hand and turned fierce eyes upon him. "I don't want to talk about my mother anymore," she growled. She fumbled with his belt and unzipped his fly before he knew what was happening.

There's a trailer park brat in all of us, Mom.

She clutched Davek's stiffening cock in her hand and lowered her face to his lap.

14

TWO MOUNTAIN

Airport security at Thornburg remained tight in the wake of the Death Curse. Folk, Light or Dark, of any age were scrutinized and sometimes detained. The tiny airport in the college town of Mayersville, downriver was far more lax.

One of the Three flew into Mayersville from New Ashbrook on the eve of Hunter's Moon. They walked unchallenged through the sleepy checkpoint, then a hired car took them to a private dock on a tributary of the Thorn River.

They boarded a skimmer, a modest but comfortable boat favored by pleasure cruisers and smugglers alike. Its owner, a stocky man with sun-ripened skin and a thick white beard discolored by a lifetime of pipe smoking, had no idea who his passenger was, nor why they were traveling to Thornburg overnight. He didn't appear to care, as long as they paid in cash—and plenty of it.

His passenger retired to a private cabin for their upriver journey to the Swamps.

Thornburg's commercial docks occupied just over a kilometre of riverfront, south of the Frontier Bridge. To the north, towering granite bluffs reared over a sharp bend in the river. Their sheer slopes supported a verdant pedestal studded with the opulent private homes of the city elite. Downriver, as the prime waterfront decayed into treacherous swampland, lay the source of some of that wealth, perhaps more than even the most well-informed citizen truly knew.

For decades after the Empire conquered Novomond, their active administrative control ended at the Thorn River. The dry and rugged western half of the continent appealed less to farmers and those with capital to exploit them. Displaced Folk roamed with disgruntled freedom, although not without military supervision, until population pressure herded them onto reservations. Thornburg remained the busiest "frontier town" well into the previous century, until the flamestone-assisted mining boom in the southwest created the metropolises of Gerino and Longhorn Park. Year by year, Thornburg's commercial traffic dwindled. Although still far from collapse, few ventures ran a healthy profit, so most augmented their income with trade of a less-than-legal nature.

The Empire's relentless demand for illicit drugs, unpaid laborers, and more specialized contraband knew no limits. Those looking to supply that demand had co-opted Thornburg's well-established distribution network. However, even with local authorities and law enforcement in their pockets, illegal operations in the commercial docks made little sense. Instead, tens of pleasure marinas bloomed like windblown seeds throughout the southern Swamps. Smaller craft could navigate the shallow, treacherous waterways that commercial barges could not. Shipwrecks weren't unheard of, but the trade was so lucrative that losing a cargo of Shade or Axlian sex slaves was little more than an annoyance.

Everyone minded their own business in the Swamps. As long as you kept the right people on the payroll, you could do as you wished—and that could be taken advantage of.

One of the Three emerged from their cabin as the skimmer picked a careful route through the winding channels. The Day End Bell had long since rung, but only the brightest stars contended with the city's nocturnal glow. A single LED lamp illuminated their progress, its narrow beam almost grazing one or two craft moored at haphazard wooden docks. A desultory drizzle misted the already humid air but failed to deter the thousands of chirping insects who had called this place home since before even the Folk first arrived.

The pilot saw no one as he nudged his boat into a private side channel, cut into a stand of reeds over two metres high. No one saw him tie it up and cut the engine. No one cared as his passenger handed him a large envelope stuffed with used bills, then cut his throat as the man counted greedily. No one would find the pilot's body, decaying several paces beneath his skimmer's hull, nor would they understand who killed him or why.

One of the Three wrapped their bloodstained knife in ceremonial cloth, its intricate pattern hand-woven by their ancestors before the Conquest. After washing their hands, they undressed, stuffing their "respectable" garments into a brand new duffel bag, along with a flashlight and an antique clock. Over the side it went, sinking briefly before coming to rest on the chest of a fresh corpse.

Clouds above the western horizon parted for a moment, revealing the modest silver sheen of an almost full Second Moon. The passenger squinted upward, tracking the satellite's almost imperceptible descent towards the horizon. se-Vana made almost two circuits of the world for each made by its larger companion. First Moon had long set. Their next appearance in the sky together would culminate in perigee just after midday tomorrow. The Hunter would, almost, catch their prey.

The passenger ducked back inside the cabin, grazing their scalp. Few boats were designed for someone of their height. They donned a simple black cloak, then wrapped a cloth mask over their nose and mouth. They sat on an unpadded bench behind a plain wooden table in the skimmer's tiny cabin, and waited.

They tensed when the boat rocked under soft footfalls, hand straying towards the wrapped knife where it lay on the table.

Knuckles rapped on the door three times, paused, then twice more. The passenger relaxed, although they didn't withdraw their hand.

"Come," they said in the guttural dialect of the One Eagle clan, now all but forgotten, along with most of those who had spoken it. One Eagle once dominated the southern half of the eastern coast, when thousands of people fished the waters and farmed the land. Other clans owed them fealty, or at least honored their authority.

Within twenty years of the first Empire ships sighting that coast, fewer than fifty One Eagle people remained, scattering westward, homeless and haunted. The old tongue almost died with them.

Almost. Like the hopes of their people, some yet carried its memory. The passenger treasured it like a memory of what was once lost, but could be again.

The door opened and two others entered. Both wore black cloaks and hoods matching their host's. Masks covered the lower half of their faces, leaving only the pale gleam of wary eyes. The passenger knew the shorter of the pair was female, the taller one male, but few other observers could have guessed that.

It no longer mattered. They were the Three. Individual identities were irrelevant.

Well, not entirely. The woman sat further down the same bench, somehow making the action elegant and dignified. The taller newcomer remained standing as if addressing an audience.

"The Three are gathered, as was foretold," the Pathfinder intoned. The others bowed their heads as the ancient dialect flowed from his tongue like rock-churned river water through rapids. "We gather on the eve of the seventh Great Year since humans defeated our ancestors and began The Great Injustice. This day, se-Vana clutches at on-Vana, determined to avenge their imprisonment. They resist. As do we. *Aliach emor'i*!"

"*Aliach emor'i*," they responded, in quiet adulation.

"The Thirteen are already in place. The Seven will follow. Their places have been chosen. The time approaches."

The passenger waited until certain the Pathfinder had finished speaking. "Can the Seven be trusted to fulfill their responsibilities?"

The Pathfinder did not move, but somehow conveyed irritation all the same. "The Seven will play their part. Look to yourself, child of Chaos."

"And our place?" the woman asked, sparing the passenger further embarrassment over his reprimand. "It is secure?"

"It is. The humans have approved the official Hunter's Moon celebration led by the One Water clan." A sneer entered the Pathfinder's voice. The woman flinched. "The LightFolk will enjoy their festivities in the largest of Thornburg's parks, under the suspicious eyes of many human soldiers. Nearby, forgotten and neglected, lies the mound where Two Mountain once laid their dead to rest. Forgotten by all without Two Mountain blood running through their veins."

Abruptly, the Pathfinder lowered his hood. Swirling and jagged tattoos in black ink covered his bald, wrinkled head, winding down his neck and disappearing under his cloak. They told the story of Two Mountain, a story passed down from shaman to shaman since the origin of the clan. Fervent eyes burned above bone-pierced nose and lips, and his gaze was terrible to endure.

"Today, Two Mountain rises again! Today, we will join se-Vana in their hunt! *Aliach emor'i*!"

15

MORNING CHORES

Pralik rarely struggled to get out of bed. Today was an exception.

Silencing the bedside alarm, he kissed his dozing wife on the cheek, then sat up, legs still under the covers. Dawn's first light seeped through cracks in the window blinds, picking out furniture and decor that had changed little in twenty years. Their bedroom was an island of stability in a growing torrent of uncertainty.

Pralik hauled himself out of bed and into the shower. He washed mechanically, soaping a body that remained hale despite his middle years, and ran through the mental checklist for the day. Hunter's Moon. The seventh since the Conquest. There was a lot to do. But even before the Festival in New Ashbrook, which the Elders of One Raven were hosting, he had to make it through breakfast with his family.

Laida was already downstairs, wrapped in her house robe and frying range bread. The thick scent of corn oil greeted Pralik even before he stepped into the kitchen. He and his wife maintained a healthy diet, rarely eating meat, let alone fried food. But his stomach rumbled at the traditional dish, which was probably more oil than bread.

"Smells good, *ieika*," he murmured, wrapping his arms around her waist and kissing the back of her neck.

She shrugged him off with amused irritation. "Go on, you. You'll make me splash oil everywhere, and then the kitchen will reek for days."

Pralik chuckled, then turned to the breakfast table. Chiana slumped in her usual chair nearest the back door, her untamed hair almost entirely shielding her expression as her thumbs swiped at her phone. Davek, true to form, was last to rise and had yet to join his family.

First task of the day.

Pralik poured himself a cup of cherryroot tea from the pot in the middle of the table, before sitting opposite his daughter as usual. Other than a brief flick of her eyes in his direction, she didn't acknowledge his presence. Nothing unusual there.

"Good morning, Chiana," he said, his tone light but with an undercurrent that caught her attention. She looked up from her phone and swept aside some wilder strands of hair.

"Hi Dad. What's up?"

He sipped his tea, and recalled the plan he'd devised for this conversation before falling asleep last night. "I read your opinion piece in the Nomad yesterday. Or do I say 'on the Nomad'? Is it a newspaper or a website?"

Chiana's eyes narrowed, and she waved her phone at him. "It's both, Dad. Papers aren't just print anymore. Most have gone fully virtual—especially the local ones."

"A pity. Seems like that makes it harder for some people to access."

"I agree. But if you've seen printing costs lately, you'd know it's become prohibitive to publish and distribute physical copies without wealthy donors or corporate sponsorship. *Collette's Journal* may get plenty of those, but the Nomad doesn't."

No, indeed. There was little perceived return on investment from a LightFolk owned news source targeting New Ashbrook's LightFolk community. Or any Folk, in theory, although few DarkFolk paid close attention to the thoughts and actions of their "assimilated" brethren.

That was a task for later, to greet and accommodate a One Snake delegation from their Black Hills reservation.

Laida set a plate of the fried dough on the table, then gave Pralik a significant look. He stifled a sigh.

"You've written a few pieces for them recently," he went on. "Are you on their staff now? Do they pay you?"

Chiana rolled her eyes. She dropped her phone on the table, forked a hunk of steaming loaf, and dumped it onto her plate next to a slice of icemelon. "They don't really have much of a staff. Uian Two Water owns it, and I'm just one of many writers who contribute. He does pay me a nominal fee, but I do it mostly for practice and to get my name out there as a writer. It's good for my portfolio."

"Is it? Because I'm not sure picking a fight with Senator Brogan Castlewood is good for anyone."

Chiana sawed off a corner of bread and chewed before replying. The kitchen's sudden tension could not be cut so easily. "I think it's good for our people to see someone articulate what we're all thinking. We've rolled over for the Empire for seven Great Years, suffering one indignity after another. That needs to stop. And it won't stop if no one speaks out."

"I don't disagree," Pralik said, selecting the smallest portion, but making no move to eat it. Strange how his daughter echoed the very sentiment he'd expressed to his fellow Elders after the Leavetaking ceremony. Before... whatever it was he'd experienced. "Others are speaking out, and you're welcome to join us. But perhaps you need not do it so... acerbically."

"Really?" Chiana gave him the kind of patronizing look endured by parents of adult children everywhere. "Do you think formal objections to the Senate, or quiet words in the corridors of power, will work? When have they ever worked? The Folk are tolerated at best. But if we raise our voices, if we show our worth, maybe we can be respected too."

"Or someone decides those voices must be silenced," Laida interrupted, standing next to the cooktop with her arms folded over her chest. "More Purists walk the streets openly now than ever before. Assaults on the Folk are increasing. Just yesterday, they knifed that One Bear protest leader in Longhorn Park. The night before, a mob in Thornburg stormed a bus taking DarkFolk back to their reservation, beating the men and raping the women. We walk on a knife edge, Chiana."

Chiana looked up at her defiantly. "Then those with courage should embrace the blade. Don't ask me to bottle up my outrage and love for my people. You raised me better than that."

"We're not asking anything of the sort," Pralik assured her. "We see your heart, Chiana. We love you for it, as in everything. But because of that love, we urge you to choose your words and pick your battles with care."

"What are we talking about?" Davek asked, slipping into the kitchen and plopping himself onto his usual seat at the table. "Ooh, range bread!" He seized the largest piece and bit into it with gusto.

Chiana looked both revolted and relieved. "Nice of you to join us, little brother." Her voice dripped with false cheer.

Davek didn't rise to the bait for once, content to eat in apparent blissful ignorance of the conversation he'd interrupted. Pralik supposed he should be grateful for that one small mercy.

"You got home late last night," he observed. "I hope you're rested enough to help me today."

"'Course, Dad," Davek said, still chewing. Laida tsked.

"Is she okay?" Chiana asked.

Davek blinked, then gulped down the rest of his mouthful. "Who?"

"Your classmate. Ariadne, isn't that her name? I heard the New Ashbrook police arrested her for assault after defending you from some Purists at Segard. Didn't you and Elder Khavrik bail her out last night?"

"Menzies isn't a Purist," Davek muttered. "He's just a dick."

"What is this?" Pralik demanded, annoyed by Chiana's deflection, and alarmed by her accusation. "Why are you involving Khavrik in anything?"

Davek continued to scowl at his sister. "How do you know about that anyway?"

"Oh, baby brother, you're not nearly as discreet as you think you are—about this or other things." Chiana returned Davek's momentary horrified expression with a smug one of her own.

"Davek?"

His son wrenched his gaze away from his sister and attempted to meet Pralik's eyes. "There was an incident between lectures. A human classmate stepped in before I got into a fight with some racist jerk. I guess his family is rich and connected enough to get her arrested. I felt guilty that someone should spend the night in jail on my behalf, and Khavrik agreed."

Pralik frowned. Presumably this was Ariadne West, the BFA agent's daughter. What had Davek entangled himself in?

"I suppose I should be grateful you weren't arrested for brawling yourself. But, again, why Khavrik? Why not bring your concern for Ariadne to me? Or your mother?"

Laida snorted, but otherwise stayed out of the conversation.

Davek licked his lips. "I thought you were still at the Academy. Khavrik called me. I guess he heard about what happened, probably from Keralek. My friend, who witnessed the whole thing. Khavrik wanted to make sure I was okay."

"How paternal of him." Pralik broke his own rule, dug out his phone from one of his robe's inner pockets, and sent Khavrik a terse text. *Bail?* "And you didn't see fit to tell me, another One Raven Elder and your father?"

Davek's eyes widened in silent appeal.

Pralik waited, hoping for contrition, or even one of his sister's spirited justifications.

Instead, Davek's face shut down. He shrugged. "You know now, don't you?" he mumbled, shoving the rest of his range bread into his mouth.

Pralik rubbed his temples. He could feel a headache coming, and the day had only just begun.

16

HOPE OF MY PEOPLE

K'uelle ti-Lan'ot bade her last farewell to her daughter alone.

She'd sent her mother to buy bread and stock up on synthetic baby food. S'ondra had clung to her mother's milk at first, but over the last few months she'd grown to tolerate, then developed a taste for pureed yam and calf liver. The fact that every jar was officially past its expiry date didn't appear to bother her.

The stench alone nauseated K'uelle. Maybe the jars smelled better when fresh. She struggled to summon more than the bare minimum of gratitude for the human charity, which provided a steady supply of such "infant nutrition" to the reservations. At least they might keep S'ondra alive for a little while longer.

"I love you, *hope of my people,*" K'uelle crooned. Her husband, who'd disappeared from her life mere days before she discovered she was pregnant, had favored that name if they ever had a daughter. The memory was doubly bitter.

K'uelle stood amidst the gloom of Ai'aial's shack, clutching S'ondra to her breast and swaying gently in place. Her daughter had slept fitfully after a restless night, likely from gas, if her swaddling was anything to go by. Normally, K'uelle wouldn't have been around for most of it, arriving home from work in the heart of darkness, but she'd skipped out on her last shift at the brothel.

Madam Two Mountain would have been annoyed, but her girls needed the money more than she did. She employed plenty of them. If any didn't show up to work, well, they were the ones who'd starve. She'd have taken an even larger cut of Kit's next night's earnings and called it even.

K'uelle didn't care. Her narrow escape at the bus terminal settled a dilemma. She wouldn't work that one last shift after all. She wouldn't try to blend into Thornburg's overnight shadows until the day of Hunter's Moon dawned. She'd spend her last hours with the only thing on this Mother-forsaken earth she still cared about.

"Mama's going away," she whispered to her heedless babe. "I wish things could be different. I wish you could have been born in a better time, a time before the humans came. There was a time when our people roamed free over these lands. Those times weren't always easy, but we controlled our own destiny. With the blessing of the Mother, of course."

The Mother who'd allowed her people to be slaughtered and enslaved. K'uelle fought off the urge to spit on the floor.

"I wish you could have known your father, dear one. He was a fine man, a brave man. He was the last man to love me for me, and to love me well, in all the ways a husband should. He would have loved you in all the ways a father should too, though he never knew you. They took him from us, as they took everyone and everything else. They took your uncle, my brother. They took your grandfather. And, in their way, they took your grandmother too. She wasn't always as she is now. But there is only so much loss one person can endure before they lose themselves. She loves you, dear one. I hope she remembers it before the end. For the end is coming."

And still, the tears wouldn't come. Ai'aial had cried rivers of tears as her kin were cut down, defending their people after yet another human outrage. K'uelle, horrified, desolate, and furious, had failed to shed a single tear. And now, bidding her heedless infant daughter farewell for the final time, her eyes remained dry.

What kind of demon am I?

"A demon who walks with Chaos and vengeance," she breathed, so soft even she could hardly tell if she spoke the words aloud.

S'ondra stirred. K'uelle cooed over her, before realizing the coos had become a chant. Not understanding at first, as if another agency guided her, she embraced Chaos and inscribed a traceless sigil on her restless daughter's forehead.

"May the Mother protect you," she whispered, laying S'ondra down on her cot. She wrapped her snugly and kissed her warm brow. "Until we meet again, dear one."

She tossed the tiny chip of flamestone in the stove, erasing evidence of the spell. She turned away before the embers flared once in vivid green.

The door opened, spilling morning light into the shack. Her mother shuffled inside, carrying a bag handwoven from dried reeds. Glass jars clinked when she set it on her wobbly table.

"You leave us early today, *papita*," Ai'aial remarked, glancing over K'uelle's cloak. "Is there so much work to be done for the festival?"

K'uelle bit her lip. Part of her wanted to confess, to tell her mother not only what she really did in Thornburg but where her path led her today. Her secrets burdened her. Surely her own mother would understand?

In the end, she could think of nothing special to say. She lingered in Ai'aial's embrace a little longer than usual, inhaling the fuel oil and cherryweed scents of her mother's brittle grey hair. Ai'aial didn't comment, but something in the way her arms tightened around K'uelle's back suggested she knew this was no ordinary farewell.

K'uelle kissed her mother's wrinkled cheeks and stepped towards the door. "Goodbye, mama," she said.

The state police stopped the bus at their checkpoint. Two young officers, likely the same pair who'd manned the post the previous day, boarded and paced up and down the central aisle. They said nothing, but their hands rested on their holstered semi-automatic pistols. K'uelle didn't have to fake a look of cowed fear. She kept her left hand palm down in her lap.

Allowed to proceed, the bus lurched forward and rumbled towards the Northern Continental Expressway.

K'uelle rarely paid attention to the uncharitable landscape of tumbled treeless hills that dominated the southern half of the Thorn River Reservation. This journey, she peered through the grimy window with a strange mix of fondness and contempt. Bright sunlight picked out subtle nuances in the reds and browns of the rock, in the shades and textures of the scrub.

She remembered days not so long ago, tramping through those hills with her parents and brother, usually to find one of the few watering holes along the Piamuat Creek. Papa and Minot loved to fish, but K'uelle was always terrible at it. Mama used to lie on her back in the shade of the reeds and laugh.

This land was harsh. Her ancestors had farmed their homelands back east for as long as they could remember. Before The Great Injustice, families and small communities sustained themselves with ease. Game had been plentiful, before the Empire slaughtered it all. Even the remaining Black Kine were but echoes of the majestic herds legend described as blotting out the land as far as the horizon. Many other species had not been even that fortunate.

The Empire had herded the vestiges of the Three Mountain clan west for days, ferried them across the Thorn River, and dumped them with little ceremony in this pocket of unwanted territory. Little grew here, and if any Black Kine yet roamed, they did so much further west.

Meanwhile, the human city of Thornburg thrived. Built with stolen magic on stolen lands, it stole DarkFolk dignity and their future too.

But theft could not go unpunished forever. The Empire would learn that today.

K'uelle tensed as the bus turned into the city transit center. She half expected a mob of Purists to be waiting for them. Instead, it was strangely quiet. Other than sheets of fiberboard spanning some shelters until their broken glass could be replaced, there was no evidence of the attack two nights before. The few buses she saw were all idle, and the only humans in sight were a pair of homeless men nursing their liquor bottles in one of the furthest shelters, at least until they were discovered and moved along.

Her fellow passengers also noticed the change, and a wave of unease passed through those standing in the aisle, awaiting their turn to disembark. It was as if the city knew. It waited for her. It knew its fate, and accepted it. Welcomed it, perhaps. Thornburg had seen untold horrors. Maybe it was ready for peace too.

Away from the transit center, the Dockside streets retained their usual traffic and character. The lunchtime crowd, drawn mostly from the nearby business district, was more respectable than their evening counterparts. Restaurants and coffee bars welcomed groups of smartly dressed men and women, most of whom would flee to the suburbs after the tenth bell, but not all. Even now, as lunches concluded and workers returned to the afternoon grind, a few sought out the seedier pleasures of the district. Pleasures found at establishments such as Madam Two Mountain's. Pleasures that Kit Three Mountain had once provided.

No more. Kit Three Mountain had died two nights ago.

K'uelle began her resigned trudge in the general direction of the brothel, on the off chance someone was paying attention.

But instead of turning right on Fourth Street, she continued straight. She kept her head down and tried to look invisible.

Her route, chosen with care over recent days, was not direct. Others of the Seven had likely ridden the same bus from Thorn River, and the last thing they wanted was several DarkFolk to be seen heading the same direction with unknown purpose. She wondered who they were.

By design, her path took her past the entrance to The Mews. At its end, the bar called Black Star remained boarded up. Indecipherable graffiti had been spray painted over the sheets of fiberboard blocking the door. Given the sour tang that assaulted her nostrils, she mistook the low piles lining the storefront—heaped like tidal debris—for garbage. Then, as she paused, stretching the limits of caution, her sharp eyes picked out photographs and faded flowers.

Tributes, then. Tributes to the fallen.

"Jek One Raven, I remember you," she murmured, too quiet for even the nearest fellow pedestrian to hear. She had never met him, but his picture had been everywhere, including the front pages of the few newspapers that made it to Thorn River. "You are one with the Mother."

K'uelle had mixed feelings about the impulsive LightFolk boy. He had drawn unwanted scrutiny upon Thornburg, giving the Castlewood clan the excuse they needed to tighten the noose around the Folk's necks. Even humans who claimed to dislike or disown the Purist movement viewed every LightFolk and DarkFolk with mounting suspicion. Jek One Raven's Death Curse had made daily life more difficult for the Folk, no question.

Yet, she admired him too. He had stood up against The Great Injustice, if only in a small way, for personal reasons. He had reminded the humans that the Folk magic they harnessed for their industry and technology, and for the energy to fuel it, could not always be tamed. It could be used to defend. If more of her ancestors had chosen as Jek One Raven had, perhaps The Great Injustice would never have happened.

K'uelle moved on. She couldn't linger, there or anywhere. The time was fast approaching when she would make her own choice. The choice of the Twenty-Three.

Four blocks further into the city, its background hum of car horns, revving engines, and snatched conversation surged in volume. Many voices, calling, shouting, chanting, vied with the mechanical growl of military trucks. Down a street leading to Empress Catarina Park, soldiers huddled, so weighed down by armor, weapons and other tactical gear, they almost didn't look human.

An amplified voice echoed between the office and apartment buildings. "Festival goers, you must present identification before entering the park at the approved checkpoint by the north gate. No identification, no entry. Protesters must stay in the designated area behind the barricades. I have authorized the use of force against anyone failing to comply!"

Boos and jeers rang out in response.

K'uelle adjusted her hood and walked on. Her usual black cloak identified her as one of the Folk, of indeterminate clan. Few of her people wore their traditional purple outside the reservation, mostly those peddling their intricate jewelry and other trifles at the Tenday markets. They snatched some vestige of pride in doing so.

Pride was of no concern to her. Stealth and speed were. Observers might think she was bound for the Hunter's Moon celebration, even if she headed south. But this close to the park, if you weren't participating in the festival or protest, you were likely inside, sheltering from what was clearly a volatile situation.

K'uelle saw no other black cloaks as she approached her destination. Thornburg residents called it Pilgrim's Hill, an unspectacular low mound overlooking a polluted tributary of the Thorn River. Surrounded on its other three sides by towering condos, past their prime, yet still out of reach of most family budgets, the mound had once been sacred to the Two Mountain clan. Generations of Elders and warriors lay entombed within, including, so it was rumored, Ran'ot, leader of Two Mountain's final failed rebellion against the Empire.

The humans built a chapel to their Brothers on top of it. Now disused, only the occasional surprised tourist paid it any attention at all. Folk objections hadn't prevented Pilgrim's Hill from being built over; objections from the condo owners' associations over spoiling their view had.

K'uelle squinted with derision at the chapel as she took her assigned position under a beetle-ridden wormroot tree at the southeast edge of the mound. She thought she'd glimpsed movement, perhaps a twitch of black. Other than a man walking his dog around the perimeter, and an elderly couple picnicking from a vantage point over the river, the mound was deserted.

As she waited, still and silent, she saw two more black clad figures arrive, each sheltering beneath their own tree. Two more of the Seven. The mound blocked her view of the others, but senses other than sight confirmed their presence. Ignoring distant chants of celebration and protest, disregarding the cloying reek of fuel oil wrapped in humidity, she found them all, nodes in a web spun from the top of the mound above.

The Three at its summit. The Seven around its base. The Thirteen encircling Pilgrim's Hill up to two blocks away.

The last thing K'uelle saw before closing her eyes were storm clouds swarming to the west. Hidden behind them, likely too faint to see in the light of day anyway, se-Vana approached on-Vana, now mere heartbeats away from perigee. As she yielded more of her individual consciousness to the Twenty-Three, humming tunelessly, she felt the satellites' steady pulse of energy, stronger than the heat of the Sun.

Thunder rumbled. Mother was angry. It was time to honor her with vengeance.

It was time to Walk with Chaos one last time.

Aliach emor'i!

She heard the Pathfinder not with her ears, but with a part of her mind she never knew existed. A part designed to share with other Walkers.

The strands of the web grew taut, throbbing in time with the rhythm of the Hunter and the Hunted. Invisible pulses of energy rode the vibrations, zipping not only from the nexus at the chapel, but also from others of the Seven, and of the Thirteen too. The web buzzed like the humans' high-voltage power lines, singing in tune with the hum of K'uelle's incantation. They were one and the same. She fed her vitality, her spirit, into the web, and the web magnified it. The spell, an ancient working, taboo, forbidden, multiplied her essence with the rest of the Twenty-Three, harnessing the true power of Hunter's Moon. In the last moments before perigee, the web buckled under the strain, held together by the Pathfinder's indomitable will.

At the edges of K'uelle's fading perception, a dog howled. Its owner rubbed his temples, wondering at the sudden headache. The elderly couple cast nervous glances at the darkening cloud cover and hurried to pack up their picnic, fearing a lightning strike.

Too late. It was far too late.

K'uelle's last thought was not of S'ondra, her daughter, cursed to be born on the cusp of her people's annihilation. It was certainly not of Ai'aial, her mother, who had yielded to grief and despair after her husband's death, and now chose to lose herself in medicated euphoria. It wasn't the faces of Ruian, her husband, or Minot, her younger brother, that she saw at the end. It was, of all things, a human man, a man called Xavier, the only human who had ever shown her kindness for kindness's sake, not indifference or brutality.

She hoped he had made his peace with his gods, whoever they were.

At the instant of perigee, the web snapped. K'uelle's body disintegrated in a blinding flash of sickly green, a spray of glowing embers and tree ash towering above her. Six other fountains of deadly flamestone erupted around Pilgrim's Hill at the same moment the mound vaporized. Stone of chapel, earthen blanket, and bone of a once proud but forgotten people fed the spell's hunger, and the spell unleashed Chaos upon Earth.

Those few in Empress Catarina Park who happened to be looking south, as the festival teetered on the edge of riot, might have seen the plume of debris moments before the loudest sound ever heard in the history of the Empire deafened them.

Eardrums burst. The shockwave arrived before most recognized the pain, and certainly before anyone realized they were dying. As cruel and precise as a spinning saw blade, the expanding circle ripped through everything in its path. It sliced people in two, men, women, and children—humans and Folk alike. It sheared tower block supports and load-bearing walls, concrete and glass tumbling like an elaborate pattern of dominoes. Dust and debris billowed up to meet the storm clouds, which kissed the obliteration of Thornburg with lightning.

Far above, se-Vana retreated once more, beginning a new Great Year in pursuit of its larger companion and betrayer. But perhaps, as on-Vana slid from its grasp yet again, the spirit of Eleiach looked down at what their devotees had wrought, and approved.

17

THE TIDE

Without the cycle of light and darkness to mark its passing, Xavier soon lost track of time altogether.

He dozed on and off. Each time he woke to the sinister red glow of the emergency lamp—standard issue on any "working" in the mine—he fought off claustrophobia and panic, tugging uselessly at his buried lower legs, trying not to sob in despair.

Inexplicably, he craved a cigarette. His mouth was so dry his tongue threatened to cleave to its roof, but he told himself a fleeting hit of tabac would soothe his terror.

Uraol ti-Lan'ot, who had spoken to him before, appeared to be their foreman—when he spoke, the others listened. He and Xavier exchanged names when Uraol passed over a canteen of water.

"One mouthful only," Uraol warned as Xavier tipped the canteen greedily towards his lips. The tepid liquid had a strange metallic taste, but it was one of the best things Xavier had ever drunk, even though his thirst clawed back almost immediately.

The second company man had regained consciousness only once, calling out a name no one understood, and he hadn't spoken again.

"Are we just waiting for someone to try and rescue us?" Xavier asked at last.

Each time he woke, the miners appeared to sit in the same positions, backs to the tunnel wall. Some chuckled grimly at his question.

"They know we were here," rasped Uraol, his voice the soft scrape of sandpaper over wood. He gestured towards the rockfall. "Radio buried. No way to contact."

"There must be something we can do." Xavier almost laughed at his use of "we". What could he possibly contribute, imprisoned and helpless as he was?

The foreman started to shake his head, then froze. The other DarkFolk startled, then sat up straight, as if listening to something. Xavier tried, but all he heard was his own heart hammering in his ears. His body vibrated and he sensed, rather than felt, the rockfall shift above him.

Brothers, is this an earthquake? If so, part of him wanted it, embraced it. Better to die quickly than to suffer from drawn out asphyxiation.

Whatever it was passed. Xavier heard the DarkFolk exhale as one, then stir with what appeared to be excitement. Uraol slid closer, and they huddled around the emergency lamp, whispering in their own incomprehensible tongue. Their silhouettes twisted against the jagged walls—ghouls from a bedtime story, huddled around a fire meant to burn the wickedness out of children.

Drowsiness threatened to overtake him again when Uraol returned with another figure. Xavier recognized the younger miner who'd flashed his defiance at him before the explosion. The two DarkFolk conferred in harsh whispers as they hunched down to study the rocks imprisoning Xavier's lower legs. He waited as long as he could before his patience completely frayed.

"What's going on? Did something happen? Was that an earthquake, or another mining operation?"

The younger miner shook his head, as if dismissing an ignorant or petulant child. Uraol stilled him with a hand on his shoulder, then turned to Xavier.

"Not earthquake. Something greater. Much greater."

"I don't understand."

The foreman paused, as if weighing how much to say. "We have talked. No one comes for us. We must risk all to save some."

No one comes for us. Dread settled over Xavier like a stone-weighted blanket.

"We should wait," murmured the younger miner, pointing at Xavier's legs. The last two fingers were missing from his left hand. "If we disturb these rocks, the tunnel may collapse. We should wait. Find the other tunnel."

Xavier peered up at the miner's face, but it was too silhouetted to read his expression. "What other tunnel?"

Uraol grimaced. "Many other tunnels surround us. Humans make us burrow through the mountain like worms through breadfruit. Older shaft runs near here. Deeper. Abandoned."

"And you think you can find it?" Xavier's voice cracked with a sharp, incredulous edge.

"We are ti-Lan'ot," said the younger miner with pride. "Three Mountain in your tongue, human. We all worked that vein. We read the mountain as you read the devices made from our cousins' forced labor."

Xavier raised a hand in placation. He spent his life tiptoeing around the awkward realities of his people's subjugation of others. "I don't mean to offend. I just don't understand. If, when you find this old tunnel, you think we can use it to reach the surface?"

"It will be blocked, of course," Uraol acknowledged. "Perhaps we have strength left to unblock it. It is best hope. Only hope."

The miners rose together and rejoined their companions. Xavier settled down to wait, stifling the kernel of panic that whatever they tried would bring the roof down on them all. Or, despite Uraol's apparent consideration of his predicament, that they would leave him behind.

The first explosion surprised him: a deep thump reverberated through the tunnel floor as if a massive fist had punched the rock. Pulverized rock dust billowed over and past the DarkFolk, obscuring most of the weak red light.

Xavier closed his eyes and shielded his nose and mouth as best he could. There was nowhere for the dust to go. He felt it settle on his exposed skin, over his eyelids and the back of his hand. He tried not to imagine it as soil tossed into his grave.

The ringing in his ears faded. Propping himself up on one elbow, he wiped his eyes and blinked cautiously into absolute darkness. No, not quite. Thirty steps down the tunnel, the faintest glow suffused the grainy air.

"Hello?" he called, spitting out dust with some of the little saliva he could summon. "Are you—is everyone good?"

"Patience." The word floated out of unguessable distance, echoed, and died.

Xavier groaned, tugged feebly at his trapped legs, then slumped to the ground again. Patience was not his strong suit.

Another explosion rattled the earth, followed by deathly silence and then another. What toll did each "working" take on the miners? How many could they perform, without any way to replenish their strength?

What were they doing with all the flamestone?

Utter darkness had returned. The DarkFolk had taken the solitary emergency lamp with them, and had progressed too far down their new shaft for its feeble light to leak back to Xavier. The dust, however, had no such difficulty. He kept his nose and mouth covered, and his eyes shut tight. There was nothing to see anyway.

Deprived of sight, smothering taste and smell, unable to move, Xavier listened to the speech of the mine. Buried deeper than ever before, he would have expected silence punctuated by the occasional thump of DarkFolk workings, now coming further and further apart. Instead, he heard whispers.

He convinced himself that air from outside had percolated through the unimaginable weight of rock, filtering and rejuvenating the stale atmosphere of the blocked tunnel. Maybe there was a gap through the initial explosion's rockfall after all.

And yet... He swore he could hear whispered words in his imagined air currents. Words in a language so ancient its speakers gave no thought to the tiny creatures chipping and digging into the mountain's flesh. A language of sibilant susurration in which words took hundredths and sentences whole tenths to speak. The language of the mountains, and of the earth itself. Xavier listened, as captivated and faintly ashamed as a child listening outside a closed door while the adults spoke.

What are they saying? What conversations are worthy of the very bones of the world?

"Xavier West?"

His eyes flew open before he could stop himself. Grit immediately stung his eyeballs, and he cursed as he tried to clear them with dust-coated fingers. By the time he'd shut his eyelids tight again, the pain at least endurable, he wasn't convinced he'd heard anything at all.

"H-hello?"

"Xavier West?"

The voice was human, male, but dry and cracked. Each stress syllable ended in a high-pitched whistle, as if a hole punctured the speaker's throat.

"Who's there? Are you one of the miners? Have you found the other tunnel?"

"Xavier West, attend. This vessel decays. We do not have much time."

This vessel?

The company man. The other human who'd survived burial in the initial explosion, but who'd suffered what sounded like a severe head wound. Xavier hadn't heard him breathe, much less speak, since the DarkFolk set off on their desperate quest. He still lived, then.

"The DarkFolk are trying to find another way out," Xavier told him. "They're trying to save us all. I'm sorry, I don't know your name."

"They try to save those beyond salvation," the voice declared. There was something odd about it, beyond the whistling. An odd cadence that made Xavier's skin crawl. "They seek hope for their people, yet hope will be found by another. They seek to join with those who lift up the fallen, even as they themselves fall. In search of hope, they seek to lift up and to tear down. Will you join them, Xavier West?"

Xavier once watched a documentary on religious cults, officially prohibited by the Empire. The filmmakers portrayed the wildest of the fringe groups in a scathing light, which irritated Xavier even though he had little empathy for the Carrollites or followers of the Tangled Way. He remembered a segment heaping derision on pop-eyed adherents of the New Moon Church as they foamed at the mouth while speaking in tongues. "Channeling the word of their god?" mocked the narrator. "Or saturated with narcotics?"

The company man hadn't taken any drugs since the explosion. He hadn't done anything but lie prone amidst the rubble, as comfortable as the miners could make him. But whatever his religious persuasion, the words he spoke sounded as if they were not his own.

So whose were they?

Xavier's flesh prickled. He was suddenly aware of the pressure in his bladder.

Don't go out like this, pissing your pants and cringing on the floor. Have a little dignity, man.

"Who are they joining?" he croaked. "What hope? Lifting up? Tearing down? I don't understand."

There was a long silence, during which Xavier began to suspect he'd imagined the entire exchange.

"The tide is turning, Xavier West. Long have the waters receded before forces too great and terrible for them to withstand. Those forces exist still. But hope will be found. The tide turns. Will it reclaim its former shores? Will it vanquish those who stand in its path? Will it lift up even as it tears down?"

"I don't... Are you talking about the DarkFolk? Who are you?"

The voice faded to a sepulchral whisper, air escaping a punctured balloon. "I am the tide, Xavier West. And I need you."

Silence fell once more. Xavier knew, without knowing how he knew, that whoever had spoken would speak no more.

He was so confused. And he was terrified.

A distant thump sent vibrations through the tunnel, jostling the loose rock and scree surrounding him. Suddenly, he felt something shift in the rock pile, trapping his legs. A loose boulder tumbled to the floor, so close that rock chips stung the back of his hand.

Holy Brothers! The tunnel's collapsing!

Desperate, he tugged at his trapped feet, and was shocked when his legs shifted a little. He'd long since lost feeling below his knees, but as he renewed his efforts, searing pain spiked through his calves once more. Boulder and stone jostled, a couple bouncing off his chest, mercifully on the smaller side. With a fractured, defiant yell, Xavier summoned all his remaining strength and yanked his feet away from the crumbling rock pile.

It was still too dark to see, but he felt the moment when they sprang free. Rock grated upon rock, and something, perhaps the mountain itself, groaned.

He heaved himself over the debris-strewn floor as if he were dog-paddling through the ocean. All he could think of was the new tunnel the miners had created, in search of escape. He flailed at the tunnel wall as he dragged himself forward, scraping off skin and bloodying knuckles.

Behind him, the grating of jumbled rock rose to a sudden roar. At that moment, his fist punched thin air. The new tunnel. With the last of his waning strength, Xavier heaved himself around the corner as a tsunami of angry stone washed past him. Cringing, utterly spent, he awaited his certain doom.

And waited.

Fresh dust and grit billowed over him, caressing his skin with the tenderness of volcanic ash. He huddled in a fetal ball, as feeling poured back into his feet and calves, agony yielding to a dull ache.

He didn't register the padding footsteps until they were almost upon him. Brushing off what seemed like a finger-width layer of dust from his face, Xavier cracked his eyes to see the red glow of an emergency lamp, bobbing from side to side in Uraol's hand.

"You survived," the foreman observed, sounding neither surprised nor particularly glad. "Can you walk? We found other tunnel."

18

THE BRIDGE OF NO RETURN

Sharol rolled over and reached for her phone, braying with
its obnoxious alarm. She fumbled the damn thing, but the
attached power cord stopped it from falling all the way to the
floor.

"Shut *up*," she muttered. She tossed the now silent device
back onto her bedside table and contemplated lying back down
for another five hundredths. Just five hundredths.

A hand brushed her shoulder and dusted her spine.
"Morning, petal," said a gruff voice.

She shivered, more from awkwardness than desire. "Gotta get
up, Jace," she said, rebuffing him without turning. Her lovers
never looked as appealing in the morning as they had the night
before.

Jace chuckled, a deep, guttural laugh that was lucky to escape
his mountain man beard. He gave her ass a playful squeeze, then
the bed shifted as he settled back on his side. Great.

Sharol slipped out from under the tumbled covers before
picking up her phone again. She dismissed the usual flurry of
social media notifications, looking in vain for a text reply from
Xavier. It wasn't like him to go dark, especially before a busy day
like this one promised to be.

"I've said it before and I'll say it again," drawled the tanned
and tatted biker she'd hooked up with last night—again.

"You're a fine looking woman, Sharol Kostellan. You let Jace know if you ever wanna settle down, breed some rugrats and all that shit."

Sharol snorted, the ghost of a grin flitting over her mouth. She was no runway model, too big boned and muscular from regular workouts. But she knew she looked good naked, particularly in profile, and especially to men who wanted more from a woman than eye candy on their arm. Petal, indeed.

"Sure, Jace. When I lose my mind completely, you'll be the first to know." She cast a critical eye over her tiny bedroom, a double bed bobbing in a sea of discarded clothing, not all from the night before. Daylight leaked in around the ragged curtain over the single small window, but gave up at the entrance to her shambles of a walk-in closet. *Definitely family material, Shar.*

"I'm gonna jump in the shower. Alone. Either leave or find something edible in the kitchen and make me breakfast. I gotta go to work."

This was her first Hunter's Moon Festival as an agent for the Bureau of Folk Affairs. It should have been a day of forced pleasantries, liaising with dignitaries from both Empire and LightFolk. In the light of recent events, it promised to be a tense balancing act, heading off the potential for vitriol and violence at every turn. She dreaded it.

Especially since her boss was ghosting her.

Jace left her two slices of buttered toast and a hastily scrawled note. She ate the toast, tossed the crumpled note into the trash, then left for the BFA office.

Thornburg didn't have a subway or light rail system, although the construction of one had been hotly debated by the city government for as long as she could remember. Cars and buses choked the streets at the best of times, especially downtown. Late last night, the city had erected barricades that formed a pedestrian-only perimeter two blocks around Empress Catarina Park, the site of the main Festival celebrations. The

BFA office was just inside that perimeter, her apartment just over a kilometre outside. It was quicker to walk.

At first, she noticed nothing different. It was a workday like any other. Her inner-city neighborhood of Blacktown had resisted gentrification. Many of its businesses came alive at night: biker bars and tattoo parlors blended seamlessly with brewpubs and Three Rings halls. The hole-in-the-wall cafes and food trucks were just opening up. Sharol wove a lonely path through narrow, barely maintained streets between plain buildings of soot-blackened stone. The old coal plant had closed decades ago, but its aesthetic legacy lived on. Blacktown was affordable, quirky, and mostly suited Sharol's temperament.

An entrenched hostility to the Folk was the neighborhood's only downside. Graffiti on highway overpasses, Purist recruitment posters pasted onto bus shelters, and "517" signs in the windows of too many businesses spoke more loudly than ever before. Sharol sported a vibrant hairstyle for many reasons. A distraction from the triangular shape of her chin and the unusual slant to her eyes was not the least important.

As she neared the freshly erected perimeter, vehicles and pedestrians clotted the streets and sidewalks. The morning commute's tension simmered, its invisible lid rattling with a stronger than usual boil. Sharol used her height to her advantage, slipping through seams in the foot traffic unseen by others. Coffee spilled and curses grew louder and uglier.

The flash of a BFA badge earned her a frown and passage through the perimeter, and she hurried to Zellers Tower like a bullet shot from a gun. The elevator up to the seventh floor may have stank like something died in it overnight, but she rode it alone.

"Has anyone seen or heard from Xavier?" she demanded as she stormed through the front door of the Bureau for Folk Affairs, Thornburg office.

Carli, the venerable and long-suffering receptionist, glanced up from her usual morning vent session with Aemon,

Thornburg's longest serving BFA agent. He blew out his ruddy cheeks, clearly irritated by the interruption. Sharol didn't care. Aemon was one of the old guard, a fossil remnant of a time when the Bureau had become little more than a tool of those who sought to keep the Folk in their place, away from civilized people. He'd never liked Sharol, and the feeling was mutual. She generally avoided him, but her need to find her partner was greater.

"Not since yesterday morning," Carli answered, face expressionless. She'd been part of the old guard too, although she'd adapted to the slightly more progressive times readily enough. "He hasn't shown his face here yet. I assumed he'd gone directly to the Festival. He didn't tell his partner?"

Sharol gritted her teeth at the offhand rebuke. "I haven't heard from him since Fourday evening." Since he'd accompanied her to the transit center, and spirited two young DarkFolk women to safety. "I thought he was headed to Thorn River yesterday, to inspect the mine. Did he ever report back?"

Carli frowned. "Not that I ever heard. Come to think of it, he never responded to my request for last tennight's expense report. I assumed he was neglecting paperwork as usual."

"I've got a cousin who works at the Thorn River mine," Aemon said slowly, as if reluctant to say anything that might be at all helpful. He scratched at the edges of the lesion on his bald scalp. "Didn't come home last night, according to his wife. She was asking around, family and friends. I assumed he'd pulled overtime, or he's doing something or someone he shouldn't be on the side. But I heard he's not the only one who didn't come home."

Sharol stared at him. Aemon might be a bigoted old fart, but he knew everyone. It was likely the only reason the Bureau kept him on the payroll.

"You think something happened at the mine?"

He shrugged. "That I can't say. Thorn River Mining are a secretive bunch. They don't do press releases or shit like that. Pay's good though. My cousin, he just built a lake house—"

"I don't fucking care about your cousin's lake house," Sharol spat. "I want to know if something might have happened to my partner at the mine."

Aemon's expression chilled. "Then perhaps you should drive out to Thorn River and find out for yourself. Ain't no one gonna volunteer that info to..."

He stopped himself, but Sharol completed the sentence in her head. It did not improve her temper.

"You know what, Agent Derrick, maybe I'll do just that. I'm sure you and Carver can handle the Festival by yourselves." She turned away from his spluttering face. "Carli, can I take the company car, please?"

The older woman's lips turned upward with amusement as she slid an unlabeled black key fob across the desk. She might be in casual cahoots with Aemon, but she loved a display of girl power when she saw it.

Sharol's smug satisfaction at scoring a point against Aemon soon evaporated. The company car was parked in a garage within the Festival perimeter. The two young policemen patrolling the barricade refused to let her through.

"I'm going *out*, not coming *in*," she insisted, over and over.

Finally, several fruitless phone calls and almost a tenth later, a senior officer stomped over and told his colleagues to let her through.

"Shouldn't you be at this damn Festival, keeping the prims in line?" he sneered.

"I would be if you'd let me through when I first tried to leave," she snapped back. "Have a nice fucking day, officer."

She decided to stop at a cafe before heading over the Frontier Bridge. She was flustered, hungry, and her phone was low on charge. That was the kicker. The company car was an older model, without an outlet suitable for charging phones or other devices. The service might be spotty on the reservation, but the prospect of a dead phone was even worse.

Hunkering down over coffee and a Kelian pastry, she stared at the lunchtime pedestrians through the window. Most were office workers, uninterested in the Festival if not irritated by the inconvenience it brought to their daily routine. As she sipped the last dregs, she noticed a figure wrapped in a black cloak pass by, then another on the opposite side of the street a couple hundredths later. DarkFolk rarely ventured this far from Dockside, a few blocks west of the cafe. Perhaps they were headed to the Festival, although it seemed strange they'd do so individually.

Sharol's thoughts returned once more to the other night at the transit center. The cloaks concealed most identifying characteristics, but she thought the second DarkFolk passerby was female for sure. Were either of them survivors of the mob attack? Would they be walking by themselves if they were?

Perhaps they had little choice. The Empire had taken almost all of those from the DarkFolk long ago.

Enough musing. She needed to get going if she hoped to drive to the Thorn River Mine and back before sunset, especially since it looked as if a brewing storm barreled in towards the city from across the river. Fantastic.

Heavier than usual post-lunchtime traffic snarled the approach to the bridge. Sharol cursed, flipping through one radio station after another without finding anything she cared to listen to. She should have stayed at the damn Festival. What was she thinking? Xavier was a grown man. He could take care of himself. The bastard had probably just lost his phone.

Wide wings of crackling black cloud swarmed the river as Sharol finally escaped Thornburg's clutches and drove onto the bridge. That was gonna put a dampener on the celebrations, but maybe it would defuse any tensions too. She chuckled at the idea of Aemon Derrick defying the downpour with his tired obstinacy, likely cursing her name. She'd hear about it tomorrow, for sure.

Her car had almost reached the western bank when she saw a flash in her peripheral vision. Stuck behind one eighteen-wheel cargo truck as another attempted to overtake it with painful slowness, she glanced in her rearview mirror. Traffic already snaked behind the passing truck, but that didn't even register. The rising tower of furious, glittering smoke did.

Her mind couldn't make sense of it at first. Was there a fire of some kind? Had the Festival turned violent, arsonists setting police vehicles and perhaps the entirety of Empress Catarina Park aflame? Had one of the soaring skyscrapers become a towering inferno?

Flashes of putrescent green tortured the roiling cloud. A deep, rolling boom drowned out the radio. Her stomach lurched with sickening realization just as the car shuddered, the suspended roadway of the bridge vibrating as if plucked like a viol string. A rising cacophony of car horns erupted around and behind her. Then the first of the eastern cables snapped.

Adrenaline flooded Sharol's body, every hair on her bare arms as stiff as the green spikes on her head. She had to get off the bridge! She had moments, perhaps ten rapid heartbeats, to clear the last span before reaching the scrubby tumbled headlands rising from the Thorn's west bank.

The two trucks, cab smokestacks belching furious columns of black smoke to rival the destruction behind them, plowed forwards side by side, admitting no room for the line of increasingly panicked trailing drivers. The bridge's eastern tower snapped in two and the roadway buckled, flinging cars traveling in both directions skyward.

She only had one slim chance. She gunned the engine, half rising from the seat as her foot slammed the accelerator into the floor. Jerking the wheel to her right, she slotted into the narrow shoulder and crept past the truck on its inner side. Less than a hand's width separated the car from the truck to her left and the low concrete wall to her right. The chassis vibrated as the wheels thudded over the rumble strip along the painted white line.

If the truck veered even slightly toward her, she was dead. If debris waited on the shoulder, she was dead.

Eyes bulging, fingers locked on the wheel in a death grip, Sharol bellowed every profanity in her considerable vocabulary. Cars smashed into each other behind her, twisted metal and shattered glass spraying in the wake of the two trucks. The western bridge tower crumbled, not sliced in half like its counterpart, but simply pulled down by the weight of the wreckage.

Time slowed down. She was level with the truck's cab, almost past it. Was that a dead animal on the shoulder ahead? Cars vanished from her rear view mirror, dropping into the scree of concrete destruction piling on the western river bank below.

She was gonna hit that fucking corpse! Was she clear of the truck?

"Fuck!"

At the last possible instant, she veered out of the shoulder, tires screeching in protest. Braced for a collision that never came, she recoiled from the harsh glare of the truck's headlights, flooding her car as its blaring horn drowned out her scream.

Then it was gone. Stunned, Sharol fought to keep the tortured company car on the roadway as she tried to understand. Half-blinded, she caught the last moments of the truck's demise, along with its companion, the cab-less container flipping upwards as the last stretch of roadway buckled and collapsed underneath, missing her rear wheels by less than a car length.

Where was the cab?

Oh, shit.

The highway made a sharp turn to the right as it climbed around an outstretched arm of rocky bluff. Cringing, she trusted a sudden instinct and swerved back into the shoulder. It saved her life.

Dropping from the angry black sky, the fume-belching cab smashed into the roadway not ten metres behind her left taillight. It landed upside down, its roof crunching with a sickening thud. The twin exhaust pipes splintered as the windshield erupted in a geyser of glass. Then the gas tank ignited in a dazzling fireball.

Sharol tore around the curve, fighting for control of the car, and braced for the concussion. Even partially shielded by the bluff, the shock wave propelled her airborne. Shrapnel pummeled the trunk, cracking the rear windshield, but all her attention stayed on the car's trajectory around the curve. She couldn't turn in the air, and the concrete divider loomed with implacable menace. The car landed in the middle of the two lanes, its front bumper touching down with a hideous metallic scrape. She forced herself to wait until both tires grounded before leaning into the curve again.

"Stay with me, you bastard!" she screamed. Her door smacked the divider, smearing the concrete with black paint, but she kept control and veered back into the outside lane. As she feathered the brakes, decelerating to a more manageable speed, she glanced through the small remaining patch of clear glass in the rear windshield. The weed-puckered bluff hid most of the destruction, except for the boiling cloud of burning diesel that billowed behind it.

As the road straightened, running parallel to the river for a short stretch before plunging westward, a sign promised a scenic viewpoint ahead. Despite the first drops of what promised to be an epic rainstorm splashing her windshield, Sharol pulled into the small parking lot.

Three other cars were already there. An older couple stood in front of their pristine sport utility vehicle, while a younger man stood behind his open car door, clutching it for dear life. They all stared in horror at the view. Sharol left the engine running, got out of the car on shaky legs, and joined them.

Thornburg was gone. Where office and condo towers had scraped the sky, where elevated roads had threaded their way through bustling neighborhoods, only smoking rubble remained. Nothing had been spared.

Debris poured into the churning river, already choked with the wreckage of cars, trucks, and boats, clogging around the broken fangs of the Frontier Bridge supports and the detritus from the docks.

At the heart of the desolation, not far from where the Bureau of Folk Affairs office had once stood, not far from Empress Catarina Park and its Hunter's Moon Festival, the rubble glowed red around the edges surrounding a tiny core of yellowish green. Thick black smoke spread in a smothering pall until the onrushing storm embraced it.

No one said a word. There were no words for their shock, their horror, their inability to truly comprehend what their eyes were telling them.

Gusts of wind tossed the stench of burning fuel into Sharol's face, her skin now plastered with diluted hair gel washed from her scalp by suddenly torrential rain. She hardly noticed.

Only when the storm's dense curtains swept over the bluffs, drawing a merciful veil over Thornburg's violent demise, did she finally escape the downpour and slump back into her driver's seat. She took three long, slow breaths. Then she reversed out of her parking space and turned west, toward the Thorn River Reservation.

What else could she do?

19

HUNTER'S MOON

"C'mon, Ari! You know you want to!"

Ariadne grinned, infected by Maya's good-natured laughter. Barrett and Simone, fixtures of her tenuous social circle, chuckled too.

Lanky Barrett Vale peered at her with intense brown eyes as he sipped his third plastic cup of beer. Simone Dupris, sporting a vibrant yellow-and-orange sundress that exposed an eye-catching amount of pale cleavage, clung to his arm. They'd been a couple since early in their first year at Segard. Ariadne suspected Maya sometimes slept with Barrett, and maybe with Simone too.

"I think I'll leave it to the younger generation," she replied, gesturing back at the stage. "My dancing days are done."

Days that, honestly, had never existed. She'd never had the desire to pursue ballet or Fenuian step dancing, or whatever other class her mother had signed her up for. Only fencing and its thrill of single combat had sustained her interest. It was a dance too, as graceful in its way as what they watched on the small stage set up in the northwest corner of Victory Plaza. LightFolk girls who couldn't have been older than ten demonstrated a selection of traditional dances, while their mothers coaxed audience members to join in.

Everyone was having a good time, humans and LightFolk alike, and wasn't that the point of the Festival?

Maya threw up her hands in exaggerated defeat, then linked arms with Ariadne as they walked on. New Ashbrook's capricious late-spring climate had dealt a warm, sunny day that lured families, college students, and many more to the four-square-block plaza in the heart of the city's Harbor District. Tens of white marble statues studded paved areas, in which miniature parks, ponds, and playgrounds nestled. It was a sanctuary for those who lived and breathed urban life.

"I've never seen the Plaza look so colorful," Maya observed, gesturing at all the LightFolk craftspeople's pastoral flourishes. Flowered vines twisted around light poles and white marble statues while ranks of tubbed trees and multihued foliage marched between them.

"That's One Raven's doing," Ariadne murmured. "Davek says it was all like this once. Before the Conquest, this space was sacred to the One Raven Clan. There was a real grove in the old growth forest that our ancestors cut down when they built the city. The Empire's victory was the Folk's defeat."

Maya pursed her lips. "Kind of ironic they chose to hold their festival here then, given all these statues honor heroes of the Empire that conquered them. Or maybe it's ballsy. I can respect that. What is Hunter's Moon anyway?"

"The start of a new Great Year. Second Moon's orbit takes it closest to First Moon once every twenty-three regular years. That happens today—any hundredth, actually." Ariadne shaded her eyes, but the bright sunlight obscured any hint of either moon. "Davek says much of his people's lore is related to the moons, and their Mother."

"Maybe we should go find him so he can tell us more," Maya said with a mischievous grin.

Ariadne laughed, although her heart fluttered. "Good luck finding him in this chaos!"

Except for the broad north–south avenue that bisected the plaza—reserved for the imminent parade—stalls, stages, and tents crowded every metre. Beguiling scents of smoked meats and delicately spiced root vegetables competed for the attention of the Festival goers. They could wash their meal down with plastic tumblers of *i'eina* beer, brewed from the sour grain of desert corn. They could observe and try out traditional crafts still practiced in Folk communities nationwide, although mostly by older LightFolk matrons or on the DarkFolk reservations. And they could enjoy cultural demonstrations, everything from dancing to range hunting.

They could even watch magic.

Under the largest tent in the plaza, five LightFolk women in formal, amber-colored robes took turns coaxing seeds into woven garlands of flowers before a rapt crowd. The tent was packed, mostly with families. Young children nearest the demonstration table oohed and ahhed, astonished by the marvelous spectacle.

Maya climbed onto Barrett's shoulders to get a better look from the edge of the tent, while Ariadne bounced on her toes and read the room. Most of the adults appeared as fascinated as the children, their exclamations blending into a low buzz. A few glanced darkly at Istilla One Raven, who chanted softly, teasing the first green shoots from the seed in the palm of her hand. Ariadne spied at least four police officers in black tactical gear hovering a not-so-discreet distance away.

Memories of the Thornburg Death Curse remained fresh.

"I want to see," Simone pleaded, tugging on Maya's bare calf where it dangled over her boyfriend's chest. Ariadne grimaced. No boy would be hoisting her onto his shoulders anytime soon. The distraction delayed her reaction to the minor commotion behind her, so she was unprepared when someone called out her name.

"Ariadne? Is that you?"

She turned without thinking, then froze as she saw her mother striding toward her.

Senator Daphne Braeyer remained a striking woman. Dark, intelligent eyes burned within a round face unravaged by age and framed by an artful tangle of chestnut-brown curls. A sharp midnight-blue suit enshrined her femininity without emphasizing it. As usual, her shrewish chief of staff, Val, scurried in her wake, along with what looked like a pair of reporters, a cameraman, and a police officer who couldn't be older than Ariadne herself. Daphne bestowed benevolent smiles on those constituents who greeted her. It looked like she'd had her teeth whitened again.

"Hello, Mother," Ariadne said. Her reply was intentionally cool—they hadn't spoken since the night before, when Daphne had refused to post her daughter's bail.

Simone shrank against Barrett, still clutching Maya's leg.

The senator from New Ashbrook North spared them a glance devoid of curiosity, and focused on her daughter. "How pleasant to run into you. You didn't return my call this morning."

"Yeah, well, I was busy. Catching up on the studying I missed yesterday." *Because you let me stew in a police holding cell*, she refrained from adding. She knew her mother had heard it anyway.

Daphne raised an eyebrow. "I'm glad to hear it. I hope you'll continue to keep your head down and avoid childish altercations in the future."

Ariadne bit her lip. Part of her wanted to start another childish altercation right there. She gestured to the tent. "I'm surprised to see you here. You never used to like LightFolk festivals or celebrations when I was growing up. Is this a photo op?"

"Of course," Daphne admitted, with a thin smile. "But I'm not immune to such a momentous occasion. The LightFolk are my constituents too, after all. I think it's time to temper the hysteria and scale back the overreaction of my colleague, Senator Castlewood. There's no reason both races cannot continue to work together for the good of the Empire."

"Spare me the campaign speech," Ariadne snapped. Then she paused, frowning.

People were streaming from the tent, not in the disorganized drift of bored tourists, but with the sharp, hurried movements of a herd sensing a predator. Low, animated conversations replaced the laughter. Then she noticed the silence. No one was cheering. Instead, heads were bowed, faces illuminated by the glow of screens, expressions twisting from curiosity to horror. Simone stared at her palm, her face pale.

"What's going on?"

"Something's happened in Thornburg," Simone whispered. Her wide eyes met Ariadne's, then flicked up at Barrett.

"Like what?" Maya asked, gripping his arms. "What's happened in Thornburg now? Not another Death Curse?"

Simone shook her head and passed her phone to Maya. Barrett craned his neck, trying to read the tiny screen too.

Ariadne turned back to her mother. The senator's practiced smile had vanished, leaving her face slack. Val whispered urgently in her ear while the camera crew and police officer exchanged nervous glances. Ariadne missed most of what Val said, but the words "emergency session" and "massive casualty event" drifted through the sudden quiet.

"What's going on?" Ariadne demanded. Gasps of shock reverberated through the increasingly restless crowd. "Can someone please tell me what the fuck is going on?"

Daphne frowned at her daughter's profanity, but it got her attention. She fixed Ariadne with a hard stare, but Ariadne didn't miss the flash of fear in her eyes. "There's been an attack," she murmured. "I've got to go. You should go too. Go somewhere safe, you and your friends. We're under attack."

She turned to leave, then paused. "Have you heard from your father recently?"

"No," said Ariadne. A pit formed in the bottom of her stomach. She hadn't tried to call Dad that morning, too busy planning her festival visit with her friends, rather than studying. "Why?"

Senator Daphne Braeyer, for once, appeared at a loss for words. In the end, she just shook her head and retreated the way she'd come, the bemused camera crew in her wake.

The police officer hesitated, one hand cupped to his ear, presumably listening to an earpiece. His face had drained of color.

"I would do as she said," he advised, turning to follow. "Find shelter now. Brothers save us!"

Pralik wasn't panicking. Not yet. But the arrival at Victory Plaza's southern edge of a fleet of emergency vehicles alarmed him. Most were police cruisers, pulsing red and blue like the opening screen of one of Davek's sci-fi shooters.

That was a disturbing analogy.

"Elder Pralik, what do we do?"

The question hung in the air, brittle with panic.

Pralik took a moment to force a calm expression before turning towards the speaker, a short man whose pale blue cloak could not disguise a heavyset build bordering on obesity. Eglente One Sky was closer to Davek's age than Pralik's, although his watery eyes and almost vanished hairline suggested otherwise. Eglente had been raised to an Elder of his clan just this past Midwinter, on the supposed strength of business acumen and diplomatic prowess. Strength of character and decisiveness in the face of adversity were not qualities he possessed in abundance.

"We tell everyone to gather their belongings and return home," Pralik said quietly, unable to entirely mask his bitterness. The festival had taken months to plan.

"But the parade!" Eglente protested, gesturing at the almost two hundred Folk of several clans lined up in formation, awaiting Pralik to join and lead them. Musicians and dancers, garbed in the flamboyant hues of each clan's ceremonial dress, poised to sweep northward up the avenue in celebration of their once vibrant and now barely tolerated culture. The crowd's growing shock and unease had infected the celebrants. Despite that, he noted with pride, none sought to dig out any phones they may have secreted within their costumes. They looked to the One Raven Elder, awaiting direction.

Pralik shook his head. "We cannot proceed. The crowd is restless and dispersing. The arrival of the police may help prevent widespread panic, but to start our parade now would be insensitive and possibly provocative."

Eglente stared back open mouthed and Pralik abruptly ran out of patience. "Think, man! This happened to Thornburg! Rational or otherwise, you surely know how emotions run in our own city right now. Start at the middle of the line and pass the word back. I'll begin at the front."

"Yes, Elder," Eglente muttered, and turned to do as he'd been told.

And act like an Elder, Pralik wanted to add, but bit his lip. Nothing good would come from injuring the pride of another clan, especially now.

A city implodes, homes and offices crumble, skyscrapers collapse. Dust and debris billow up and out, enveloping all. Thousands upon thousands of people, humans and Folk alike, sliced in half as if by a giant scythe. No screams, no time to even draw their final breath. Blood and smoke and a sickly green glow that enshrouds the wreckage, cooling to a malignant red as the heavy air clears.

His vision after the Leavetaking ceremony at the Emori Cadrach temple continued to haunt him. Had it been the True

Sight after all? Had he received forewarning of Thornburg's demise?

Could I have done anything to stop it?

He took a deep, shaky breath and shunted those thoughts aside. There would be time to dwell further on the matter, to seek the advice of those better learned in his ancestors' most mystical traditions. Right now, a more pragmatic response to the unfolding disaster was required.

He frowned, following Eglente's shambling progress towards the group of Two Water dancers halfway along the line of celebrants. There was supposed to be a contingent of One Snake DarkFolk there, dancers and musicians both. He'd seen them arrive, and had spoken to Ai'aina *chiek'la* herself. Now he couldn't see her or any of her people in the parade line or elsewhere. Where had they gone?

And where in the name of the Mother was Khavrik? Istilla, the third One Raven Elder, was supervising the magic demonstration. Khavrik should have been floating around the plaza, offering general help and support to his people where needed. Pralik hadn't seen any sign of him, his increasingly irritated texts remained unanswered, and his attempts to call had been shunted to voicemail. His usual cordial dislike of his fellow Elder blossomed to simmering fury. How dare Khavrik abandon his duties today of all days.

"Davek!" Pralik spied his son hurrying past with his friends from Segard, all waving their phones and talking over each other. Davek looked up and stumbled to a halt, almost tripping over the shallow curb marking one side of the main avenue.

"Did you see, Dad?" Davek pointed to his phone with his free hand, his voice rising. "They're saying Thornburg's gone! The entire city destroyed—"

Pralik cut him off. "Have you seen the DarkFolk? No? Then I need your help. You, and your friends too. Start at the front of the line and tell the celebrants that the parade is canceled.

Tell them to find their families and to go home, as quickly and quietly as possible. Do you understand?"

Davek gaped at him with wild eyes. If others saw that, it could start a real panic.

"Son," Pralik said in his calmest voice, just loud enough for Davek to hear over the crowd's disquiet. "I need you to be One Raven. Master your alarm. Control your fear. Be the man you are becoming. Lives may depend on it."

Davek swallowed, then straightened his back and took a deep breath. "C'mon, guys," he told his friends, who watched the exchange warily. They all nodded and headed for the start of the parade line at a brisk walk.

"Good boy," muttered Pralik. He called his wife as he headed towards the square patch of green in the plaza's southwest corner, known mockingly as "The Grove" since a lonely pair of middling sized trees grew in the middle of it. The One Snake DarkFolk had staged there, those participating in the parade and those demonstrating ancient crafts and dance.

The true grove, once a source and focus of One Raven power, had lain elsewhere and been hacked down a long time ago. Its ruins lay buried beneath Empire concrete. Pralik and his people mourned it still.

"Laida, where are you?" he whispered urgently when she picked up. No one in the crowd he politely shouldered through appeared to pay him any attention, but better safe than sorry.

"At the magic tent," she replied. It was difficult to detect nuance over the phone, but there was an edge to her calm voice. "We're helping Istilla break it down. She decided no one would be interested after the parade, or... Is it true? What they're saying about Thornburg?"

"I don't know. I only know what I've been told. I've canceled the parade, and I'm sending people home. Until we find out more, I don't want to give the city's more excitable elements an easy target for their frustrations."

"Oh, Pralik!" Laida said nothing more for a few moments. Pralik gained his first sight of The Grove through the turbulent throng. He glimpsed the maroon colors of One Snake: there were definitely some DarkFolk sheltering under the trees, under the suspicious eyes of at least ten riot police.

He cupped his phone and spoke with more urgency. "Is Chiana with you? Good. Go home, Laida. Take our daughter and go home. I'll find Davek and join you soon. Go home and stay safe."

Pralik paused ten metres from the police line, replacing his phone inside his amber robe. For now, he had to suppress concern for his family. It was time for him to act like an Elder.

He found the policeman with the most lethal weaponry and black boxes of unclear utility dangling from his uniform. "I'm Pralik One Raven," he announced. "The One Snake Folk are my guests. I wish to speak with them."

The officer peered at him from behind oversized dark glasses that dominated his pale, rugged face. "We're just trying to keep things orderly," he said in a flat voice. "Help us by doing the same."

Pralik inclined his head in a minimal show of polite respect, then approached the DarkFolk. Twenty, maybe twenty-five, including what looked like some of the parade contingent. The dancers, mostly teenage boys and girls, were still dressed in multilayered strips of cloth, mostly maroon twisted with just about every other color imaginable.

Where were the older dancers? Where were the other twenty or so DarkFolk who'd ridden the bus from the Black Hills reservation this morning? He could see it—an old model of scratched and faded black—parked on a side street a stone's throw away, beyond the police line. Other than the dancers, only a pair of older women and a handful of children huddled together, fearfully watching his approach.

"Where is Ai'aina *chiek'la*?" he asked, addressing the sterner-faced of the two matrons. She retained hints of youthful beauty but deep lines etched her face and brittle white hair marked too many years living too hard a life. "I need to talk with her immediately."

She exchanged an unreadable glance with the other matron, and clutched her robe tight. The dancers and children drew closer, like travelers gathering around a campfire.

"We are all that are here," she replied in a wheezing voice, spreading her hands in feigned regret. "We wish to go home."

Pralik shook his head. Something didn't feel right. "Where is Ai'aina? Where are the rest of you? You can't leave until you're all here."

The matron cocked her head. "We are not welcome in your city? We may not come and go as we please?"

"It is dangerous, especially now. Has no one told you the news? Of course you should be able to come and go as you please, but now may not be the best time. You may not be safe."

Pralik glanced at the cordon of riot police encircling The Grove. Was *he* safe?

"The young ones wish to leave," said the matron, a glint in her dark brown eyes. "If you care about their safety, *chiek'la* of the One Raven Clan, you will let us take them back to our homes."

"But where did the others go?" Pralik hissed in frustration. One Snake were notoriously secretive, even for DarkFolk. But what were they thinking? Even before this latest devastating news, those who clung to life and work in New Ashbrook had bigger targets on their back.

"Is such knowledge the price of our departure, *chiek'la*?" The matron softened her voice and held his eye in silent appeal.

Obstinacy. Secrets. Pralik blew out his cheeks and rubbed his forehead, trying in vain to ease the throbbing headache he'd been unable to shake since breakfast. The day, once full of promise after months of planning, continued its inexorable slide into chaos. In the words of his son, it had turned into an utter shit show.

"Fine," he told her, then raised his voice. "Gather your belongings. I'll escort you to your bus."

As he turned to lead them through the ring of police, the officer he'd spoken to cupped his ear.

"Copy," the officer barked into a microphone pinned to his lapel, then made a slicing gesture with his hand. Instantly, all the police surrounding The Grove stood up straight and clutched their rifles menacingly.

"Is there a problem?" Pralik asked, stopping short as the officer stepped in his path.

The man didn't smile. He just thumbed the safety off his rifle.

"Tell your people to take a seat. Relax. You ain't going anywhere for a while."

20

A Rescue, Of Sorts

Xavier had heard many sayings about the "light at the end of the tunnel." Some were positive, some whimsical, but the metaphor was so rooted in popular culture that he was unprepared for the literal experience.

He sank to his knees, weeping, as the first pinprick shafts of daylight finally penetrated the boarded-up opening of the disused mineshaft.

The three-fingered miner, who'd grudgingly helped Xavier hobble along this last stretch of dust-shrouded darkness, sat with his back to the wall nearby, next to Uraol, his foreman. Only five other miners remained. Two had died as the DarkFolk blasted their path towards this old tunnel, simply dropping in place. No one would tell their human tagalong, but Xavier suspected they'd burned themselves out—maybe literally—after one spell too many.

No one had the energy to bring their bodies to the surface. They scarcely had strength enough for their own.

"Leave them to the mountain they dishonored," Uraol had declared, his expression unreadable in the waning red glow of the emergency lamp.

Xavier was surprised his body still had moisture enough for tears. As it was, the drops just welled in the corner of his eyes, before the grime coating his skin absorbed them.

He was so thirsty. He could barely move his swollen tongue. His nostrils were so clogged with dust that he had to breathe the stuffy air through his mouth. His head throbbed with every brittle heartbeat. His left leg was sore, but at least he could put some weight on it. He suspected his right ankle was broken.

He would have crawled down these tunnels, clinging to the fading hope that he'd ever see daylight again. He would have crawled, the mystifying words spoken through the last company man's lips reverberating around his brain, making less and less sense.

And yet, the DarkFolk had helped him. Uraol had half supported and half carried Xavier all the way up the gentle incline of the newly blasted tunnel. Neither had spoken a word. The miners had found the old shaft, but not perfectly: its floor intersected the new working at waist height, tangled iron rails snapped in half and ready to impale the unwary. The three-fingered miner had helped haul Xavier up the scree of rock, while Uraol pushed from behind.

"Why?" he'd croaked, flopping onto his back, panting with exertion and stabbing agony from his ankle.

The two miners had exchanged a strange look, but they didn't answer. They probably didn't know why they were bothering to help him either.

Now, huddled within blissful sight of the outside world, they and their kin gathered for one last effort. This must be an ancient shaft, for unless Xavier missed his guess, it emerged directly onto the surface, maybe through a natural cave. They'd climbed steadily ever since finding the shaft, stumbling over rocks and mining debris, avoiding the rails that could destroy an ankle if stepped on.

One last effort, then freedom.

Xavier listened, but try as he might, he heard nothing but the ponderous groaning of the mountain. No human voices, or evidence of heavy machinery, of rescue efforts underway. Maybe the Thorn River Mining Company had focused on the site of the initial explosion. There had been another working, the one that likely caused the blast. Maybe they'd found survivors from it. But if they'd hoped to find Harran Latham, they'd be disappointed. That image would haunt Xavier forever.

Without a word, the seven remaining DarkFolk stood. Xavier considered doing likewise, then thought better of it. He watched from his knees as they shambled into a semicircle facing the barricade. One of the older miners could only stand with the help of another, but there was little point in resting further. The mine offered nothing to replenish the body, and the water canteens were empty. It was now or never.

Uraol led the DarkFolk in another low chant. Xavier didn't hear it so much as he felt it, a strange tremor vibrating in his teeth and ringing his skull. He shut his eyes, but the sensation intensified, a rising pressure that demanded release, until—

The tunnel barricade blew outwards, shards of disintegrating wood and pulverized stone billowing from the hillside. Late afternoon sun breached the tunnel for the first time in years, piercing the cloud of dust and dazzling them. Xavier shut his eyes until the echoes of the blast faded, along with the buzzing inside his skull.

They were finally free!

A deep, dissatisfied groan reverberated further down the tunnel, as if the mountain itself was shifting in its sleep. Time to get out of there.

Xavier didn't wait for assistance. It looked like the miners were busy helping each other, although at least one appeared beyond help. Xavier crawled, allowing his stinging eyes to adjust to the daylight as he skirted boulders and other debris.

A soft breeze struck up as he emerged onto a level patch of pockmarked scrub between two barren slopes. He turned his face and submitted to the wind's gentle caress, then groaned and collapsed onto his back.

He could sleep for a tennight.

Someone shook his shoulder as he began to doze. He startled awake to see Uraol's dirt-smeared face hovering above him. Powdered rock choked his hair and turned it gray. Yet the thick lips set above his hard angular chin twisted in a relieved smile.

"You did well," Uraol said, his hoarse voice scarcely louder than the breeze. He rose up on his knees and surveyed the area. "Seven survived. Perhaps that was Mother's will."

"What next?" Xavier whispered. "Will they come for us?"

The foreman snorted. He held out his hand. Xavier took it and allowed himself to be hauled into a sitting position.

"Barracks are not far. Can you walk?"

"I'll walk to get away from this damn mine."

"Good," Uraol said, and his smile warmed. "Mother favored us."

The bullet took him right between the eyes.

Gunfire crackled, kicking up dirt and chipped stone as bodies fell. Xavier froze in horror as Uraol's lifeless body toppled onto its side, then flung himself back down to the ground as the fusillade stuttered to a halt.

"—shooting, you fucking imbeciles!" roared a voice. A female voice. He knew that voice. "That's a BFA agent! Lower your weapons!"

"Sharol?" Xavier croaked, too soft for anyone but himself to hear.

"Xavier?! You still alive up there, partner?"

All he could do was raise a shaky hand in the air. But it was enough.

○··●

Thorn River Mine's medical bay occupied a prefab trailer not much larger than the nurse's office at the Metropolitan Academy in New Ashbrook. Xavier and the three-fingered miner shared the bare steel examination table. A young, prematurely balding medic, whose dangling badge proclaimed him to be Dane Vallance, treated the two other survivors for bullet wounds as they slumped in the only chairs. The wall fan labored noisily to replace the hot stuffy sweat-sour air with anything remotely breathable.

Sharol had bullied the security guards into helping those still alive after their panicked assault. Two of them, scarcely older than Ariadne, had supported Xavier on each side as he hobbled back to the Command Center. Other guards and company employees stood around, listless and fearful. Few were older than his assailants turned helpers. None met his eye.

"What were they thinking?" Xavier demanded, clutching his second plastic bottle of tepid water to his chest. He'd never tasted anything better in his life.

He'd shed his tattered pink vest and exchanged his radiation monitor for two chunky pale blue tablets. Dust and dirt still caked his exposed skin and torn clothing. Medic Vallance had splinted his left ankle, believing it was only sprained and not broken. Xavier avoided looking at the crimson spray that stained the front of his shirt.

"They heard an explosion and panicked," Sharol murmured. She leaned against the rear wall, next to the ineffective fan, as out of the way as she could be. She'd tossed her jacket on the table next to Xavier, and bare muscular arms hugged herself over her sweat-dampened black vest. Red-rimmed eyes blinked slowly within her haggard face. There was something more going on here.

"Where's the rest of management? I want heads to fucking roll. And where's the rescue operation?"

Three Fingers snorted. Vallance shook his head, but left the talking to Sharol.

"There wasn't one. I expected to find some sort of effort when the guards at the gate finally admitted there'd been an accident. They wouldn't or couldn't tell me why no one was trying to help the miners buried in the blast. As I understand it, the Director himself was down there."

"Harran Latham," Xavier confirmed, shuddering at the memory. "He didn't make it."

Vallance glanced up, licked his lips, then returned to bandaging a wounded man's arm.

"I figured. They let me through the gate, but no one seemed to know what to do with me. A lot of the senior managers left this afternoon. I passed them on the way, I guess."

It was Sharol's turn to shiver, her eyes focusing on something only she could see.

"What are you doing here?" Xavier asked gently. "Don't get me wrong, I'm elated to see you, especially after you stopped those trigger-happy assholes from killing us all. But why are you here? Didn't you call ahead?"

"Tried that, from the office before I left. No answer. So I came myself. And..."

"And what, Sharol?"

Tears welled in her eyes, and she bit her lip. Given his partner's usual unflappable demeanor, Xavier knew something was terribly wrong.

"Oh, Xavier! It's gone. Thornburg's gone!"

The room froze.

"Then it's true?" Vallance's voice, barely a whisper, echoed in the deepest vaults of Xavier's brain. The medic gripped one end of the bandage, poised to pin it in place. The DarkFolk stared at Sharol as if seeing a human for the first time.

"Tell us," Xavier said quietly.

So she did, in a lifeless monotone that couldn't conceal the terror and trauma of the moment and its aftermath. When she finished, describing her drive away from the scenic overlook towards the reservation, Xavier reached out and took her hand. He couldn't tell which of them he comforted.

"Could anyone have survived?" he asked quietly. His sister Alira and her family lived in North Kennerly, seven kilometres east of downtown Thornburg. He couldn't imagine not seeing her again, sharing awkward holiday dinners or beers on the deck while their two young sons played in the yard. How could any of that be gone?

Sharol shrugged. "I suppose it's possible. I don't know how far the devastation reached. It's like an earthquake leveled the city, every building flattened. If anyone survived the blast, they'd be buried underneath it all. I saw planes and copters in the sky before we heard you guys blast your way free of the mine. It'll be dark soon, but maybe someone will start looking."

She paused, casting a wary glance at the miners. "But Xavier, even if someone survived the blast... It wasn't a normal explosion. I don't know if it was an attack or an accident, but the smoke was riddled with green light. Flamestone green light."

The previous awestruck hush was nothing compared to the silence that followed. It was a vacuum, heavy and suffocating, as if the air itself had been sucked out of the trailer. To even draw a breath felt like a violation.

Vallance pinned the bandage and sat back on his knees, putting as much distance between himself and his patient as the confined space allowed. The miner murmured something in his native tongue that caused the DarkFolk next to him to flinch. Three Fingers shook his head, but the others didn't appear reassured by his rebuttal.

"What is it?" Xavier hissed. "Do you know something?"

The young DarkFolk rewarded him with a scathing expression. "How, agent? Even when we're not buried by explosions in the tunnels, we're cut off from the world outside the mine. Cut off from our people." A fire kindled in his dark eyes. "Even though many of us may wish such death and destruction on those who have enslaved and slaughtered our people, how would we do so?"

"Magic?"

Three Fingers shot Sharol a look of the utmost contempt. "If indeed your ancestry is cursed with the blood of my people, no knowledge came with it. The spell to commune with another—even one of my own kin in ti'Lan-ot City—requires a personal token and energy too great to conceal from our jailers."

He turned his implacable gaze on Vallance. The medic cringed as if struck. Then Three Fingers sighed and deflated. "No. None here had any knowledge or involvement with what happened to your city. I have never heard of any spell that could do what you said you saw."

The bandaged miner grimaced, but remained silent.

"If there was a flamestone reactor in the city, I could believe some catastrophe might be responsible," Xavier mused, keeping his horror at a distance until he was ready to deal with it. "But there isn't. Wasn't. Could someone have weaponized flamestone?"

Sharol just shook her head. She sniffled and wiped her nose with the back of her hand, and that's when the panic hit Xavier.

"Ariadne! Shit, I need to call my daughter! I need my phone."

He slid off the examination table, almost pitching onto the third miner, who pushed him back with two strong hands to his chest. Xavier hardly noticed. He couldn't think about Alira and her family, or the very few other people in Thornburg he cared about. He couldn't worry or begin to mourn. But he imagined Ariadne hearing the devastating news back in New Ashbrook and trying to call him, only to get no answer. She wouldn't know he'd been trapped in a mine disaster while Thornburg died. She'd be distraught!

He brushed off Sharol's first attempt to lay a comforting hand on his shoulder, but she was undeterred. "The phones are down. Why do you think people have been leaving? Cell network's out, land line is dead, and some asshole took the emergency sat phone with them."

Xavier gripped her arm. "I've got a satellite phone in my car. BFA issue. Just need to charge it. Gotta drive somewhere."

"Alright," Sharol said after a long pause. "Where do we go?"

The DarkFolk eyed them warily, but Vallance spoke up first. "Can you get us help? Find out what the company wants us to do?"

"Sure. Give us a number to call." Xavier looked at each of the miners in turn, landing on Three Fingers. "I don't know your name. Mine is Xavier. Xavier West."

Three Fingers inclined his head. "Ruian ti-Lan'ot."

"Thank you, Ruian. Thanks to all of you. You saved me down there. I'll never forget it. I'm in your debt." He grimaced. "And I'm sorry that not all of us who escaped the mine survived."

Vallance flinched, but Ruian simply inclined his head again. "I will remember it. I acknowledge your debt."

His words had a formal ring to them. *Maybe that's how it should be.*

Xavier and Sharol emerged into darkness, punctuated by the harsh glare of spotlights that the night confined to narrow cones. Clouds had long since swallowed the stars. The pleasant breeze of late afternoon had escalated into a dispassionate chill, with frozen gusts of real bite. Only a couple guards braved the elements, standing in the lee of the Command Center. They raised their weapons as the BFA agents approached.

"Don't fucking start that again," Sharol snarled. One guard lowered his rifle guiltily, but his older companion was undaunted.

"You're guests here," he said in a sullen growl. "Don't try telling us what to do."

"Guests? You're a bunch of trigger-happy sadists. We should report all of you. But right now, we're just trying to figure out what's happening. Who's supposed to be in charge?"

"I'm going to plug in my sat phone," Xavier told her. He liked this Sharol, determined and confident and unwilling to take any shit.

Miraculously, his car keys had survived intact in the zipped inside pocket of his torn and stained jacket. He popped the trunk and glanced at Sharol's company car parked alongside.

Even in the dark the damage was clear: dents, pits, shredded paint, and random chunks of metallic shrapnel embedded in the chassis. Cracks in the rear windshield sprayed out in starbursts, making it impossible to see through, and the right rear tire was flat.

"Guess you're riding with me," he muttered, fishing out the briefcase-sized box containing the old satellite phone. It amazed him how much more compact technology had become in the last two decades—and versatile. This phone was designed to be charged only from certain car models. Even had he wanted to wait around and charge it from a standard wall socket in one of the mine buildings, he didn't have an adapter. They didn't even make them anymore. Planned obsolescence.

Hearing raised voices, he plugged in the phone and limped back towards the Command Center. Sharol stood toe-to-toe with a man sporting a chest-length ginger beard just inside the open front door. The two guards stood gaping a discreet distance away.

"Try it," the bearded man blustered. "As far as I know, they blew up the mine themselves. They were trying to escape justice. That's what will go in *my* report."

"Good luck with that." Sharol didn't blink. She noticed Xavier's approach and turned away from the other man with casual dismissal. "Let's get out of here, Xavier. This place reeks of sweat, incompetence and bigotry. Oh, we'll have to take your car. Mine is trashed."

"I noticed." He sagged while he walked around to the driver side as Sharol climbed into the passenger seat. Exhaustion seeped through his bones, and he wondered if he should be driving, especially at night. He probably only had to make it to ti'Lan-ot City though. The satellite phone should be charged enough by then.

○··●

Back in the medical bay, Dane Vallance slept peacefully on the examination table. Two DarkFolk miners dozed in their chairs. Their three-fingered companion was nowhere to be seen.

21

EMERGENCY SESSION

"An emergency session of the Senate is scheduled for 1.50 tonight," Val confirmed, peering at her tablet through stray auburn bangs. She held the device close to a narrow face whose features jostled for room like an overlarge family crammed into a tiny apartment in one of New Ashbrook's south-bank ghettos. Her watery eyes seldom blinked as she scanned articles and documents with rapid efficiency. Daphne could never persuade her chief of staff to wear glasses or contacts.

"I guess that's to be expected," Daphne sighed. "That would be early morning for the Emperor in Earia. Or is he traveling?"

"He is not, senator. Can I confirm your attendance?"

Daphne waved her hand in assent, then settled back into her desk chair. She never understood how something so padded and "ergonomic" could be so damned uncomfortable.

She picked up a glass of whiskey and swirled the rich brown liquid, watching it leave viscous residue near the rim. It reminded her of the medicines her mother would force on her as a young child at the slightest hint of a sniffle or cough. She'd hated them as much as she once loved whiskey. She set the glass back down on the massive wooden desk that occupied a third of her office.

This pour had lasted eight days. She doubted it would last the night.

"Is that all, Val? Do I have time to grab dinner somewhere?"

"Just two more things, senator." Apparently not. "Senator Castlewood would like a brief word before the emergency session."

Daphne's eyebrows shot up in surprise. "Really? About what?"

"The message doesn't say. Just asks when it would be convenient for him to stop by."

"He wants to come here?"

Even stranger. Brogan Castlewood preferred to play with home-field advantage, in his cavernous office that was palatial in comparison to hers. But then, he'd joined the Senate almost thirty years ago. She was two years into her first term, a rookie on the team he all but captained.

What could he want? She suspected it wasn't anything good, not for her anyway.

"Sooner is better than later, I suppose. Just let me know. What else?"

"Chancellor Palmer of Segard Law School called. He wishes to speak with you urgently."

"Urgently? Today? After one of our cities was wiped off the map?"

Men, honestly. No matter what was happening to anyone else in the world, their problems always took center stage, demanding immediate attention.

Val frowned, squinting down at her tablet. "Shall I tell him you'll call back in the morning?"

"No, call him now. Maybe I'll interrupt his evening meal."

Her chief of staff punched in the number on the ancient black speakerphone that squatted next to the sleeping computer monitor. Daphne wanted the caller ID to reflect her office, not her personal line.

"Good evening, senator," answered Chancellor Maven Palmer. His voice scratched and hissed through the tinny speaker. "I appreciate you returning my call so late, especially on what I'm sure must be a difficult day."

"It is, Chancellor," she said, trying not to grit her teeth. "How may I help you?"

"Ah yes. Well, this is a courtesy call of sorts. Are you aware of the incident involving your daughter yesterday morning?"

Daphne picked up the glass of whiskey again. "I know Ariadne was involved in a minor scuffle between classes, and that some overzealous parent decided to press assault charges leading to her arrest. I have not heard of any effort from your institution to bring even a semblance of rationality to the situation."

"Well, ah yes, that is of course why I am calling. I have spoken to Dean Collins and we believe it is in the best interests of all concerned if Miss West is suspended from classes for the remainder of the term. Should she show appropriate contrition, she will of course be welcome to return at the start of next academic year."

Fuck it. Daphne downed her whiskey in one long swallow, savoring the glorious burn it inflicted on the back of her throat. "Val, do you have that Menzies file handy?"

Ever the professional, Val showed no emotion as she sifted through the manila folders stacked near one corner of the desk. She extracted one and laid it open in front of Daphne. A black and white photograph of two men sat on top of a thin sheaf of papers.

"Thank you, Val. Now, Chancellor, what is Segard's official position on anti-Folk discrimination and racism?"

The line crackled to itself for a moment before Palmer returned, his tone considerably cooler. "I don't think that is relevant to our conversation. Your daughter—"

"The acceptance of the school's first three LightFolk students made headlines last year. Segard, quite rightfully, earned praise for its progressive policies. You wouldn't want to lose all that goodwill by caving to Purists, would you?"

"What are you talking about, Senator Braeyer?"

"I'm looking at a photograph taken from security camera footage last tennight, outside a known Purist meeting in the Little Haven district. Aleister Menzies and his father, Aston, were seen leaving that meeting. I have other evidence of Aston's long involvement with the Purist cause."

"Are you trying to blackmail me?" Palmer spluttered.

Daphne rolled her eyes. "I've made handsome contributions to the Segard Foundation. I have been, and am, publicly proud that my daughter studies at such an esteemed law school. Segard benefits greatly from my association. I suspect it would not do nearly so well from its association with the Purists."

More crackling silence. Daphne waited, resisting the urge to refill her whiskey glass.

"Perhaps we can moderate our response," Palmer said at last. He sounded like a sulky child. "An official sanction, but no academic restrictions."

"For both Ariadne *and* the Menzies boy. And I want those charges dropped, Chancellor, for the good of Segard as well as my daughter. I let her stew over her poor decisions in a police station holding cell, when other parents may have bailed her out immediately. I see no reason to further involve the authorities."

She stabbed at the "End Call" button and slumped back in her chair. This wasn't her first duel with the privileged establishment, of which Segard was unmistakably still a part despite its flirtations with progress. Privileged *male* establishment. She wondered if such lengths would have been necessary had Menzies' assailant been another male student.

"Senator Castlewood is waiting outside," Val murmured, cupping a hand to one ear.

Daphne sighed, and closed the Menzies file. "Perfect. Let's hope this is quick. Show him in."

"Daphne! Thank you for seeing me," Brogan Castlewood declared as he marched into her office. It was a shorter march than he was likely used to. He stopped just short of her desk and offered Daphne his hand. She stood and gripped it, meeting his firmness with power of her own. A lazy grin slid over his bearded face.

"It's always a pleasure to converse with a senator of such distinction," she replied, polite but guarded. "I'm told you had something to tell me before the emergency session."

"Indeed I do." Brogan's grin faded, and he covered her hand with both of his. "Has there been any word from your ex-husband?"

"No." She had called Xavier every quarter tenth since returning to her office following the parade. The maddening, if polite, recorded voice continued to assure her he was unavailable. She'd even texted Ariadne, but her daughter hadn't heard anything either. Daphne wasn't ready to deal with the implications and their ensuing emotions, especially not in front of Brogan Castlewood.

He grimaced, then released her hand. "He's a fine man. Let's not give up hope. Please let me know if you hear he is safe."

"Thank you, but I suspect that isn't why you troubled to visit my office."

"It is, in part, but not all. I'll keep it brief, as I suspect you also wish to dine before we endure another night of debate with our esteemed colleagues." His eyes twinkled, but it looked more like malice than merriment. Daphne noticed he had dispensed with his usual suit jacket, and had rolled up the long sleeves of his impeccable white shirt.

She gestured to one of the two chairs he stood between, but he shook his head. "I'll stand, thank you. I came to tell you two things. First, that I admire you. That's neither flattery nor idle simpering praise. It's only your first term, but you've proven yourself capable and, more relevant here, willing to confront me in policy debate. Your arguments are sound, even if I disagree with most of them. You're an effective foil and restraint, more so than almost anyone else in the Senate. The Empire is better for it."

Daphne tried to conceal her surprise and any foolish blush. She had to remember where she was and who she was dealing with. "Thank you, senator. Debate without opposing voices is no debate at all. We owe our citizens rigorous examination of every issue."

Brogan's sincere smile turned grim. "Which brings me to my second point. No. In fact, we do not."

"Senator?"

"While I might ordinarily agree with you, certain times, certain events, demand prompt decisive action. In times of national emergency, latching onto debate for debate's sake is counter to the Empire's interests."

"What are you saying, Brogan?" Daphne bristled, guessing what was coming next.

"Evidence will be presented tonight of an existential threat to Novomond, and to the Empire. A course of action will be proposed. I'm asking you, and other senators of like mind, to temper your desire to oppose me at every turn. I'm asking you to think of the Empire first, and the ongoing safety of its citizens."

Daphne bit back her instinctive rebuttal. Brogan wasn't a tall man, but his personality towered over the Novomond Senate. Even with the opening he'd given her, she'd be a fool to walk willingly into his trap.

She met his glittering eyes and pondered for a full hundredth before speaking. Brogan waited, his face a mask of self-assured patience.

"It is my duty, as it is every senator's, to prioritize the Empire and our citizens' safety," she said slowly. "I appreciate your forewarning and will consider carefully all evidence that is presented and all that is proposed. And then I will do my duty."

The corner of Brogan's mouth twitched, then he nodded and took a step back. "That is all I ask, Senator Braeyer. It is time we all did our duty."

○··●

Technically, the Novomond legislature was the Lesser Senate, a colonial echo of the Greater Senate back in Earia. The building where it met, an imposing white marble and stone homage to classical architecture, overlooked the old harbor at the heart of New Ashbrook. Inside, once a ring of offices and smaller meeting rooms had been breached, the architects had designed the main chamber to mimic the amphitheater style of the famous Administratum. A gigantic projection screen behind the Proxy Chair and between the statues of the two Brothers was a modern addition. The Proxy Chair itself was the real difference between the Greater and Lesser Chambers.

In most matters, the Lesser Senate operated independently of the Greater. Novomond's legislators knew Novomond better than those east of the Finemian Ocean, who focused on the Empire's territories in the huge continent of Earia. The Emperor nominally approved every decision and signed every law, but in the Lesser Senate the Proxy almost always performed that task. The Proxy was, to all intents and purposes, the Emperor's hand-selected voice in Novomond.

There were exceptions, of course. Significant decisions and world events warranted a joint conclave, presided over by the Emperor himself. As Daphne entered the Lesser Chamber with ninety-nine other senators and took her back row seat, she noticed the soft blue glow of the projection screen. The Emperor would join them soon.

Daphne exchanged polite greetings but few smiles with her neighbors, many of them also junior senators. Everyone was on edge, their collective unease simmering like a cauldron from one of her grandma's old folk tales. She poured herself a glass of water from the pitcher she shared with Bryn Hammond—about the only thing she shared with the boisterous former professional Mauler and Castlewood protegé—and folded her hands on her section of the semicircular wooden tabletop. No materials had been allowed into the chamber for this emergency session, so her water glass's only companion was the mechanical Voter, a squat black box the size of her phone with two buttons: green for "Yes" and red for "No".

How long would it be until she had to press one of those buttons? Would she be happy with the decision she made?

It was Brogan Castlewood's visit, not the whiskey, that had left a sour taste in her mouth.

A bell clanged three times. The acoustics magnified its deep resonant tones as they would the voice of the Proxy, for it was the deceptively frail white haired man in his billowing scarlet robe who rang in the traditional opening of the session. All conversation died before the third ring faded, and a few remaining senators scurried to take their seats.

"All rise for His Imperial Majesty, Valiant the Fourth!" The Proxy's querulous voice permeated the chamber as the screen flickered, and then the face of their ruler appeared.

Valiant IV had been born not long after his Proxy in a tiny fishing village in Iliea, one of the southernmost states in the Empire. His deep brown eyes burned with vigor and intelligence above a square jaw. Short, tidy silver hair framed a sun-bronzed face surprisingly devoid of lines and wrinkles. Or, as some would have it, compassion. The Emperor hadn't ascended to his station by choosing any path but the most ruthless.

Daphne stood with everyone else in the chamber and crossed her fists over her chest in salute.

"Hail to the Emperor!" they cried. A twitch of the imperial lips was their only acknowledgment.

"Be seated, my friends," Valiant said, in his sing-song sibilant accent. "We are convening the Greater Senate as we speak. An attack on Novomond is an attack on the Empire itself. We wish to be guided by this chamber tonight. But first, is Senator Gravell present?"

"I am, Your Imperial Majesty," said the senator from Thornburg, a heavyset man of late middle age. He struggled to rise again from his seat several rows in front of Daphne. She could only see the silvering black hair on the back of his head.

Valiant pursed his lips in a grim line. "You have our deepest sympathy, and that of all true citizens of the Empire. We understand your wife, son and daughter were in Thornburg today. We can only imagine what you are going through. If you need time away to grieve, no one will fault you."

Gravell shivered, then drew himself taller. "Thank you, Your Imperial Majesty. But my place is here, to serve the Empire at this dark time. It's what my family would have wanted."

Would they though? Daphne thought. *I'm pretty sure they'd prefer to be alive.*

"Then we will honor your wishes and those of your family," said Valiant gravely, with the slightest of nods. "Should you need anything, please forward the request to our desk directly. We understand a search for survivors is underway?"

"Thank you, Your Imperial Majesty. Yes, two Army regiments have been dispatched to coordinate the search, although, ah, expectations are low. First responders from nearby townships have graciously offered their assistance. It is too soon to abandon hope."

"Indeed. We will all pray to the Brothers that some, at least, have survived this terrible catastrophe."

The Emperor bowed his head and closed his eyes. Daphne and the Lesser Senate followed suit. She heard Bryn Hammond's whispered prayer and others from neighbors too sanctimonious to keep it to themselves.

Brothers, let humility and wisdom guide us, not only strength and righteousness. Whose prayers would they hear, or listen to?

"Now, what do we know about the cause of this unthinkable tragedy?" Everyone raised their heads once more at Valiant's words, which took on a harder edge. Daphne noted he avoided the word "attack". That term had buzzed through the corridors all afternoon and evening like a swarm of angry bees. "Senator Castlewood, we understand you possess the latest intelligence."

Brogan rose to his feet like an eagle surveying potential prey. "I do, Your Imperial Majesty. I have, of course, shared much of this with you already. Now I wish to share it with my esteemed colleagues, with your permission of course." Valiant nodded, although Daphne thought she detected a hint of impatience. Perhaps she wasn't the only one weary of her fellow senator's pomposity. "Thank you, Your Imperial Majesty. Screen on, please."

Gasps of horror erupted from the floor as the image of their Emperor was replaced by an aerial shot of the smoking ruins of Thornburg. Clouds of dust and soot swirled amid the mist from a late afternoon storm. Daphne gritted her teeth and tried not to think about Xavier as she watched the silent footage, presumably taken from an Army helicopter as it circled the devastation.

She'd visited once, to serve divorce papers to her ex-husband. She remembered looking out the window from much the same vantage point, as the airplane banked around the western edge of the city towards the airport on its northern outskirts. While not approaching the grandeur of New Ashbrook, the downtown skyscrapers had stood tall and proud next to the iconic suspension bridge crossing the River Thorn. Now, she couldn't distinguish one building from the next. The crumbled remains of what might once have been an office tower blended into what was left of a one-story convenience store. She could only guess where the bridge had been from the northern extent of a debris field washing downriver.

Someone, somewhere, sobbed.

"Few of you have seen the scale of the destruction," Brogan murmured. "It is one thing to be told, to hear or read the words. It is another to see it with one's own eyes. Over one million men, women and children lived, worked, and followed their dreams in Thornburg. No more. We will remember them."

The senator's voice grew louder, carrying an unmistakable undertone of outrage and anger. "But who is to blame for this atrocity? Was it an accident, perhaps? No analyst or scientist I have spoken to can devise any explanation for such widespread damage. No space rocks were detected, and no telltale crater has been seen.

"What of a weapon then? Were we attacked? Such weapons have been conceived, but the Empire's early field tests show we are a long way from using them. Kelia and the Peripirian Autonomy deny such capabilities, denials supported by satellite evidence. Imagining that another rogue actor could successfully wield such terrible technology stretches the boundaries of belief."

"Who then?" Senator Gravell interrupted. "Who attacked my city? Who slaughtered my family and millions of other innocents?"

"Who indeed." Brogan's voice was grave. "Switch to the drone, please."

The screen flickered, momentarily showing the Emperor's impassive face. Then it darkened, except for a shaky pale green glow in the center.

"Remote-controlled drones are still in their infancy," Brogan continued. "Other than military purposes, whose nature I obviously cannot divulge here, we've used them at other natural disasters to help first responders assess the situation. This was taken two tenths after the event, just after sunset. It shows the epicenter of the blast, near enough. The drone failed moments after this image was captured. There is only one substance I know that emits light of such a color."

"Flamestone?" Gravell sounded like he didn't believe—or didn't want to believe—his own answer.

"That is our assessment." Brogan's voice hardened. "This was not a conventional attack by outside forces. The enemy has been among us all along. They are among us now. This was a DarkFolk magical assault."

Pandemonium erupted in the Lesser Chamber. Some raised their voices in objection; others screamed their outrage. Daphne gripped the edge of the table and waited. She knew there was worse to come.

"Silence!"

The din ceased as abruptly as it had begun. The Emperor's scowling visage reappeared. Those who had leapt to their feet hurried to retake their seats like unruly schoolchildren.

"You are Senators of the Empire," Valiant said coldly. "Lesser Chamber or not, you will act with the proper decorum, or you will be expelled. Senator Castlewood, please proceed with your proposal."

"Thank you, Your Imperial Majesty. Such a heinous act cannot go unpunished. We must be swift, decisive, and just. The measures the Senate recently enacted at my recommendation have proven insufficient to prevent this day. Perhaps we focused too much on the LightFolk, on those with whom we share the bounty of our great civilization, and whose troubles affect us more immediately. But make no mistake. The true enemies are the DarkFolk, those who brand themselves Chaos Walkers and those who support them. Is there anyone here who would dispute that this was a Chaos Walker attack, using foul magic unseen in more than a century?"

The question hung in the air like a venomous snake, poised to strike any who dared object under the Emperor's baleful regard. Daphne saw a handful of heads bowed in shame, a shame she struggled with herself. While the horrifying possibility was all too real, she wanted to demand more evidence, certainly before taking any punitive action. Which, knowing Brogan Castlewood, was sure to be emphatic.

She looked back at the senator, who'd risen to a prominence almost rivaling the Proxy himself. She found Brogan staring at her, a grim smile on his face. *It is time we all did our duty.*

"I thought not," he said with uncharacteristic softness. Then he straightened his back. "There will be time enough over the next few days to work with the Army and other military commanders to devise a long-term strategy for eradicating

Chaos Walk and its adherents. What we need first is a statement—a warning to those who would destroy our beloved Empire from within.

"The nearest DarkFolk reservation to Thornburg is Thorn River, likely a hotbed of Chaos Walkers. I ask you to join me in unanimously authorizing our vengeance. Come the dawn, our enemies will pay the price for this vicious insurrection."

22

A DANGEROUS SANCTUARY

Tension spiked in the crowded One Raven parlor at the scrape of a key in the front door. Wedged beside Maya on the sofa, Ariadne looked up from her phone. Opposite her, Davek sat rigid between Keralek and Jair, staring at the hallway's double doors.

When his father appeared, Davek sagged in relief.

"Pralik! Thank the Mother." Laida, Davek's mother, rushed from the corner of the elegant room and threw herself into her husband's arms.

Pralik staggered, then wrapped her in a fierce embrace. Over her shoulder, he studied his guests, forehead creasing. Ariadne forced herself not to fidget.

"I am well, my love," Pralik murmured. "Things are... difficult. But I am well. I see we have guests."

"Davek thought this was a good time for a party," Chiana said from the shadows. They were the first words Davek's sister had spoken since they'd arrived over a tenth ago. She stood in the corner, scrutinizing the human guests as daylight faded. Half-hidden outside the glow of the wall sconces, she reminded Ariadne of a wolf evaluating prey.

"It's not a party," Davek snapped without looking at his sister. "These are friends from school, Dad. They were at the

Festival. We ran into them as we left the Plaza and offered to escort them home. Things were getting vexy."

"Vexy?" Pralik raised an eyebrow.

"People started to panic." Maya's voice was uncharacteristically quiet, her words brittle. Ariadne wanted to take her hand, but Maya had been oddly distant since they'd squeezed into the parlor. "When they heard about Thornburg, some thought New Ashbrook would be next."

The words hung heavy. Laida shrank against Pralik, whose expression turned grim.

"I heard there'd been looting," he murmured. "And some idiots decided to burn cars. Is that what you call 'vexy'?"

Davek gaped, then glanced at Barrett of all people before answering. "We didn't see that. But we saw fights break out, and women having their purses stolen, and no one was doing a damn thing. I don't know where the police were. There was a stampede at the subway."

"It was horrible," whispered Maya.

Ariadne shuddered in agreement. They'd been staring at the crush of festival-goers choking the stairwell of Victory Plaza station when Davek and his friends found them. The screams—especially the children's—would haunt her forever.

Pralik muttered something in the One Raven tongue, then kissed Laida on the forehead. She whispered something back, something intimate. Ariadne turned away, embarrassed.

"Where have you been, Dad?" demanded Chiana, stepping forward into the room and standing behind Davek's couch. She towered over her brother, who flashed her an irritated glance.

Ariadne couldn't meet her eyes. The only other time they'd half met, Chiana had walked in on her sprawled naked on this very couch with Davek's head between her legs. Yet Ariadne couldn't help but admire the way Chiana's sleek amber robe accentuated her figure and the poise with which she carried herself. She wished she had half the beauty and bearing of the young LightFolk woman.

Pralik sighed. "I have been trying to help our One Snake guests. Many, including Ai'aina *chiek'la*, appear to have vanished into thin air. The rest, mostly children, claim ignorance. The authorities don't buy it and neither do I. Ordinarily, it would be an irritant. Today, it is a problem."

"Because of the rumors?" Chiana asked.

"There are many rumors. We would do well not to give them air until we know more." Father and daughter locked gazes until Chiana gave a tight nod.

"So, Davek, can you please introduce our guests?" Pralik favored Ariadne and her friends with a benevolent smile, but she sensed his unease.

It was all she could do to force a smile in return, and not flee into the night. Davek hadn't introduced her to his family. This was not the occasion she would have chosen.

Davek recited their names, starting with Barrett and ending with Ariadne. He placed no particular emphasis on her, leaving her both irritated and relieved. Perhaps there would be a more auspicious moment for him to claim her as his girlfriend.

But Pralik's eyes narrowed. He'd heard her name before. A hint of alarm crossed his features, before compassion smoothed it away.

"Miss West, we meet at last. I know your mother, of course, and I met your father recently. He gave me sound advice, for which I am very grateful. I hesitate to ask, but have you heard from him today?"

Ariadne's lip trembled. She'd lost count of her unanswered texts. Every call met the same automated voice telling her Xavier's number was unavailable. Even her mother claimed to have heard nothing.

"No," she whispered, shaking her head. "Not since yesterday."

She bit her lip. Now was not the time to bring up her arrest—though she suspected Pralik already knew.

"I haven't heard from my uncle either," Maya interrupted. She was trembling. "My dad's worried sick. He and Uncle Johanne are tight. He taught me how to fish, and... and now the DarkFolk—"

"You don't know that," Davek hissed. "That's just a rumor from people like Menzies."

Maya stared him down. Tears welled in her eyes as she glanced at Ariadne, looking more helpless than she ever had. Guilt slammed into Ariadne. She'd been entirely absorbed in worry for her own father, and for Davek. What a shitty friend she was.

"I'm so sorry, love," she murmured, finally taking Maya's hand. Her friend gripped back hard. "I didn't know."

Maya sniffed and nodded. She glanced at Davek, expression inscrutable, before her eyes fixed on his father. "Why wouldn't the DarkFolk be responsible? Especially the Chaos Walkers. Their magic is as they are, isn't it? Much darker than what you LightFolk use. Forbidden. Evil."

Chiana scoffed, her lips twisting in disdain. "Fool. LightFolk, DarkFolk—those are just names you humans gave us in your ignorance."

"Peace!" Pralik stepped between his daughter and Maya, palms raised. Chiana met his frown for a moment, then folded her arms and looked away.

Pralik turned to Maya. "Names have power, and should never be used lightly. The Art comprises several disciplines. Those who choose to live among our human conquerors favor the disciplines that produce truesilver in honor of First Moon. Those who live apart—clinging to their meager freedom—prefer others. Flamestone honors Second Moon, but the Art that produces it is not evil."

A pleasant veneer masked his steely authority. Not even his children weathered his gaze in comfort. "Chaos Walk recalls who our people once were, the lives we once lived. It embraces many ancient disciplines, few well understood. Any magic may be used for good or ill. Dark deeds are done as often in the full light of day as during the night. As are deeds of honor and renown."

Maya stared back at him, then bit her bottom lip and nodded, as if acknowledging a Segard professor's firm but polite correction. Then she squeezed Ariadne's hand again. "I don't want to be here, Ari. I don't want to be alone, but I don't want to be here."

As much as she craved the comfort of Davek's arms, Ariadne agreed. "Let's get a rideshare."

Barrett snorted, waving his phone. "Nothing available for at least a tenth. And that's better than it was when we got here."

"Then let's try the subway," said Maya fiercely. "That must have calmed down by now. Where's the nearest station?"

"River Road on the blue line is three blocks away, near the Bottleworks Bridge." Chiana studied Ariadne as she spoke, looming over her disgruntled brother. Heat rose in Ariadne's cheeks, and she wondered if Davek would try to keep her there.

He didn't. His father did.

Pralik cleared his throat, sounding for all the world like a lecturer demanding their students' attention at the start of class. "While I understand your desire to return home, I would urge caution. The city is still, as my son would say, vexy. It may not be in your best interests to be seen leaving the residence of a prominent LightFolk family."

Laida stirred alongside him. "What do you mean? Are we in danger?"

Pralik drew her closer, but kept his attention on his four human guests. "Not as long as we stay inside, for this evening at least. I saw a group of Purists in the Circle just now, and many others gathered nearby. I fear vandalism of our monument is afoot."

"How dare they!" Davek leaped to his feet. Keralek and Jair exchanged uneasy looks, but stayed seated. "We've gotta stop them!"

"No." The One Raven Elder shook his head. "Marching outside now and confronting them with righteous indignation is exactly what they want. There are too many of them, unless you're willing to break the law on use of magic. And that will make a bad situation worse."

Ariadne didn't recognize the word that came out of Davek's mouth, but she guessed its meaning from the way his mother recoiled. Pralik frowned, but Chiana interrupted before he could reprimand his son.

"If only Elder Khavrik were here. I heard he can conjure a small army capable of taking on such a mob without resorting to magic." Davek scowled at her, which she returned with an innocent smile.

Something was going on between those two, and Ariadne wasn't the only one who thought so.

Pralik glanced from one to the other through narrowed eyes. "Whether or not that's true, it wouldn't be my preferred course of action. And I haven't heard from my fellow *chiek'la* today. Have either of you? Davek?"

"Why me?" Davek asked sullenly.

Ariadne squirmed. She remembered the charismatic LightFolk who had bailed her out of jail at Davek's request. *Brothers, that was only last night!* It was easy to imagine others following a man like Khavrik to battle. No offense to Pralik, who seemed better suited to the negotiation table, but Khavrik was a warrior. He got things done. "Maybe Elder Khavrik had to follow up with the police after posting my bail," she interjected.

Everyone turned to look at her, some shocked, others curious. And some, like Chiana, calculating. Ariadne flushed, but returned the attention with quiet defiance.

"Maybe," Pralik murmured. "But your public show of support for my son will not have endeared you to the gathering mob outside."

Barrett slid over to the nearest window. At a gesture from Davek, Jair joined him. The two drew back the floor-length russet curtain just enough to peer through the glass.

Jair repeated Davek's profanity. "There's at least twenty of them around the pillar," he said over his shoulder. "Waving flashlights. One guy is speaking to the rest."

"What are we going to do?" Simone asked in a small voice, her first words since arriving at the One Raven house.

Ariadne's phone buzzed in her lap. An unknown number. She declined the call.

"We're not afraid of them," Maya insisted. "They're just assholes using mass panic to sow more discord."

Pralik nodded. "Agreed. But that doesn't make them any less dangerous. I'm guessing they might deter any rideshare driver."

"Is there another way out?" Ariadne asked. "We're grateful for your hospitality, Elder and, um, Mrs. One Raven. And for your help, guys. But I think we should go. Back home, where our families know we're... know where we are."

Where they know we're safe. Brothers, she'd almost said it out loud. Pralik's grim expression suggested he'd heard it anyway.

"There's the back way." Chiana locked eyes with Davek, who flashed her a sudden grin like the boy he'd been not so long ago.

"We haven't used that way for ages," he said. "Or at least I haven't."

Laida frowned at them. "What are you talking about? The back door leads to our fenced-in garden. Do you expect your friends to fly?"

Chiana's smile turned enigmatic. "Not exactly. I wasn't thinking about the door. My bedroom window opens onto the balcony too, remember?"

"What? Chiana, no!"

Pralik shook his head, but chuckled as only the father of mischievous children can.

"What's going on?" Ariadne demanded, silencing her phone again. Now was not the time.

Davek turned his grin on her. "When we were kids, me and Chiana used to slip out at night sometimes. All the houses on this row have second-floor balconies. You can jump from one to the next easily. You'll be halfway to the subway station before anyone out front notices a thing."

She couldn't help but grin back. *I'd love to run across balconies and rooftops with you, Davek.*

The insistent buzzing of her phone ruined the moment. With a soft and very unladylike curse, she snatched it up. It was the same damn number. Her thumb hovered over the screen, poised to dismiss it again.

"What's the matter?" Davek asked.

"Someone keeps calling me. I don't know who."

"Maybe you should answer it, love," Maya suggested.

Ariadne sighed. No voicemails. Usually she'd dismiss it as spam.

Fine.

She swiped accept, and held the phone to her ear. "Hello?"

Static crackled. Then a scratchy, desperate voice. "Ariadne? Thank the Brothers! It's me. It's Dad."

23

STOWAWAY

"Dad? Holy shit, you're alive!"

Xavier laughed—a ragged sound born of fatigue and worry-induced hysteria. He couldn't help it. There was little else to laugh about right now.

"I am," he said, cupping the microphone of the chunky satellite phone despite being alone in the car. Outside, Sharol leaned against the hood, arms folded in casual insouciance as she kept watch. "However unlikely it once seemed."

The connection crackled with heavy static, but it couldn't hide the relief in Ariadne's voice.

"But where are you? Not in Thornburg, obviously, or…"

"No. Not in Thornburg." Xavier licked his lips, wincing at how cracked they were. "I'm on the Thorn River Reservation, in ti-Lan'ot City."

"ti-Lan'ot City?"

"One of the main towns on the reservation, although town is a kind word. I had business at the nearby flamestone mine yesterday and, well, let's just say I was delayed. I didn't learn about Thornburg until late afternoon from Sharol, my partner. Sounds like she might have been the last person to escape the blast."

"Holy shit," Ariadne repeated. For once Xavier didn't chide her for the strong language. *Holy shit* barely covered it.

"I'll tell you the full dramatic tale next time I see you. But what about you? How are you taking the news? What's the mood in New Ashbrook? What are people saying?"

Now it was her turn to give a shaky laugh. "How am I? Did you lose your phone?"

"No, but there was no cell service at the mine, and now there's no cell service anywhere around Thornburg by all accounts. I'm using my emergency satellite phone."

"Great. Well, heads up, when you get service again, you'll have like a million messages from me. Probably some from Mom, too." She paused. Voices murmured in the background. So she was with people. Good.

"I tried calling Aunt Alira. No response, but like you said, the cell service is down."

Alira. His sister was next on his list of people to call, but without much hope of response. And not just because of the damaged cell network.

He couldn't let himself think more about Alira, not yet. He wouldn't.

"And you?" he prodded softly.

Ariadne took a deep breath over the line. "I'm safe, but things have been crazy. Are crazy. I have my own dramatic tale to tell. Right now I'm trying to figure out how to get back to my apartment. The city's been on edge since the news broke."

"I bet. Are you at a friend's? You might want to stay put if you can. Shelter in place and all that."

"Well, it's complicated. We're actually at the house of someone you know. Pralik One Raven."

Xavier blinked. He tried to imagine what chain of events could have led his daughter to the home of one of the pre-eminent LightFolk in New Ashbrook. He didn't want to pry, and he only had so much charge left on his satellite phone.

"Well, do what you think is best," he said lamely. "What do people think happened? I'm sure there are lots of theories."

Ariadne lowered her voice. He couldn't hear background voices anymore. "There are. But some people are blaming the DarkFolk, saying it was some sort of badass spell, like a death curse on steroids. Davek denies it, but it's got the LightFolk rattled."

"Davek? He's Pralik's son, right? The one who goes to Segard with you?"

"Yeah. Umm, Dad? Pralik wants to talk to you."

Xavier glanced at the row of LEDs on the bottom of his sat phone handset. The last red light had begun to blink. He had a couple of hundredths, no more. "Okay. Take care, Ne Ne. I'll call you again tomorrow, once I've recharged this thing."

She tutted at his use of her childhood nickname, and he chuckled as he imagined the roll of her eyes. "Bye, Dad. You take care too."

Then there was silence until a new voice came on.

"Xavier West? I am very pleased to hear from you. Almost as much as your daughter."

"I'm glad you're hearing from me too, Elder Pralik. It was a close run thing."

"I can only imagine. My condolences for any family and friends who may not have been so fortunate."

"Thank you. What can I do for you, Elder?"

Pralik spoke with an urgency suggesting he knew time was short. "I gather you're calling from a DarkFolk reservation. As your daughter mentioned, there's a growing belief they are responsible for the destruction of Thornburg. I spent over a tenth this afternoon persuading New Ashbrook police to allow old women and children to return to their One Snake reservation. We need help from the Bureau of Folk Affairs now more than ever. Please prepare those whose company you currently keep for hostility, if not outright violence. And there's something else. I have reason to believe—"

Crackling overwhelmed the LightFolk's voice, and then the line went dead.

"Dammit," Xavier cursed softly.

He stared at the dead handset, then plugged in the charging cable and tossed it onto the passenger seat. It wouldn't do any good until he ran the engine. With less than half a tank of gas, he couldn't risk idling for long.

He rubbed his sore eyes, then the bridge of his nose.

I'm too tired to think.

He opened the car door and used its frame to haul himself out of his seat, standing without putting much weight on his throbbing ankle. A chill northerly breeze nipped between the dark rows of shacks, as foreboding as the shadows.

Shivering, he shuffled around the car to stand next to Sharol, or more accurately to half-sit on the hood. First Moon's full light was just enough to see by. His partner trembled, and he suspected not just from the dropping temperature.

"How's our boy doing?" Xavier murmured.

Sharol shrugged and glanced at the nearest shack, a one room affair whose interior they'd only glimpsed. "Still coming to terms with being a father, I imagine."

Halfway through the drive from the Thorn River Mine, a frantic thumping from the trunk had startled them both. When Xavier pulled over and popped the lid, they'd found Ruian ti-Lan'ot curled inside.

"I want to see my people again," he'd told them with a defiant glare. "Take me back to the mine tomorrow if you wish. But let me see my wife and my da one more time."

Their stowaway had ridden the rest of the way in the back seat. No one could break the uncomfortable silence until Xavier eased his car into the city's ill-lit dirt streets. They'd found Ruian's father's shack empty, and no one appeared to answer their questions. They saw no one at all until they'd stopped before the fiberboard home he'd once shared with his young wife.

Ruian rattled off an impassioned torrent of words Xavier couldn't understand, then banged on the door for almost a hundredth. Finally, it had opened to reveal a short, wizened woman with unkempt white hair, clutching an infant to the shapeless smock covering her chest. They'd stared at each other for the time it took Xavier to remember to draw and release breath. Then Ruian had simply stepped inside and closed the door behind him.

Xavier had decided it was time to call his daughter.

It really was getting cold out there. An occasional curious face peered out from a neighboring doorway. The chill air held no danger, merely a lack of welcome.

Pralik's last words reverberated around his brain. These people's lives were hard enough. Now they could become even worse?

Of course, what if they were responsible for what happened to Thornburg? To his sister, to his colleagues, to a million people he'd never known. What would he think of them then?

"Xavier West."

The two Bureau of Folk Affairs agents turned towards Ruian, who stood in the open doorway of his former home. He held the swaddled child tenderly, his expression serene.

"'Congratulations' feels like the wrong word," Xavier murmured. He remembered the first time he held Ariadne in his arms, at Sandfield General Hospital. An age ago.

Ruian grimaced. "They took me away before I even knew my wife was pregnant. I came here hoping to find her, and discovered my daughter instead. She's just over a year old. Isn't she beautiful?"

It was too dark to see more than a hint of the infant's face, but Xavier and Sharol both agreed that, yes, Ruian's daughter was beautiful. The beauty of new life, of promise, in a harsh world.

"Is your wife not here?" Sharol asked gently.

A shadow passed over Ruian's face. "She is not. Her mother tells me she works in the city now, afternoons and evenings. She returns home on the last bus."

No one spoke. What was there to say? There would be no more buses from Thornburg back to the reservation.

Xavier remembered the two Darkfolk women he and Sharol had helped evade a Purist mob, who he'd hosted in his now-destroyed apartment overnight, and brought back here himself.

Brothers, that was only yesterday morning!

Whether or not the DarkFolk were responsible for what happened to Thornburg, his heart went out to Ruian and to the wife he would likely never see again, not in this life anyway. No wonder the man cradled his daughter as if she was the most precious thing in the world. To him, she was.

How could they even think of taking Ruian back to the mine?

Xavier yawned involuntarily, setting off Sharol, who at least remembered to cover her mouth.

"You are both weary," Ruian said. It was a statement, not a question.

"We should get back on the road, recharge my sat phone so I can call our boss and let them know we're alive," Xavier muttered, trying to convince himself and failing. "But between an ankle that screams every time I shift, and eyes that won't stay open, I'm not sure that's the best move. Unless Sharol wants to drive."

His partner snorted. "Dude, the only reason I'm still standing is that I'm too tired to lie down."

"We don't have much room, but we have a roof, a stove, and clean blankets," Ruian offered. "It may be a better option than your car."

Xavier and Sharol exchanged a brief questioning look, then she nodded.

"Thank you," he said.

24

OVER THE BALCONIES

Davek hurdled the side rails of two adjacent balconies, tapping the first with his fingers only as a guide. Chiana still led, halfway back to their house from the street corner where they'd bid Ariadne and the others farewell.

"Race?" his sister had challenged, eyes glinting with the rush of a childhood dare. She'd gotten a half-balcony lead before he could react, but he'd gained back a couple steps. He wanted to whoop with exhilaration, but aside from disturbing their neighbors, he didn't want to attract the attention of those gathered in Kulish Circle.

Chiana's robe flared behind her as she vaulted onto the next balcony, sweeping her legs sideways over the rail. She looked like one of the Old Folk warriors from the animated shows they'd watched as kids.

For all that he sometimes resented his big sister, Davek admired the woman she'd become. Not that he was about to tell her that.

He was running out of balconies to erase her lead, despite his shirt and pants making it easier to clear the waist-high railings. Just as he prepared his good-natured *unfair head start* defense, Chiana stumbled on her next landing. With a stifled cry of pain, she pitched forward, skidding to a halt just shy of the balcony's edge.

Suppressing his competitive instinct, Davek dropped into a crouch beside her. The lights were off in the adjacent second-floor room, but that didn't mean it was empty. He kept his voice scarcely above a whisper. "You okay? What happened?"

"I fucking fell," Chiana hissed. She sat up and clutched her right ankle, grimacing as her fingers probed the joint. "Dammit, I was smoking you, too."

He returned her arrogant grin. "I was closer than you think. I would've caught you."

"Sure you would."

He frowned, gauging their options. They were three balconies from home. Between First Moon's glow poking through the clouds, and New Ashbrook's ambient light pollution, he could clearly see Chiana's beckoning open window. The low hum of insects and ill-tempered traffic almost obscured the yelling and cheering of the vandals in the park.

"Do you think you can put weight on it?"

Chiana's nostrils flared, as if irritated that anyone must show her consideration, especially her baby brother. "Help me," she murmured, grabbing the nearby railing with one hand and reaching for him with the other.

Davek grasped her forearm and hauled her up. She grunted, limping several short steps to the far end of the balcony before leaning heavily against the railing with a look of utter disgust.

"Give me a minute," she said.

He sidled over to join her. "It's been a while since we raced over the balconies. I can't remember the last time I beat you."

That earned a soft chuckle. "Did you ever? Hurdles were my specialty at Metropolitan. I should have made the school team."

Her expression soured. Who would they have competed against? None of the human high schools wanted any part of LightFolk "magic-assisted" athletics.

"I hope that lot makes it home okay," he said, eager for a change of subject. "This was a good idea."

"I have my moments, little brother. Ariadne seems nice enough, for a human. Not sure about the rest. That Maya's one to watch."

Davek frowned. "Maya? What about her? Everyone loves her. Well, almost everyone."

"Exactly," Chiana replied, but didn't elaborate. She shot him a shrewd look. "Ariadne was relieved to hear from her father. Are they close?"

He shrugged. He didn't want to talk about it, but refusing point-blank would only fuel Chiana's curiosity. It was best to toss her scraps and distract her.

"I guess? He moved to Thornburg a few years ago after her parents divorced. I don't think they're as close as we are with Dad, but then, we still live with our parents. Yay, us."

"He's a BFA agent, right? Bureau of Folk Affairs?"

"I know what BFA stands for," Davek huffed. He glanced pointedly at Chiana's open window, but she ignored the hint.

"Are they on our side, or just shills for those in the Empire who want to suppress us and milk us for our truesilver?"

"Wow, sis. Are you going all hard-hitting reporter on me?"

Her stern expression told him he wasn't getting out of this easily. He bit his lip. "Yes and yes. It sounds like her father is one of the good ones. He worked with Dad, after all. But he's butted heads with others in the BFA who *are* your Empire shills. Depends which way the wind blows in the Senate, I guess."

"That's right, her mother's our senator," Chiana murmured, nodding to herself.

Had he told her that? Davek couldn't remember. It sounded like his wannabe-journalist sister was investigating his semi-secret girlfriend. He didn't like it, and prepared to say so.

"Is that why Khavrik had you hook up with her?"

Davek froze. He forced himself to relax, offering a puzzled smile. "What does Elder Khavrik have to do with it?"

"That's what I'm trying to figure out," Chiana said, her stare implacable. "I know you and Khavrik are tight. I've seen you together, including when you didn't think you were being noticed. You'd make a terrible spy, little brother."

His joy at their evening escapade faded. *Leave it to Chiana to spoil everything.*

"He's an Elder," he said with a careless shrug. "If I want to follow in Dad's footsteps and become one someday, I need to learn from the others, too. And he had nothing to do with me and Ariadne."

He pushed off the railing, standing tall. If she wanted his help getting back to their house, she'd have to seek it now, on his terms.

She gave him a wry grin and struggled to her feet. "One more question," she said, sweeping a stray strand of hair from her face. "Do you love her?"

He returned her intense gaze. As much as he understood such things, he wrestled with that very question. "I don't know."

Her smile broadened. "Finally. An honest answer."

Then she leapt forward, springing over the balcony rails with the effortless ease of a wild forest creature. Davek's mouth hung open in indignant astonishment as she skidded to a halt in front of her window. She gave him a cheeky wave before slipping inside.

25

RED DAWN

Exhausted as he was, Xavier didn't sleep much.

He'd gathered only a fleeting impression of the cluttered one-room home after ducking through the doorway. The old woman, Ai'aial, Ruian's wife's mother, huddled on a pallet in a far corner and scowled in silence. The pungent odor of what Xavier recognized as the narcotic cherryweed was strongest there. Most of the light and all of the heat emanated from the solid cast-iron stove that squatted in the center of the floor. A pair of blankets had been laid out to its left, next to a tumble of plastic tubs holding clothes. They shared space with a pair of hot plates and cardboard boxes of cooking utensils and other tools.

Xavier had half-collapsed and covered himself with his blanket. Then he stared at the dark roof of Ruian's home and drifted in and out of fitful sleep.

The child woke once, crying in a way he thought he'd long forgotten. His paternal reflexes hadn't. To the accompaniment of Sharol's soft snores, Xavier watched through half-closed, dark-adjusted eyes as Ruian struggled to clean and change her. The old woman wheezed sleepily next to Ruian's pallet, while he cooed and repeated his daughter's name, over and over in a sing-song voice. *"S'ondra. S'ondra. Ezh lain, papita,"* he soothed.

Xavier wished he'd subsided as easily as the DarkFolk child.

His back hurt. His ankle throbbed. His nose was clogged, a possible reaction to the pervasive cherryweed. He squirmed under the blanket, which barely compensated for the ground's chill, the stove's embers long since burned out. Finally, after Ruian's measured breathing suggested he'd found sleep again, Xavier couldn't stand it anymore.

Besides, he had to pee, and there was nowhere inside the stuffy room to do so.

As quietly as possible, he unlatched and opened the front door. It was still dark. First Moon had set, revealing the glittering canopy of stars in all their glory. He stared open-mouthed at the pinpricks of light nestling within the narrow cloud of the Belt, stretching from horizon to horizon and passing almost directly overhead. Astronomers claimed it was a view of their galaxy, an incomprehensibly vast structure of which the Sun and the world were but a part. *Mother's Necklace*, the Folk called it. Xavier doubted such a display had been seen for decades, marred by Thornburg's ever-increasing light pollution. It was beautiful.

The chill breeze still wafted idly around the modest homes of ti-Lan'ot City. All was quiet, except for the steady chirping of some sort of insect. He should know what they were, but he'd never been much of an outdoorsman. He limped on his stiff ankle to the outhouse, did his business, and hobbled back to his car. Knowing he wasn't going to fall back asleep, he eased into the driver's seat and left the door open to let in the fresh air. Then, because he felt guilty for not contacting DeArei last night before his sat phone ran out of juice, he started the car to charge it, at least enough to where he could leave a voicemail if she wasn't up yet.

The engine growled, momentarily disturbing the night's peace, before settling into a low purr. No one looked out of their homes, not even Ruian. He wondered what Sharol might think if she'd woken to hear his car running. Would she think he was abandoning her? But everyone slept, everyone but him.

He started awake to see the second LED on the handset flashing. Cursing himself for dozing off, he turned the key and killed the engine. The last thing he needed was to run out of fuel.

The first hints of light seeped into the eastern sky as he frowned, trying to remember DeArei's number. His own phone had long since given up its search for a cellular network and shut down. He keyed in a number on the sat phone and hoped for the best.

DeArei answered on the third ring. "Hello?" She sounded out of breath. Maybe he'd interrupted her early morning workout. At least he hoped that's what he'd interrupted.

"DeArei, it's me. Xavier."

"Xavier? Brothers on a bike, is that really you?"

"It really is. It's a long story, and I don't have enough sat phone charge to do it justice. But I wanted to let you know that me and Sharol are alive and well, for the most part."

DeArei let out a long exhale. "I look forward to hearing that story. Sharol too? That's better than I dared hope when I finally went to bed last night."

"Yeah. Sorry about that. I needed to call my daughter first. And I ended up talking to Pralik One Raven for a bit."

"Did you now? What did he have to say?"

"Not much. The sat phone died while he asked me to warn the DarkFolk they can expect even more hostility than usual."

"He's not wrong," DeArei murmured. Then she gasped. "Wait. Where are you right now?"

"ti-Lan'ot City. We hadn't decided where—"

"ti-Lan'ot City? Fuck! Is it dawn there yet?"

"Um, no, but it's starting to think about it."

"Listen to me, West," DeArei said, suddenly all business. "You need to get out now. You and Sharol. Get out of the city, get off the reservation, get as far from it as you can as quickly as you can!"

"Why? What's going on, DeArei?"

"Just fucking do it, man! They're sending in the Air Force at dawn. Revenge strike."

Fuck. Fuck fuck fuckity fuck.

"I'll call you from the road," Xavier snarled.

He ended the call and lurched out of the car. He staggered to Ruian's door, thought about banging on it, and decided that was a good way to get jumped. Instead, he shoved it open and stood in the doorway, staring blindly into the dark interior.

"Sharol!" he hissed. "Ruian! Get up!"

"Fuck, dude, is it even dawn yet?" Sharol grumbled. Shadows moved next to the cold stove as she struggled to her feet.

"What is happening?"

Xavier flinched as Ruian loomed from the darkness to stand right in front of him.

"Airstrike," Xavier said. "My boss just warned me. Airstrike at dawn. We've got to leave, right now!"

The DarkFolk blinked once, then turned and shook the old woman awake. "Ai'aial. Gather S'ondra's things. Prepare to leave." She muttered sleepily, and Ruian spoke urgent words in their own tongue. Then he turned back to Xavier and Sharol. "Help me rouse the town, man and woman of the Bureau. Give my people a chance."

Then Ruian pushed past them both and ran into the street, yelling at the top of his lungs. Xavier and Sharol shared a questioning glance, then followed him, turning the other direction. Sharol crossed the street, cupping her hands around her mouth as she bellowed almost incoherently. Xavier limped along the near side, screaming "Get up! Get out!" until he was hoarse. There was so much more light in the eastern sky now, red and angry, revealing the telltale glow where the sun lurked just below the horizon.

He stopped for a moment and listened. He knew what planes sounded like, what military jets sounded like. He'd watched plenty of air shows in his time. He knew they'd hear them before they saw them, this close to dawn. When they heard them, it would be too late.

He'd say this for the DarkFolk: once roused, they moved with purpose and efficiency. It was as if he had kicked open an ants' nest, the workers swarming with one mind. Only these people weren't protecting their nest; they were fleeing it. As Xavier stumbled back to his car, he watched families with bags, mothers carrying infants, fathers with children riding on their shoulders. Some packed into the few working vehicles and headed north, away from the checkpoints and the Expressway. More fled on foot. The young helped the old, streaming into the low hills to the west, away from their meager homes. From their lives. His heart sickened for them, no matter who had done what.

He desperately hoped DeArei had been wrong, but he couldn't take that chance.

And he and Sharol needed to get out too.

She met him back at the car, eyes bulging and spiky green hair flattened on one side. Ai'aial hovered in the doorway of her home, Ruian's daughter in her arms. A camping backpack rested on the ground by her feet. She stared at Xavier with wary eyes. *Where was Ruian?*

With a shout, S'ondra's father came running back. He scooped up the backpack, and made to take his daughter from Ai'aial. She shied back, and they shared a rapid, incomprehensible exchange in their own tongue. Then Ruian turned to Xavier.

"My wife's mother cannot walk far, Xavier West. If destruction is imminent, she cannot walk to avoid it."

There was no time.

"Get her in the back," Xavier barked, opening the driver's side door. "You too. Everyone, get in the car. We've gotta move."

This is the part of the action movie where the fucking car doesn't start, he thought wildly as he turned the key in the ignition. The engine rumbled into life. As soon as the last door closed, he sped through the gears, weaving around the last stragglers hobbling towards the hills. The southernmost buildings were in view when he caught a flash of something low in the brightening southern sky.

Xavier stamped on the gas pedal. Wheels spun on the dirt as the engine roared. He gripped the wheel tighter than he'd gripped anything in his life, straining forward in his seat like those last few inches would make all the difference.

They'd barely reached the road out of town when the first bomb hit.

Xavier had just registered the menacing roar of an overhead bomber jet when furious white light blossomed in his rearview mirror, followed an instant later by a window-rattling boom. He cringed in his seat, but the blast was too far away for the shockwave to reach the speeding car. More explosions followed, lighting up the loose grid of ti-Lan'ot City's streets.

By the time the road curved around the last outstretched arm of the Teeth, roiling plumes of black smoke towered into the morning sky.

The Empire had taken its first revenge for the destruction of Thornburg.

ti-Lan'ot City was no more.

26

DEATH CANNOT CLAIM YOU

Both the Reservation and State Police checkpoints were deserted. Only S'ondra's quiet whimpering interrupted their stunned silence as they sped through.

Xavier pulled over just before they reached the Northern Continental Expressway. He left the engine running, but flung open his car door and vomited onto the asphalt. Not that there was much in his stomach. He hadn't eaten since they left the medic bay at Thorn River Mine.

Had the mine been bombed too? Surely not; there were humans there. But what about se-Perik City, north of the ruins of ti-Lan'ot City but west of the mine? They would have had no warning.

His empty stomach heaved again. It was one thing to learn about the destruction of the city you'd lived in for the last four years, and the deaths of over a million people. It was quite another to witness firsthand the callous obliteration of a town of defenseless DarkFolk, those with least status in the Empire. Quite another to come within seconds of being obliterated yourself.

Ruian passed him a heavy flask with a crude steel cap. It was made of the hide of some animal, but Xavier didn't think it was Black Kine. Something sloshed inside as he took it.

"Water," said Ruian. "Ai'aial thought to salvage that from her home. Please be sparing. It is our only flask."

"Thank you," Xavier croaked, and allowed himself a single mouthful, as much to wash out the taste of bile as to drink. His stomach convulsed in protest. He passed the flask to Sharol, who took the tiniest of sips before handing it back to Ruian.

S'ondra started fussing in Ai'aial's arms, and the old woman muttered something unintelligible. Ruian replied in the same tongue, then glanced out the rear window. Above the low hill obscuring it, the pyres of ti-Lan'ot City merged into one tumbling black cloud, backlit by the morning sun.

"Are we safe for now, do you think?" Ruian asked, voice shaking from either fear or anger. Probably both.

Xavier leaned his head out of the car and listened. Nothing. Not even the chatter of insects or the whisper of the wind. The railroad tracks keeping pace with the expressway were just as empty. The only burning scent was the exhaust from his own car. The wind carried the smoke east, perhaps in homage to Thornburg.

"I think so," he said at last. Ruian nodded, then made space on the backseat so that his mother-in-law could lay the child down to change her.

Xavier turned to Sharol, who stared out the rear windshield in horror. Was she seeing flashbacks of Thornburg from the day before? He gently tapped her arm.

"Hey. When the sat phone gets a couple lights worth of charge, can you call DeArei back and let her know we survived? She was the one who warned me. Then maybe ask her what we should do next. Because I have no fucking clue."

Sharol took a deep breath, then nodded and inspected the handset. Her hand trembled. After a moment's hesitation, he covered it with his.

"We survived, partner. I don't know if it was luck or something else, but we survived. We'll be okay."

Their eyes met and her lips tightened. She'd known him too long to be uncomfortable with the contact. Right now they needed each other. They weren't just partners. They were friends.

"Death cannot claim you, Xavier West."

Xavier released Sharol's hand and turned back to Ruian, whose expression was a mix of awe and gentle mockery.

"Not for want of trying," Xavier muttered.

"Indeed. You survived a mine explosion, despite partial burial in a collapsed tunnel. You survived the destruction of Thornburg because you were trapped in that mine. You survived the gunfire that greeted us upon our escape. And you survived the bombing of my people's city just now. I think it was not luck."

Xavier wanted to argue, but now was not the time for philosophical debate. Besides, he remembered the voice in the tunnel, the voice he'd not allowed himself to think about.

I am the tide, Xavier West. And I need you.

The tide had a lot to contend with.

"Yeah, well a lot of others didn't survive," he said. "And the ones who made it far enough from the bombs, what are they supposed to do now?"

"You gave them a chance. You gave my people a chance, Xavier West. They are hardier than you know. They will take it."

Ruian hoisted his freshly changed daughter into the air. S'ondra let out a delighted giggle, but instead of returning her father's amazed gaze, her eyes locked onto something just past his right shoulder, as if someone sat between him and her grandmother. She giggled again, then stuck a tiny thumb between her lips.

The contented sound was so at odds with everyone's shock and despair that Xavier couldn't help but smile.

Let's see if we can give her a better chance than most.

He drove more cautiously now, conserving fuel. Which raised the question of where they should go.

Urban life paused abruptly on the banks of the Thorn River. Even had he seen a point in returning east to see Thornburg's ruins for himself, he could recall only one refueling station on the highway this side of the river. What were the chances it was still open? There had been one in ti-Lan'ot City, but he hadn't thought to fill his tank the previous night.

The wide untilled scrubland of the reservation stretched north and a little south of the Northern Continental Expressway, studded with self-sufficient homesteads and, of course, the mine. Even if he could find the road, he wasn't going that way. That left only one option.

He turned right onto the paved slip road and joined the Expressway as it plunged westward.

There was nothing much to see or comment on, but everyone kept their own counsel. Xavier fiddled with the radio, seeking a distraction from the featureless four lanes of asphalt rather than holding any real hope of finding news. Aside from one crystal-clear station playing twangy New Pilgrim that set his teeth on edge, he found only static. Finally, he gave up.

Theirs was the only vehicle on the road. He hadn't expected many, certainly not westbound. There was almost nowhere now from which traffic would come. Still, he'd expected emergency vehicles or supply trucks headed back east. Then he remembered what Sharol had said about the collapse of Frontier Bridge. Maybe relief efforts only came from the east, or the river itself.

As the sun rose high in the clear blue sky—a perfect late Spring day to mock current events—he mentally mapped out their geography. They were well over a full day's drive from Novomond's west coast. The towering mountains of the Teeth, which formed a once impassable barrier between the western third of the continent and the originally settled lands to the east, had to be half a day away. Just this side of the mountains lay Charlouth, a former military outpost with pretensions of urban grandeur. They wouldn't make it that far, not without refueling.

There had to be open gas stations, other towns, between them and Charlouth. Right?

He kept a nervous eye on the fuel gauge as it drifted towards the quarter tank mark.

Sharol cleared her throat, as if checking her voice still worked. Ruian had just passed around the water flask a second time, and everyone had taken the smallest sip possible, just enough to wet their parched mouths.

"I'm calling DeArei," she announced. "What's her number?"

Xavier recited the digits, something that was surprisingly hard to do without looking at a keypad. The phone trilled faintly as Sharol held the handset to her ear.

"Senior Administrator Bisset? This is Sharol Kostellan. I'm with Xavier West. We made it."

DeArei's response buzzed through the tinny speaker, but the only word Xavier could distinguish was "fuck." He gritted his teeth, piecing together the conversation from only one side of it.

"Completely destroyed from what we could tell. We, uh, managed to warn some of the residents. I think some of them got out, but Brothers know where they'll go."

Sharol caught his eye and glanced towards the rear seat. Xavier shook his head. She nodded, then screwed up her eyes in concentration as she listened.

"Just the one pass. We assume they did the same thing to se-Perik City, but we have no way of knowing. We're heading west on the Northern Continental." Sharol paused. "Because we have nowhere else to go, and can't think of anything better to do." Pause. "A little over a quarter tank I think. Yes. Beantown? The fuck kind of name is that? I know, I know. Yeah, we can probably make it that far. I'll tell him. Thank you."

Sharol wedged the handset into the cup holder between seats and plugged it back in.

"Beantown?" Xavier prompted.

"Right? Dumb name, but it's the first town of consequence we're likely to hit, probably within a half-tenth. Lots of jarabean farms out here apparently."

"To the south," added Ruian. Xavier glanced to his left, where the terrain flattened out. The many varieties of prairie grass stood taller and greener than their counterparts to the north. If he squinted, distant pivot irrigators glinted in the morning sun.

"Anything you can tell us about Beantown?" Xavier asked, glancing in the rearview mirror.

Ruian shook his head. "Reservation ends a day's walk east. My people don't go there."

Xavier wasn't sure what to do with that. "What else did DeArei have to say?"

"Not much. Happy we're alive. Outraged by the airstrike. Oh, and she said she'd reserve a pair of rooms for us at the Historic Beantown Hotel, so we could freshen up. And to charge food and anything else we need to the rooms. She'll be in touch with next steps when we're there."

Next steps. Xavier's stomach rumbled at the mention of food, and the idea of a hot shower made him all too conscious of how filthy he was. But then what?

He had a car, and the ragged clothes caked to his skin. He still, miraculously, had his phone and wallet. But he had to assume his Thornburg apartment was a total loss. And Alira... well, he would still try calling, but he held little hope of shelter there either.

Where was he supposed to go next? Back to New Ashbrook like a beaten puppy with its tail between its legs?

The road crested the latest in a series of gentle undulating peaks, skirting the last foothills of the Teeth's eastern hook, marking the beginning of Novomond's vast central plains.

The ribbon of black asphalt draped in an arrow-straight line for several kilometres across a shallow trough. And just for a moment, before their car began coasting down into that trough, flashing red and blue lights strobed in the distance, just over the next crest.

"Was that what I think it was?" Sharol murmured.

"If you think it was a roadblock, yeah," Xavier replied. "Probably why we haven't seen any westbound traffic. We must be getting close to civilization, at least the Empire's version of it."

In the backseat, Ruian frowned. He exchanged a few terse, unintelligible words with Ai'aial, who cradled S'ondra. The child appeared to be sleeping.

"Xavier West, I think you should let us out," Ruian said urgently, leaning forward so that he almost spoke directly into Xavier's ear.

"Out where?" Signs of agriculture multiplied to the south, but the north offered no signs of life or shelter. Maybe Ruian could survive out here, but hadn't he said Ai'aial couldn't walk far? He couldn't carry both her and the child.

"We are at the very edge of Thorn River. That is where they have blocked the road. I doubt we three will be welcome there, especially as witnesses of our homes' destruction."

"But you're with us," Sharol protested, even as Xavier slowed down, reaching the low point of the trough. "We're agents for the Bureau of Folk Affairs. If we carry DarkFolk passengers, that's our business."

"Don't underestimate the fear your people carry in their hearts," said Ruian, bitterness creeping into his voice. Ai'aial asked something in a querulous tone, and he replied in a more soothing one.

Xavier made his decision and pulled over.

"Don't take long, in case someone noticed us coming. Let's not give them a reason to look back."

He hated that he agreed with Ruian. But he couldn't blame the man, not after this morning. Not after they were almost cut down in a hail of bullets after escaping a mine tunnel collapse.

Despite the need for haste, Xavier got out of the car and extended a hand to Ai'aial as she struggled to climb out from the back seat. The old woman stared at his palm, grimy with soot but still pale, at the uncalloused fingers of a man who'd worked a desk job and lived in middle-class prosperity all his life. He braced for her to ignore the gesture, but she gripped his hand with surprising strength and hauled herself to her feet. Her dark unfathomable eyes, still glazed with a veneer of cherryweed bliss, met his for the briefest of instants.

"*U'o'ai memi,*" she declared, sweeping one finger twice across the center of his forehead. She scooped up S'ondra and cradled her tight. The child sobbed once in protest, then yawned and fell back asleep.

Xavier gaped at Ai'aial, his own fingertips halfway to his face to trace her design. She ignored him. Ruian carefully guided her off the asphalt shoulder and onto the sun-baked earth of the Thorn River scrubland.

"Where will you go?" Xavier asked, dropping his hand to his side and exchanging a puzzled look with Sharol.

Ruian paused, glancing up at the still cloudless sky. "I know of a homestead not far from here. Thank you, Xavier West. Your debt to me is paid."

Xavier stared after the old woman, and at the infant girl she carried. The sun beat down, itching his unprotected scalp.

"I was just saving my own skin," he said slowly. "I still consider myself in debt, if not to you, then to your daughter."

Ruian tilted his head in acknowledgment, the echo of a smile on his face. "Let it be so."

The DarkFolk raised his three-fingered hand in farewell, then turned and didn't look back.

27

MORE THAN ONE WELCOME

Pralik stood on the steps of the Senate building, hidden in the shadows of its towering marble columns as the rest of their delegation arrived.

Istilla had thought it best they avoid any kind of parade or spectacle that could attract Purists or other negative attention. He'd agreed, as had the Elders of One Sky and Two Water—the other two clans with a significant presence in New Ashbrook.

They were here as solemn representatives of their people, not as attention-seeking protestors.

Someone must have tipped off the news media, though. By the time Eighth Bell rang—literally, in this case, from the crenelated tower of the adjacent Saint Camara's Chapel—as many camera crews had gathered as Elders. Other clans convened in other cities today to petition their local Empire legislators, but none likely drew as much attention as those in Novomond's capital.

Pralik conceded they offered quite the photo op. The *chiek'lai* wore their finest ceremonial robes, the vivid amber of One Raven flanked by the pale and navy blues of One Sky and Two Water. The bone-white facade of the Senate building behind them added aesthetic appeal to the historic significance.

The three clans hadn't gathered here since signing the last treaty, over a century ago. The treaty that, more than any other, had split the Folk in two.

"All of One Sky are here," Istilla said, gesturing at the three Elders huddling nearby. Shalae maintained her usual imperious air, but Eglente had regained little of whatever poise he'd possessed since the aborted Hunter's Moon parade two days ago. He darted furtive looks at Pralik, the cameras, and the Senate doors, while Shalae conferred with the clan's third *chiek'la*—the equally imperious but borderline senile Ashe. It would be harsh to claim their clan was in decline, but they missed the strong leadership of Ishe, Ashe's twin brother, who had died two winters prior.

"They are," Pralik agreed. He wrinkled his nose as a gust of wind carried the characteristic stench of the old harbor inland. The salty ocean scent barely survived beneath the layers of fuel oil and organic decay. It had been decades since a ship last sailed from that harbor, and almost two centuries since the proud masts of One and Two Sky had filled it. "I note that we are two short of the nine we expect. Varin Two Water and our own Khavrik are missing."

Istilla pursed her lips. "I spoke with Liurin Two Water earlier. He has not heard from Varin since the eve of Hunter's Moon. It is apparently not unusual for Varin to go silent for days at a time. It is inconsiderate and inconvenient that he should choose to do so now."

"At least he has precedent," Pralik muttered. "I'm running out of patience with Khavrik. What Two Water tolerates is unacceptable in One Raven, and I intend to tell him so, should he ever reappear."

She smiled thinly and glanced past his left shoulder. "We may both do so, but I suggest waiting until after we meet with the Senate. Until then, let us maintain a united front."

Pralik frowned and turned. Khavrik strode toward them, lavish amber robes flowing behind him like a character from one of the Empire's frontier dramas. Two younger LightFolk in simpler robes scurried in his wake, one carrying a heavy-looking black backpack. The media cameras jostled to capture his arrival, and Pralik ground his teeth.

"My profound apologies," Khavrik murmured, halting in front of his fellow One Raven Elders. He bowed his head, though he kept his pleasant smile, the twinkle never fading from his eye. "For being late for your summons, and for my recent absence. I'm sure you are both irritated and frustrated with me. I will do my best to explain later."

"Later?" Pralik didn't miss Istilla's cautionary glance, but he couldn't let Khavrik's absenteeism pass unremarked. There was too much educator in him. "I cannot speak for Istilla, but I sent you countless messages and called you repeatedly. What was so important that you couldn't even grant me the courtesy of a simple acknowledgment? Why couldn't you provide proof of life?"

Khavrik raised a brow over narrowed eyes. "You feared for my life, Pralik? I'm touched."

"Don't evade the question. As Istilla reminds me, at this moment above all others, One Raven and the LightFolk must present a united front. I do not wish to interrogate you, nor do I expect a detailed accounting of your activities. But you are *chiek'la* of the One Raven clan. You have a duty. We need you to perform it."

Khavrik held Pralik's gaze while cameras clicked and whirred in the background. Then he lowered his eyes and spread his hands in apology. "You are right," he murmured. "I beg your forgiveness. I promise to give both of you, as you say, a detailed accounting of my activities. They are of great concern for One Raven and all the LightFolk. For now, I will say only this, since it pertains to our purpose here: I was protecting our One Snake brothers and sisters. The DarkFolk need our protection, now more than ever. Is that not our duty today?"

Pralik opened his mouth to demand clarification, but a sudden buzz through the crowd announced the arrival of Senator Daphne Braeyer.

The smartly dressed woman's entrance was less about drama and more about poise. She exited the Senate building's grand double doors, surveyed the assembled LightFolk gravely, and descended two of the wide steps toward them. The Elders, clustered by clan, walked up to meet her. The media and other bystanders scattered, rearranging into a crowd at a mostly respectful distance. Braeyer's diminutive but ferocious-looking assistant spared choice words for a photographer who approached too close.

"Is this everyone?" the senator asked, glancing at the Two Water Elders. "Very well. Does each clan wish to speak for itself? Or does one among you speak for all?"

Heads turned—with varying degrees of deference—toward One Raven. They'd discussed this. Not everyone liked it, but all understood how the Empire preferred to conduct its business.

"I am Istilla One Raven," she announced, mostly for the benefit of the onlookers. "I speak for the Folk today, Light and Dark."

Senator Braeyer couldn't disguise her grimace but replaced it swiftly with a polite smile. "Greetings, *chiek'la*. The Senate assembles as we speak. We are prepared to listen to your statement." She paused, and her smile turned grim. "However, I would caution you all to moderate your expectations. Emotions continue to run hot."

"As they do within our people," Istilla pointed out stiffly.

"I have no doubt. I'm not here to tell you what to do, or how to present your message. Simply be aware that there are those who would leverage righteous passion for their own ends. Now, if you would follow—"

The crowd stirred again, cameras swiveling toward the Senate doors. Senator Braeyer frowned, looking over her shoulder. Her lips pursed as her fellow senator, Brogan Castlewood, emerged.

It was all Pralik could do not to take a step back. Castlewood's sharp suit and immaculately trimmed silver beard couldn't entirely mask the impression of a predator leaving its lair. The predator wore a wide grin that failed to match the solemnity of the situation. Or perhaps he was simply pleased to see the cameras.

"Welcome, friends of the Empire!" Castlewood cried, sweeping his gaze over the Elders. His pale eyes lingered for a barely perceptible moment on Pralik. When they rested on Senator Braeyer, his grin faded slightly. "Many thanks to my colleague for extending an informal welcome to you. I wish to add a formal one. No matter what race or social standing, all friends of the Empire are welcome here. You are welcome."

He waited until Istilla nodded respectfully, then faced the media and other onlookers who hung on his every word. Right now, Brogan Castlewood was the most powerful man in Novomond, and he knew it.

"We live in troubling times. Our great nation trembles at the horrors we have witnessed in recent days. These tremors shake the very pillars of the Empire itself—pillars that cannot and will not fall. It would be all too easy to lose ourselves in recrimination and violence against our fellow citizens. We must do better. We must choose a harder path, but one that seeks respect and harmony, not just for ourselves but for our children and future generations."

Castlewood locked eyes with Pralik before continuing. "Today, we choose that path. We set our first foot upon it. Petitioners representing the LightFolk seek an audience, and we acknowledge their right—the right enjoyed by every true citizen of the Empire. So we will listen. We should listen to the understandable concerns of those Folk who have long shown commitment to working with the Empire and not against it."

He stepped aside, gesturing toward the yawning Senate doors. "Please. We will listen to you now."

28

PILGRIM'S HILL

Xavier thought he was prepared to see what was left of Thornburg. He was wrong.

Part of it was vertigo. As the army helicopter swept in a wide circle, approaching from the south and sweeping east of the ruins, Xavier became increasingly conscious of the open fuselage between him and the ground. It wasn't that he didn't trust his harness buckles; he just didn't trust helicopters. But as they crossed the debris-choked Swamps and the desolation of Thornburg's suburbs came into view, his unease gave way to horrified shock.

He had yet to hear reports of any survivors from the first emergency responders. Now he knew why. The only structures higher than a metre were rubble, piled high in the congestion of collapse. It looked like a miles-wide tornado had flattened the city.

Pale grey lines marked major streets, and splotches of discolored green showed where parks and sports fields lay strewn with debris. Downtown—all the way from inner neighborhoods like Blacktown to Dockside—was one huge mound of crumbled concrete. Hardly any green remained where Empress Catarina Park used to be. All that survived of Frontier Bridge was tangled wreckage caught up in submerged pylons, their broken tops protruding from the heedless river like the decaying fangs of an old wolf.

How could anyone have survived? Even if you'd been in a basement when the attack happened, you'd have been buried alive. Xavier bowed his head and hoped the end had been quick for his sister and her family, for Carli and his colleagues at the Bureau office. For everyone, human and Folk alike.

He thought of the girl again, the DarkFolk to whom he'd given sanctuary. He thought of Ruian's wife, who would never see her husband or daughter again. So much senseless loss of life. But that hadn't started with Thornburg, had it? Nor had it ended there. Xavier leaned back in his seat and closed his eyes as they descended toward the airport north of the city. It had been a physically exhausting and emotionally draining couple days.

He and Sharol had caused quite a commotion when they rolled up to the roadblock the previous morning. Theirs was the first vehicle to arrive from the east since the night before. The young highway patrolmen had plied them with questions—*Were you there? Did you see the aftermath? Did the prims really do it?*—until a senior officer took pity on them and escorted them through.

"Talked to your boss," he'd rumbled through a graying beard as mighty as his paunch. He'd insisted on spinning up his lights, leading them into the sparse and utterly unremarkable "city" of Beantown. It looked like someone had dropped a handful of strip malls at random around the railroad tracks, then filled the gaps with trailer parks and occasional cookie-cutter subdivisions. Old Beantown consisted of two parallel streets of brick buildings. The Historic Beantown Hotel, at four stories, was the tallest structure of all.

As promised, DeArei had reserved rooms. The vivacious, red-haired woman behind the front desk took their disheveled appearance in stride. She promised to send food up to their rooms before asking in an awed whisper, "Are you gonna make sure the prims get what they deserve?" Xavier had snatched his keycard, joining a silent Sharol in the elevator. Once in his room, he'd stripped, showered, eaten, and collapsed on the king-sized bed. Only when he awoke with daylight fading did he realize he had no clean clothes, no phone charger, and no idea what to do next. Fortunately, his boss came to the rescue.

"There's a big-box store in town that delivers," DeArei told him after her call was routed to his room. It had been a while since he'd used a handset with a physical cord; he'd almost yanked the phone off the end table twice before forcing himself to sit still. "Give me your measurements. I'll have them send a couple changes of clothes to tide you over. I need you back in Thornburg. Sharol, too, if you're willing. We need your expert opinions."

Both he and Sharol had mixed feelings about returning to their devastated home. It was too soon for closure, and the helicopter's approach hadn't helped.

However, they were still employees of the Bureau of Folk Affairs. When they were ready to take time off to process it all, they would. But not today.

"We need to get into the city," Xavier told the Army officer who greeted them after they landed on a clear patch of Thornburg Airport runway.

General Shae Roddicks had Sharol's athletic build and height, and the lines crinkling her pale, round face failed to soften her no-nonsense demeanor.

"So I hear," she growled. If she'd jammed a cigar into the corner of her mouth, it wouldn't have upset the stereotype. "We've kept civvies away from the city for their own safety. But I understand you're big shots with Folk Affairs, and I have orders to indulge you."

The General looked the pair up and down with overt skepticism. Xavier could hardly blame her. The hem of his new jeans ended way above his bare ankles—he'd forgotten to order socks, of all things—and the cuffs of his scarlet *Beantown Berserkers* sweatshirt protruded from under the arms of his jacket, no matter how often he stuffed them back in. *How come all Sharol's stuff fits properly?*

"I can spare Private Letissier and an ATV," she told them, leading them toward the ruins of an aircraft hangar on the southern perimeter of the airfield.

This far from downtown, the damage hadn't been absolute. Two walls of the hangar still stood, though the roof had partially collapsed, all but destroying the passenger jet inside. Still, the blast had been sufficient to toss aircraft across the field like tumbleweeds, spilling luggage, seats, and debris over the asphalt. Several planes had caught fire, incinerating those unlucky enough to survive the initial shockwave. Xavier tried not to look too closely at the charred husks of broken fuselage.

Private Armand "Armi" Letissier was a tall, fresh-faced young man with a new shaving cut on his upper lip. A bright pink full-body jumpsuit concealed his uniform, reminding Xavier uneasily of the Thorn River Mine. He stood at ease next to the "ATV," a vehicle that rivaled the flashier raised-tire monster trucks Xavier usually gave wide berths on Thornburg's highways. He doubted there was a piece of field gear the Army hadn't attached to its open frame.

Letissier saluted Roddicks and greeted Xavier and Sharol with a curious smile. He hooked a thumb at a pair of similar jumpsuits hanging off the vehicle's frame.

"You'll want to put those on," he said, a slow drawl placing his origins much further south in Novomond. He tapped his chest, where a strip of five LED lights glowed green. "Radiation monitor. Readings aren't high on the outskirts, but the General tells me you folks wanna go closer in."

"Something's not adding up," DeArei had confided to Xavier on the phone. *"We know from visual evidence and instrument data that flamestone was involved in the attack. But despite pockets of high radiation, the overall levels aren't what we expect. People are struggling to explain the scale of the destruction based on magic alone. We fear someone—internal or external—has*

figured out how to weaponize flamestone. The Army knows weapons, but you two know flamestone. See what you can find and report back to me. And only me."

Roddicks wore a pensive frown as she watched Xavier and Sharol struggle into their jumpsuits. It wasn't a warm day, but Xavier already wore a jacket, a sweatshirt, and an undershirt; the bulk strained the suit's zippers. He worried about overheating, but he'd be damned if he was leaving his meager belongings lying around the airport.

"That suit is your lifeline," Roddicks said abruptly as Letissier handed out thick white gloves and plexiglass helmets. They were going full astronaut. "You tear it, you evacuate back here. Any one of you hits three red lights, you evacuate back here. That is not a suggestion. That is an order. Do you understand?"

"Yes, General," Xavier said gravely. He had no desire to expose himself to more flamestone than necessary.

Letissier demonstrated the inter-suit communications, and Xavier followed Sharol into the back seat of the ATV.

They were off.

Xavier had steeled himself against the gruesome sights of up-close destruction as they crawled south through the wreckage. Letissier avoided debris as best he could, aiming for wider highways and sparsely populated neighborhoods. The collapsed buildings kept their grisly secrets, but many people had been outside when the attack happened. Bloody clumps of clothing littered the broken streets, occasionally gashed open to reveal picked bones.

Massive flocks of carrion birds wheeled overhead like small thunderclouds, diving down to settle on dismembered limbs as if they were roadkill. Letissier gunned the engine as they passed a cluster of corpses, but the dining birds barely twitched their spread black wings, refusing to spare the ATV a glance from their glittering eyes.

"I guess you can't do anything about that," Sharol murmured, her voice crackling in Xavier's ear with little more clarity than his satellite phone.

"No, ma'am," Letissier said with distaste. "The birds are just doing what's in their nature. We try to keep the wild dogs and other animals away, because they're a danger to us, too. But those mostly come out at night."

Xavier looked closer, then wished he hadn't. Scarlet smears decorated the clear patches of asphalt, trails leading into pockets formed by collapsed buildings—caves amidst the urban destruction. He tried to shake the impression that feral eyes stared unseen from within.

Their opportunistic passage into the heart of the city brought them just west of the Thornburg Tornadoes Maul stadium. Some of the two-metre neon letters from its main entrance had survived, protruding from the concrete slush in a poignant acknowledgment that the Tornadoes' quest for their first-ever trophy had ended unfulfilled.

Xavier's apartment wasn't that far east of the stadium, but he quickly dismissed any inclination to head that way. What would be the point? There were very few things in his bachelor pad worth salvaging, and almost zero chance he'd be able to dig them out.

Stay on task.

Brothers, it was hot in this damn jumpsuit. He should have left his jacket behind. His labored breath began fogging the inside of his helmet. It was the only sound he could hear over the ATV engine and the steady clicks of his radiation gauge. An eerie, sepulchral hush enshrouded Thornburg. Even the carrion birds mostly kept their own counsel.

"Gods, that smell." Sharol's muttered voice spat out of Xavier's earpiece. The back of her gloved hand smacked the front of her helmet in a futile attempt to cover her nose.

Absorbed by the carnage, Xavier gagged as the sweet, sickly odor invaded his suit's ventilation filter. Most decomposing bodies didn't produce a noticeable odor for days, but the process started within hours. And there were a hell of a lot of dead bodies hidden in these ruins.

"First time I've smelled it," Letissier said. He paused at what once was a busy intersection, four lanes in each direction. A wall of mangled cars towered over the northbound lanes, as if a tsunami had roared through. They were lucky they'd zigzagged west and were headed across the path of the blast. "We're at one red. Do you guys have a destination in mind?"

Xavier glanced at Sharol's suit, then his own. Sure enough, their leftmost LEDs glowed red. *Click, click click, click.*

He peered at the nearby rubble. If there were chips of flamestone around, they were far too small to be obvious.

"Where's the highest pocket of radiation?" he asked Letissier.

"Somewhere just south of Empress Catarina Park. We've already lost seven or eight drones near there."

"That could be Pilgrim's Hill," Sharol said. "Didn't that used to be an old Two Mountain clan burial mound?"

"Yeah," Xavier confirmed. *And likely a symbol for any Chaos Walkers seeking revenge on the Empire.*

Letissier turned further around. "Two Mountain? Were they LightFolk or DarkFolk?"

"Neither," Xavier said. "The Empire wiped them out before it started using those distinctions."

The glare of reflected sunlight off Letissier's helmet obscured his expression. "Copy," he said, then swiveled back and drove southeast.

In the half-tenth it took to reach Pilgrim's Hill, the clouds peeled back. The sun baked them even more. Xavier sweated out of every pore, barely able to see through the condensation misting his helmet. The terrain grew rougher; twice they had to backtrack and seek another route. The clicks of his radiation gauge gathered pace, reminding him of the first burst of raindrops on glass heralding an approaching thunderstorm.

By the time they squeezed between slabs of semi-pulverized concrete and emerged into a wide circular space, two red lights glowed on their chests.

Xavier had noticed occasional slivers of flamestone strewn through the wreckage of the last two blocks. But the gently convex disc of soil and sand that used to be Pilgrim's Hill scintillated with it—especially dense in a ring around the periphery. He had no doubt he was looking at the epicenter of the explosion.

Adjacent buildings showed evidence of being sheared clean through with precise chest-high strokes. Stone, metal, glass—it didn't appear to have mattered.

"What kind of weapon can do that?" Xavier asked.

"Nothing we have," Letissier said in awe. "Holy fucking Brothers. Look, we're all at two red, and even I can tell that's flamestone out there. We can't stay here long."

Xavier carefully climbed down from the ATV, stretching awkwardly within his suit. "Give us a few hundredths. I want to look at something. Coming or staying, Sharol?"

"Coming," she said, dismounting from the vehicle.

"Okay, but if you go three red, get out of there," Letissier warned.

Xavier grunted his assent. He approached the ring of flamestone slowly, trailed by Sharol. Even through the foggy plexiglass of his helmet, chunks of green-veined black rock as big as his thumbnail glittered amid the soil. The clicks from his radiation gauge sounded like a drumroll as he neared the ring. He couldn't just stand there.

He stepped into the ring. The gauge went crazy. Adrenalin surged. He wanted to run, flee in terror back to the ATV, back to the airport, and get the hell away from Thornburg. Instead, he forced himself forward.

After six quick steps, the gauge tailed off to a frequency scarcely more than ambient. He shambled forward a similar distance before stopping, then glanced at his chest.

Three red lights blinked back at him.

Static buzzed wildly in his ear, the suit intercom system struggling within the ring of flamestone. He'd have to cross it again and incur another dose of radiation, but he was relatively safe inside its shield. Safe from radiation, anyway.

He hadn't learned anything yet. He was the first person to visit the scene of the crime. It was his responsibility to uncover evidence that might confirm who had committed it, and why.

A voice crackled through the static. "...shit, Xavier, did we just get fried?"

Careful not to turn too much lest Letissier see his chest, Xavier glanced over his shoulder. Sharol had also crossed the ring. Three red lights glowed on her suit, too.

"We're here now," he answered. "I'm not picking up much more than background levels inside the ring."

"Me neither. Whatever the price was, we already paid it. What do you want to do now?"

"Let's look around. This mound used to be three or four stories high, with a chapel on top. I guess most of that was vaporized or propelled outward during the blast. But let's do a quick survey. See if there's anything left to help us understand what happened here."

"Gotcha. I'll take the right half."

Xavier motioned to Letissier, miming walking around the remnants of Pilgrim's Hill. Their driver lifted an arm and pointed to his wrist. Xavier signaled twenty. After a pause, Letissier raised his thumbs in acknowledgment.

The scrunch of Xavier's boots accompanied his heavy breathing as he circled the truncated mound. Very few flecks of flamestone studded the powdery soil. It reminded him of walking on sand the time he and Daphne had taken a young Ariadne on a beach vacation to Barlolos, a chain of tropical islands off the southeastern coast of Novomond. The scenery here was considerably grimmer, and that happy memory faded as his walk became a slog.

"Not finding much, partner," sputtered Sharol's voice. She was almost out of sight on the other side of the inverted bowl.

"Me neither. I'm gonna head to the summit."

Halfway up the slope, he tripped. Something solid cracked and gave way beneath his foot. He pitched forward with a cry of alarm, gloves plunging into the dirt as his knees broke his fall. Adrenaline spiked. A fresh wave of sweat broke across his skin.

Brothers, let my suit still be intact!

"Xavier! You alright, man?"

He didn't answer immediately. The fingers of his right hand gripped something solid, hard, and uneven. He slowly drew it out of the dusty soil, turning it over in his gloved hands as his brain struggled to make sense of the shape. Then, he shuffled backward to find what he'd tripped over. A pit formed in the bottom of his stomach.

"Xavier! Answer me, dammit!"

"I think you'd better come over here," he said quietly.

Sharol shuffled across the slope toward him. From the corner of his eye, Xavier noted Letissier standing next to the ATV, hands on his hips.

"What is it?" Sharol demanded, squatting next to him. "Are you hurt?"

"I'm fine. Look at this."

Xavier passed her the object he'd dug up. It was shaped like a human vertebra—one of the bones of those who'd been buried here almost two centuries before. Bright gray metal shone under the dust. And not just any metal.

"Then this one's a femur. Or a tibia. I never could keep the names straight."

Sharol glanced at the long bone, snapped in two to reveal the off-white hue of its interior. She rifled through the soil, quickly turning up other bones: fingers, ribs, fragments of skull and pelvis.

A thin layer of pure truesilver coated every one.

"What the actual fuck?" she breathed hoarsely. "What could do this?"

"I think I understand why DeArei and others are puzzled by the relative lack of flamestone," Xavier said, gazing at the devastation. "I think it was just for show. To misdirect. I think there were DarkFolk involved, but I don't think they were the ones behind it."

He took a deep breath, his mind reeling. "It was the LightFolk who destroyed Thornburg."

EPILOGUE

They didn't take off Davek's blindfold until he'd been standing in silence—and, he assumed, alone—for several hundredths. He tried not to fidget. He clasped his hands in front of him, balanced on the balls of his feet, and focused on breathing evenly.

He was inside. The air had changed. The industrial tang of the city breeze had vanished, replaced by the cloying odor of damp wood. A hand on his shoulder had guided him down a flight of creaking steps. Wafts of fresh paint replaced the wood smell, but the dampness remained.

He shivered, but he wasn't cold.

He blinked rapidly after the cloth was stripped away from his eyes. It was too dark to see much. A single candle on the floor in front of him provided the only illumination. Regular, boxy shadows lined the walls, but he spared them little attention. He fixed it instead on the three hooded and robed figures standing on the other side of the candle.

The tallest, to his left, tucked something inside their robe as they resumed their place. Davek guessed that was Elder Khavrik, the man who had blindfolded him as soon as he climbed into the black sedan. Beneath the hood, flickering yellow flame illuminated only a rounded-off triangular chin and thin lips.

No, not *Elder* Khavrik. He wasn't *chiek'la* here. He wasn't even One Raven. He was a Walker.

Time passed, measured only by Davek's thudding heartbeat and his racing thoughts. Let the humans blame Chaos Walk for Thornburg and every other infraction against the Empire. Let them try to make it a crime to stand up for who you are, to demand past treaties be honored, to seek reparation for what was stolen. To resist the Empire's increasing marginalization and subjugation of the Folk.

Using the law of the Empire on behalf of his people would never be enough by itself. He needed the Mother. He needed Chaos.

The figures in front of Davek stirred. He blinked and remembered the brief instructions he'd been given. He knelt on the rough stone floor and lowered his head until the candle filled his vision.

"Chaos awaits us all," a voice intoned. The Pathfinder. Her voice was high-pitched but sonorous, filling the claustrophobic chamber. He shivered as if savoring remembered pain.

"From Chaos we came, and to Chaos we shall return. Some live apart from Chaos. They fear it, as they should. They build walls to shut out the darkest night. But such walls also shut out the brightness of the Sun.

"Others Walk with Chaos. Those who choose and are chosen embrace the truths that only Chaos brings. For too long, the world has forgotten such truths. It is time that it remembers."

Leather scraped softly against stone, and a robed shadow eclipsed the candle flame. He caught his breath.

Be strong. You've been waiting for this moment for so long. Be strong.

"Child of the Folk, Chaos has chosen you. Do you choose it in return?"

He exhaled through his nose and slowly lifted his face. The Pathfinder's silhouette was utterly black.

"I choose Chaos," he said, and by a miracle his voice was steady.

"Then rise, child of Chaos," said the Pathfinder.

Davek rose to his feet. The hoods of the Pathfinder's companions loomed in the shadows behind her. She was half a head shorter than him. But that meant nothing here.

Movement shifted in the gloom, and a curled hand appeared in front of his face. He forced himself not to flinch. Her thumb pressed against the center of his forehead, a short stroke followed by a longer one.

"The question is asked of Chaos," the Pathfinder whispered, her voice barely carrying. Moments later, she pushed something against his lips, hard and leathery. He accepted the offering and chewed.

Mother, it's bitter!

He suppressed a sudden urge to gag and forced himself to chew the revolting meat. Swallowing too early would dishonor the Mother, and the Chaos that birthed Her. Better not to wonder what animal this came from. By the time he swallowed, the desiccated flesh had absorbed half the moisture in his mouth.

"And Chaos has answered. Chaos chooses you. *Aliach emor'i!*"

"*Aliach emor'i!*" chanted the Pathfinder's companions. She retreated behind the flame, resuming her place between them.

Davek could scarcely croak his response. But his heart soared.

"Walk with us, child of Chaos. Walk with us, and lead our people back to what is rightfully ours. *Aliach emor'i!*"

"*Aliach emor'i!*"

Davek's voice was loud and clear this time.

He resisted.

Cast of Characters

Humans

Bureau of Folk Affairs

- Xavier West - senior agent

- Sharol Kostellan - agent, Xavier's partner

- DeArei Bisset - senior administrator

- Carli Tomson - receptionist

- Aemon Derrick - agent

Senate

- Brogan Castlewood - senator for Sentarino

- Daphne Braeyer - senator for New Ashbrook North

- Val Colliano - Daphne's chief of staff

- Bryn Hammond - senator for Charlouth

- Merrick Gravell - senator for Thornburg

- Valiant IV - emperor

Segard Law School

- Ariadne West - student

- Maya Gortauld - student

- Barrett Vale - student

- Simone Dupris - student

- Ulysses Kent - professor

- Serala Kovic - professor

- Aleister Menzies - student

- Jordan Kuypres - student

- Henri Collins - dean of Segard Law School

- Maven Palmer - chancellor of Segard Law School

City Police

- Alexander Sorens - chief detective, Thornburg PD

- Chae Gallish - detective, Thornburg PD

- Gia Brady - officer, New Ashbrook PD

Thorn River Mine

- Harran Latham - director

- Dane Vallance - medic

Novomond Army

- Shae Roddicks - general

- Armand "Armi" Letissier - private

Other

- Fenner Castlewood - socialite

- Alira West - Xavier's sister

- Madam Two Mountain - brothel owner

- Jace - biker

LightFolk

One Raven

- Jek - student at Starshine Academy

- Pralik - clan elder and co-principal of Metropolitan Academy

- Laida - homemaker, Pralik's wife

- Chiana - aspiring journalist, Pralik's daughter

- Davek - student at Segard Law School, Pralik's son

- Istilla - clan elder

- Khavrik - clan elder and low income housing program manager

Three Raven

- Keralek - student at Segard Law School

One Sky

- Shalae - clan elder

- Eglente - clan elder

- Ashe - clan elder

One Water

- Loro - clan elder

- Ajan - clan elder

- Jair - student at Segard Law School

Two Water

- Varin - clan elder

- Liurin - clan elder

- Ellin - student at Starshine Academy

- Uian - owner of Nomad online journal

DarkFolk

Note: The mid-word apostrophe denotes a sound not present in languages outside Novomond. It is best mimicked by "tl", a percussion of the tongue off the roof of the mouth.

Although such words remained in LightFolk clan dialects, by the time of this story the apostrophe had been reduced to a simple "l".

ti-Lan'ot (Three Mountain)

- K'uelle (Kit) - prostitute

- S'ondra - K'uelle's infant daughter

- Ai'aial - K'uellle's mother

- Shilaiyo - prostitute

- Uraol - mining crew foreman

- Ruian - miner

on-Ara'is (One Snake)

- Ai'aina One Snake - clan elder

Unknown clan

- The Pathfinder - shaman

Acknowledgements

Writing and publishing books doesn't get easier the more you do it. Not for me, especially after leaving the relative comfort of an established series to try something different and more ambitious. Fortunately, I had a lot of help.

Early readers corrected my more egregious mistakes, especially in the early chapters. Rick Wurl read the first drafts in serial form as usual. I suspect I out-violenced my violence consultant, but his critique convinced me I was on the right track. My beta readers then took over: Geri Dreiling, Brooke Eisen, Lisa Hanhart, CC Kline, Jacki Fakhrahmad and Aimee Keener each offered invaluable insight. Some screamed when appropriate.

From there, I left the manuscript in the capable hands of my editor and formatter, Gareth Clegg. I'm not sure what he was expecting, other than the usual rearrangement of commas. He immediately latched on to "the big bad Brits" vibe of the story's Empire, which is more charming than current alternatives. As I write this, we're still arguing over how to spell "metre".

Michele Guarnieri of Khalil Covers (www.khalilcovers.com) resumed cover design duties. I challenged her for something distinct from my previous books and which would be consistent with future unwritten installments of this new series. She knocked it out of the park! Although, I wouldn't want to be on the receiving end of a spell that generated that much truesilver.

Ever since I first read *The Lord of the Rings* as a teenager, I've dreamed of creating a world deserving of its own maps. Now I have! Kate Moody (kate_moody.artstation.com) created amazing renditions of Thornburg and the continent of Novomond. You may think that a map of New Ashbrook would be handy too. I agree. Next book, perhaps.

My Instagram street team has been patiently waiting for a new book to promote, especially after we rebranded to the "Chaos Walkers". Here it is, guys! Heather Mayers, my PA, presides and works tirelessly to save me from myself on social media. She makes graphics and forms, reads early drafts and provides developmental edits, tracks deadlines, gives me story ideas and, most importantly, encourages me daily. Oh, and thanks for filling in that anthology form on my behalf.

I've found help closer to home too. My sister-in-law, Keri Ousley, continues to augment my wardrobe with book themed hoodies and sweatshirts, as well as producing much of my book swag. My older daughter, Rhiannon, often joins me at book signings demonstrating her considerable bookbinding skills, and she's just completed a very limited set of amazing, hand-bound omnibus editions of my *Of Imprints & Erasure* series! I can't wait to see what she does with this book.

You may have wondered about the symbols subtly adorning the book covers. They are Folk clan sigils. My younger daughter, Imogen, took my ideas, ran off to do a bunch of research, and created the first five for me. I'm hoping she'll add the remaining six as we meet those clans in future books.

Finally, inevitably, I have to thank the one without whom none of this would be possible: my wife, Sherri. I didn't think she'd enjoy the darkness of this book compared to my others, but she read it and gave me opinions and advice I needed to hear. The story is better for it, and I'm better for having you as my wife, my love. You'll like Davek in the end, I promise.

About the Author

Gareth Ian Davies was born and raised in the south of London , during which time he wrote many terrible things and dreamed of becoming a novelist. Instead, he earned a degree in Physics from the University of Bristol and didn't quite know what to do with it. After moving to the American Midwest he flirted with a career in nuclear engineering before taking the somewhat safer path as a software architect.

He spent the next three decades writing code and technical documentation, before finally realizing his dream by publishing his first novel. He has since completed that series, contributed several short stories to anthologies, and may be getting the hang of this author thing.

Gareth lives in St. Louis with his wife, two cats, and a cockatiel. Many empty fish tanks lurk within these walls.

ALSO BY GARETH

Stay Connected

Want to be one of the first to get all the latest news? Check out Gareth's socials and sign up for upcoming announcements, first looks, and more!

Facebook:
Gareth Ian Davies

Instagram
@author.garethiandavies

Website
garethiandavies.com